* * * * * * *

"Why don't you tell me why you are here and what it is you would like me to do for you?"

Mr. Endicott squirmed in the chair for a moment or two as he looked from me to his wife then back at me.

"I - - ah - - I would like you to find our son, Jonathan."

"Okay. How long has he been missing?" I asked.

"Well, you see, he's not actually missing."

"I'm sorry. I don't understand. If he's not missing, that would indicate you know where he is."

"I guess it would."

"So, do you know where he is or not?"

"Kind of," he replied.

"Walter, you don't mind if I call you Walter, do you?"

"No, of course not."

"Walter, if you want me to help you, you're going to have to be a little clearer on what is going on and what you want me to do."

"Our only son has run off with *some woman*," Mrs. Endicott blurted out.

I was a little surprised at her sudden outburst. However, the way she said "*some woman*" made me think she didn't approve of her son's choice of women. She was not the first mother who didn't like the woman her son had chosen.

* * * * * * *

Other titles by J.E. Terrall

Western Short Stories
    The Old West
    The Frontier
    Untamed Land

Western Novels
    Conflict in Elkhorn Valley
    Lazy A Ranch
       (a modern western)

Romance Novels
    Balboa Rendezvous
    Sing for Me
    Return to Me
    Forever Yours

Mystery/Suspense/Thriller
    I Can See Clearly
    The Return Home
    The Inheritance

Nick McCord Mysteries
    Vol – 1 Murder at Gill's Point
    Vol – 2 Death of a Flower
    Vol – 3 A Dead Man's Treasure
    Vol – 4 Blackjack, A Game to Die For
    Vol – 5 Death on the Lakes
    Vol – 6 Secrets Can Get You Killed

Peter Blackstone Mysteries
    Murder in the Foothills
    Murder of My Love

Frank Tidsdale Mysteries
    Death by Design

MURDER ON THE CRYSTAL BLUE

A Peter Blackstone Mystery

by
J.E. Terrall

ISBN: 978-0-9844591-6-2

This is a work of fiction. Names, characters, and incidents
are either a product of the author's imagination or are used
fictitiously, and any resemblance to actual persons, living or
dead, is purely coincidental.

Printed in the United States of America
First Printing / 2010   www.lulu.com
Second Printing / 2013   www.creatspace.com

Cover photo taken by J.E. Terrall

Book Layout /
Formatting: J.E. Terrall
              Custer, South Dakota

MURDER ON THE CRYSTAL BLUE

To Richard and Kim Luze

CHAPTER ONE

I WAS STANDING AT THE WINDOW of my ninth floor office looking down at the street below. The streets of Denver were wet from an early morning rain. It was still overcast, but the rain had stopped with the exception of a light drizzle. It was one of those gray days that makes a person wish they had stayed home to relax with a hot cup of coffee and the local paper, or a good book.

People were scurrying along the sidewalks dodging around puddles and each other. They looked like little ants going from place to place. From where I was they didn't seem to have any real destination, yet all of them seemed to be in a hurry to get there.

I was wondering why so many people were in such a hurry when my thoughts were interrupted by a firm knock on my office door. I turned around and saw a very well dressed couple standing in the doorway.

The woman looked to be in her mid-to-late forties. She was wearing a rather nondescript tan pantsuit that actually looked very nice on her. Her hair was sort of a mousy brown with a nice wave to it. The expression on her face was that of someone who wasn't sure whether they should have come or not.

The man was tall, which made the woman look shorter than she really was. He was probably in his mid fifties. He stood straight with his shoulders pulled back and his chin set firm as if to say "life is serious business and that is the way it is going to be".

He was wearing a dark gray suit with light gray pinstripes. His tie was bright red and contrasted sharply with his brilliant white stiff-collared shirt. The red handkerchief neatly folded in the breast pocket of his suit coat matched the tie.

Although his appearance told me one story, the look on his face told a completely different one. His eyes seemed desperate and pleading for help. What kind of help, I had no idea.

"Good afternoon. May I help you folks?" I asked as I turned and walked over to my desk.

"I sure as hell hope so," the man said.

I decided to overlook his forcefulness, at least until I found out what they wanted. I motioned for them to come in and have a seat in front of my desk. The woman looked up at the man as if she wasn't sure they should take the time to sit down, but seemed to be either afraid to say anything, or simply willing to let him have his way. The man took her gently by the arm and guided her to the chairs.

"Are you Peter Blackstone?" the man asked without sitting down.

"Yes. What is it I can do for you?"

"You're a private investigator, right?"

His questions were sharp and to the point. This led me to believe that he was used to getting what he wanted, when he wanted it.

"I've been called that," I said with a slight grin. "Are you in need of a private investigator?"

"Yes," he replied.

"Maybe it would be best if we start by introducing ourselves. As you already know, I'm Peter Blackstone. Who might you folks be?"

I watched them sit down in front of my desk, then waited for them to introduce themselves.

"I'm Walter Eugene Endicott," he said without introducing the woman.

The way he said his name made me think that he expected me to know who he was. The fact was I did know of him, although I had never met him until now. I knew him to be a fairly wealthy businessman with a string of auto dealerships up and down the Front Range from Fort Collins to Pueblo. I wondered why he would need a private investigator, but figured we would get around to that soon enough.

I nodded slightly to acknowledge that I had heard him, then turned my attention to the woman, smiled politely and waited for her to introduce herself.

"I'm Mrs. Endicott," she said, her voice timid and soft.

"Nice to meet you both. Does your visit have anything to do with your automobile businesses, Mr. Endicott?"

"No," he replied quickly, almost a little too quickly.

The way he answered my question made me wonder what he was keeping from me.

"Why don't you tell me why you are here and what it is you would like me to do for you?"

Mr. Endicott squirmed in the chair for a moment or two as he looked from me to his wife then back at me.

"I - - ah - - I would like you to find our son, Jonathan."

"Okay. How long has he been missing?" I asked.

"Well, you see, he's not actually missing."

"I'm sorry. I don't understand. If he's not missing, that would indicate you know where he is."

"I guess it would."

"So, do you know where he is or not?"

"Kind of," he replied.

"Walter, you don't mind if I call you Walter, do you?"

"No, of course not."

"Walter, if you want me to help you, you're going to have to be a little clearer on what is going on and what you want me to do."

"Our only son has run off with *some woman*," Mrs. Endicott blurted out.

I was a little surprised at her sudden outburst. However, the way she said "*some woman*" made me think she didn't approve of her son's choice of women. She was not the first mother who didn't like the woman her son had chosen.

"Let me see if I understand you. You want me to find your son when you know where he is, or at least that he ran off with a woman. Is that correct?"

"Right," Walter said with a slight smile of approval.

It was obvious by the look on his face that he was pleased I had a grasp of the situation. However, I wasn't so sure I understood any of it.

"How old is your son?"

"He's twenty-four," Mrs. Endicott said with the smile of a proud mother.

"He's twenty-four?"

"Yes," Walter confirmed.

"Don't you think he's old enough to make his own decisions?"

"Yes, of course, but, you don't understand," Mrs. Endicott said.

"Apparently you're right. Why don't you explain it to me?"

"The woman he ran off with is about forty years old. She is after him for his money, and we believe she will do him harm in order to get it."

Finally, there was a reason for me to take an interest in them. I was also beginning to understand their concern.

"What makes you think that? Have you received a ransom note, or a call demanding money?"

"No, but the woman he ran off with will not tell us where he is," Walter said angrily.

"So you have been in contact with the woman in question?"

"Yes. We think she is holding him somewhere against his will," Mrs. Endicott explained. "She won't let us talk to him."

"Did you ask the woman why she wouldn't let you talk to him?"

"Yes, of course. She said he didn't want to talk to us," Walter replied.

"And that was not a good enough answer for you, right?"

"Right," Walter said.

"Look at it from my point of view. You have a son who is old enough to be responsible for his own actions. He runs off with a woman who is, what, about fifteen years older than he is? He, or should I say the woman, says he doesn't want to talk to you, which may or may not be true. Am I right so far?"

"Yes," Walter said reluctantly after giving it some thought.

"Now the way I see it, your son may be doing something you think is foolish, and it may very well be. But unless you have good reason to believe he is in danger because of this woman, I don't see that there's anything I can do for you."

"But we have reason to believe he is in danger," Mrs. Endicott said, her eyes pleading for help.

"And what might that be?"

"Our son, Jonathan, took every cent he had out of his savings account the day he disappeared. He also withdrew a large sum of money from the business account of the dealerships he was managing for me," Walter said.

When large sums of money are involved, it becomes a lot easier for me to understand their concern.

"How much money are we talking about?"

"Over two hundred and fifty thousand dollars. A hundred and fifty thousand of it came from the business."

"I see."

"I don't care so much about the money; but if I get audited, the missing money will point directly at my son. He will be branded an embezzler. My partners will not like that. You see, Mr. Blackstone, I could be in serious trouble with my partners. The entire business could be in financial trouble if it were to leak to the press."

It appeared to me that his son was a thief, but I got the feeling there was more to it than that. If his son was branded a thief, it could possibly damage Walter's reputation. Walter struck me as the kind of a man who would do just about anything to protect his reputation.

"Which dealership did your son manage?"

"The Toyota, Lexis and the VW dealerships here in Denver."

"You said you talked to the woman. Where did you talk to her?"

"I talked to her on the phone. I tried to reason with her, but she hung up on me."

"By reason with her, do you mean you tried to buy her off?"

"I guess you could call it that. I offered her ten thousand dollars to let me talk to him," Walter said.

"I take it she refused?"

"Yes, and that's what has us worried," Walter replied.

"Do you know where the woman lives?"

"I believe she lives somewhere around Frisco. We're pretty sure of that."

"What makes you so sure?"

"I had the number traced. It's a public phone in Frisco."

Frisco is a small town in the mountains about seventy to seventy-five miles west of Denver. It is located on the western side of Dillon Lake, a rather large mountain lake. Frisco is a tourist town in the summer and a ski resort in the winter. It is known for its many high priced condos. The fact that it is located fairly close to the Denver metro area makes it very popular for the well-to-do.

"What makes you think she might live there?"

"Jonathan said she had a good size sailboat. Where in the mountains is there a lake near Frisco big enough to sail a boat on?" Mrs. Endicott asked.

"Dillon Lake," I replied in agreement. "Have you considered going up there and having a talk with her?"

"We don't know her address," Walter said, then glanced at his wife.

"It wouldn't be very difficult to find out where the woman lives. After all, Frisco isn't a very big town. I'm sure the local police could help you find your son."

"I haven't talked to the police because my attorney told us not to talk to them, or to the woman. He said it could prove to be a problem," Walter explained.

"How could talking to the woman about your son be a problem?"

"Our attorney said if the newspapers get wind of my son taking money from the company, then running off with some woman; it could seriously hurt my business," Walter explained.

I suppose that could be true, but I doubted it would make much difference. Most people paid little attention to what was in the newspaper, especially when it came to making purchases like an automobile. Most people were interested in only the bottom line cost of the vehicle.

These people had been given some poor advice to my way of thinking. If I were their attorney, I would have told them to go to the police as fast as they could. The one thing that would concern me the most was once the woman got hold of Jonathan's money, his life wouldn't be worth a plug nickel.

"How long ago did Jonathan disappear with this woman?"

"A few days ago," Walter said.

I tipped back in my chair to take a minute to think about it.

MR. AND MRS. ENDICOTT seemed like nice enough folks, so I decided I would look into what had happened to their son. I sat up and leaned forward, putting my elbows on my desk. I looked at them for a moment before saying anything.

"I will look into it for you, but I have some conditions."

From the look on Walter's face I was sure he was not used to anyone giving him conditions, especially when he was paying the bill.

"What are your conditions?" he asked suspiciously.

"First of all, I don't want a word to anyone that I'm looking for your son. I especially don't want your attorney to know you even talked to me. Is that acceptable?"

"Okay, Mr. Blackstone," Walter agreed. "What else?"

"Secondly, I want to know everything you know about the woman. Do you have a photo of her?"

"Yes, but it is not a very good one. She had her head turned to the side," Walter said.

"I think it was intentional," Mrs. Endicott added.

"I still want the picture of her. I also want a recent picture of your son."

"I'll get them to you," Walter said.

"Good. I have to tell you right up front this will not be cheap. I will need a substantial retainer. I'll need to rent a vehicle fitting of the area, something big enough to tow my sailboat. And I'll need to rent a condo on the lake."

"I understand," Walter said as he nodded his head. "Would a new Chevy Tahoe work for you?"

"Yes. It would work fine.

"Okay. You can pick one up at my dealership in Fort Collins tomorrow morning. I'll make it look like a cash deal so no one will suspect anything. I'll have the pictures then."

Walter understood the importance of appearance. He knew the importance of making me look like I belonged in such a high priced, high-class area.

"How much of a retainer will you need?"

That was another thing Walter understood, money talks. He was ready to get things rolling, and he wanted the bottom line with no haggling.

I took a few minutes to explain what my fees were and what I needed as a retainer in order to get started. He didn't hesitate one second. He took his checkbook out and wrote a check for exactly the amount I asked for.

"The check is from my personal account, an account no one working for me ever sees. Take it to the Wells Fargo Bank in Fort Collins. I'll let them know you are coming."

"Fine. Remember, not a word to your attorney. I don't trust anyone who does something that doesn't make sense."

"Do you think he might know what's going on?" Mrs. Endicott asked.

"I don't know."

"If I find out he knows what's happened to Jonathan, I'll kill him myself," Walter said angrily.

"I don't want you to do anything," I said firmly. "He might be looking out for the business and that's all. For now, treat him as you have in the past. Understand?"

"Yes, I understand," Walter said, but he didn't look like he really wanted to.

"Mrs. Endicott?"

"Yes, I understand."

"Good. If I find out he knows about me working for you, I'll pull the plug on this and go home."

"We understand, Mr. Blackstone," Mrs. Endicott insisted.

"Now, I will be in touch with you at your home. I will not contact you at your office except to pick up the Tahoe tomorrow. I'll call you as soon as I get established to let you know I'm working on it. I'll call you every couple of days after that unless, of course, I have something important to report. I will let you know about your son as soon as I know something myself. Okay?"

"Okay," Walter replied.

"I also want you to go about your daily routine as if nothing has happened. That is very important."

"We understand, Mr. Blackstone. No one is to know," Walter reiterated.

"Okay."

"I'll see you tomorrow at your dealership," I said to Walter as I stood up. "Act as if you were expecting me."

"Right."

"Thank you," I said.

Walter and Mrs. Endicott stood up. We shook hands, then they left my office. I watched them as they walked out the door.

ONCE THE ENDICOTTS were gone, I returned to my desk, sat down and leaned back in my chair to think. I had no idea what it was I had gotten myself into, but I knew it would most likely prove interesting.

After so many years as a private investigator, I had grown used to people not telling me everything I needed to know. I had the feeling it was no different this time. Walter and his wife were keeping something from me. The problem was I didn't know what it was, or what bearing it might have on the case.

I looked at the check Walter had given me. He had written it out without so much as a twitch of an eye. There was no doubt the check was good. If he could whip out a check without blinking an eye, he could probably find the money to replace what Jonathan had taken. If he did that, he could go after the woman without any concerns over what his partners thought, nor would he have to worry about an audit.

Unable to come up with any good reason for Walter's actions, I decided the best place for me to start would be at the dealerships Jonathan had managed. The best person to start with was Jonathan's secretary. Often, the secretary knew more about the boss than anyone else.

I took the elevator down to the parking garage in the basement, got in my car and headed for Broadway. It was not a long drive, but it was long enough to give me time to think about how I was going to approach his secretary and how I would explain why I was there since I was not there to buy a car. What I found out at the dealership might set the tone for the entire investigation. It might give me some idea of what I was getting myself into, and what problems I might have to deal with along the way.

CHAPTER TWO

AS I DROVE ONTO THE SALES LOT of the Toyota and Lexis dealership Jonathan Endicott had managed, I noticed the VW dealership was next door. The building was the same style and design as the Toyota dealership, which sort of made sense. Walter had said his son managed both of them. It was easy to see where it would be possible since they were so close together.

I no more than got out of my car when two salesmen came charging out of the showroom. The one who got to me first was a tall young man wearing a dark tie, white shirt and dark slacks. His hair was combed back and he looked a little too perfect.

"Good afternoon, my name's Frank. I'm sure we can find the perfect car for you. You look like the sporty type to me. We have some great deals on some of the hottest cars around, and I'm sure we can find one just right for you," he said, hardly taking a breath.

He had one of the stupidest grins I had seen in a long time. It made me wonder if he had attended smile school. If he had, my guess was he failed "Smiling 101".

"Whoa, hotshot. Not so fast. I'm not here to buy a car. I'd like to talk to the manager."

"Oh," he replied as the phony smile faded away like melting ice on a hot summer day.

"Where will I find him?"

"I don't think he's in, but you can check with the secretary. She's in the office on the north side of the showroom," he said.

"Thanks."

I went inside and walked across the showroom to where the offices were located. There were several salesmen sitting in the lounge area watching me. They were waiting for some poor guy to come in so they could browbeat him into buying a car he probably didn't really want. Since I had shot down the first salesman, the others didn't seem to have a great deal of interest in talking to me.

However, I did notice one of them watching me as I walked across the showroom floor to the offices. He seemed to be taking a special interest in me.

In the office there was a nice looking woman in her mid-to-late thirties sitting at a desk behind a counter. She was busy talking on the phone, but managed to look up at me and smile.

She was wearing a very pretty sundress. From where I was standing, I would have had to have been blind not to notice how nicely she filled out the dress.

I watched her as she wrote down something on a piece of paper before finishing her conversation. I got the impression she was very capable at her job. She hung up the phone, stood up and walked over to the counter.

"May I help you?" she asked.

At least her smile looked more like the real thing. It was friendly and looked sincere.

"I hope so. I'm looking for Jonathan Endicott. Is he in?"

The smile faded from her face. I had to wonder if she might know something, but didn't know if she should say anything. I was hoping I could get whatever she knew out of her without telling her too much.

"I'm sorry, but Mr. Endicott is not in right now."

"Oh. Do you know when he will be back?"

"No. Is there something I can help you with, or would you like to talk to someone else?" she asked very business like.

"I'm an acquaintance of his from college."

She looked as if she didn't quite believe me.

"I can see you find it hard to believe since Jonathan is much younger than I. I didn't go to college until after I served several years in the military. I used the GI bill to get my education."

"Oh," she said as the smile returned to her face.

It seemed my explanation had satisfied her. She appeared to relax a bit and the tension seemed to disappear.

"Can you tell me where I might find him?"

"I really don't know where he is."

"Do you know when he will be back?"

"No, I don't. I'm sorry."

I was getting the impression she really didn't know anything that would be of help. I thought being his secretary she might know something, but it was not the first time I had been wrong. I decided it might be best if I left before she started asking a lot of questions.

"I was in the area and thought I would stop in and say 'Hi,'" I said trying to look a bit disappointed.

"Is there a message you would like me to give him when he returns?"

"No. He probably doesn't remember me anyway. We weren't very close. Thanks just the same," I said then started to turn, but stopped.

I couldn't see where giving my number to her would do any harm. After all, if Jonathan called me, there would be no more need for me to look for him.

"Maybe I will leave my phone number. He might give me a call."

She smiled and picked up a pen. I gave her my phone number and told her that he could reach me there, but if I wasn't home he should leave a message. The number I gave her was to my answering machine at home, the one that didn't give any business information. I smiled, thanked her, then turned and headed for the door.

AS I HEADED TOWARD THE front door of the showroom, one of the salesmen in the lounge area got up and followed me. It was the same one who had watched me when I came in. I wondered if he wanted something, but decided to let him make the first move. He didn't say anything until after we were outside.

"Keep walking toward your car," he said softly without stopping.

I didn't turn and look at him. The way he spoke gave me the impression he didn't want anyone to know he was talking to me. Since he had initiated the contact, I would play it his way, for now. There was always the possibility he knew something that might be of help.

"Don't look at me or turn your head. Get in your car and meet me at Perkins down the street," he said as he continued to walk a pace or so behind me.

When I turned to walk to my car, he continued on down the sales lot. It was obvious he didn't want anyone to hear what he had to say, or for anyone to see us talking. I had to wonder why the secrecy. The only way to find out was to do as he said.

As I turned and reached down to open the door, I glanced toward the salesman over the top of my car. He continued walking on down the row of cars toward a new Camry.

I got in my car and drove the few blocks down the street to the Perkins Restaurant. As I drove off the sales lot, a quick look in my rearview mirror showed me that he was going the wrong way to meet me at Perkins. I thought he might be going the long way around to make sure no one would figure out we were going to meet.

I could see no reason not to go to the restaurant and see if he showed up. If he didn't, I was no worse off. The most it would cost me was a cup of coffee and a few minutes of my time. If he did show up, it could prove to be worth the trouble.

AFTER PARKING MY CAR in the restaurant parking lot, I went inside and asked for a table in the back. I was seated away from the windows, but where I could see anyone coming into the restaurant. I sat down to wait. While I was waiting, I ordered coffee.

It was several minutes later when the salesman walked in the door. He stopped and looked around the restaurant before he came over and slid into the booth across from me. He was the one who wanted this meeting so I waited for him to speak first.

"I heard you talking to Mary, the secretary. You're looking for Jonathan Endicott, aren't you?"

"If I am, I don't see what business it is of yours."

"I know who you are."

"Really?"

"Yeah. You're Peter Blackstone, a private investigator."

"Okay, you know me. What's your name?"

"Jess Nolan."

"What's on your mind, Mr. Nolan?"

"Well, I know you are not looking for Jonathan because you were old classmates in college, or because you want to buy a new car directly from him."

"What makes you think we weren't classmates?"

"Because I went to college with Jonathan and I never met you before."

"Do you know every class Jonathan took?"

"As a matter of fact, I do. We majored in the same subjects and took the same classes all the way through college."

"Okay. For the sake of argument, let's say you're right. Why do you want to talk to me?"

"If you're looking for Jonathan, I have some information that might help."

"What makes you think I am looking for Jonathan and that I would be interested in anything you have to say?"

"Because I think Jonathan is in trouble and so do you. He's my best friend and I think his old man has hired you to find out where he is."

"How do I know your information is any good?"

"I've been a friend of Jonathan for a good number of years, since high school, in fact. That should be easy enough for you to check out."

"Okay. Let's hear what you have to say."

"Jonathan has been gone from work for almost two weeks. He's never been away that long without being on vacation, or having a damn good explanation."

"How do you account for his sudden disappearance?"

"Jonathan has a good head for business and does a damn good job of running the two dealerships. Jonathan could sell an ice cube to a freezing Eskimo, and he can run a business as well as anyone and better than most. But when it comes to women his judgment goes to hell."

"How so?"

"A couple of months ago we went to a sports bar in Larimer Square. We were watching a game on the big screen TV when a rather sexy woman came up and started flirting with Jonathan. She made a play for him and he fell for it hook, line and sinker. I tried to tell him that she was hustling him, but he wouldn't listen. He fell pretty hard for the woman and they started dating. That was two months ago."

"Was the sports bar a place you visited often?"

"Yeah. After that night she started coming into the office at all times of the day. Whenever she came in, Jonathan would drop what he was doing to talk to her. Sometimes he'd leave with her in the middle of the day. He even provided her with a new car and would go out with her every night after work. It wasn't more than a week or so and she had moved in with him. I could see where it was going."

"And where was it going?"

"He was going to give her everything she wanted; and when she got all she could get out of him, she would dump him for her next sucker."

"That sounds pretty cynical?"

"Maybe, but I've been there."

I wasn't sure what he meant by that comment, but I was not interested in his life experiences. I was interested in Jonathan.

"Tell me about the woman."

"She had a figure any eighteen year old girl would kill for, but she was hardly eighteen. She had to be in her late thirties, but probably more like forty. She had at least fifteen years on Jonathan.

"There was no question she was pretty. She had long blond hair fresh from a bottle, dark brown eyes and expensive clothes. She knew how to play a guy like Jonathan. It was obvious to me that she had been around the block a few times."

"What do you mean a guy like Jonathan?"

"Jonathan didn't have much experience with women. He was an easy mark for a broken heart. He had been burned several times in college. Unlike most of us, he never seemed to learn from it."

"Did this woman give a name, or did Jonathan tell you what her name was?"

"He said her name was Bonny Ford and she lived in Littleton. I tried looking her up in the phone book, but I didn't find any Bonny Ford, or anything even close in Littleton or in the entire Denver area. I told Jonathan, but he just got mad at me for sticking my nose into his business. All I was trying to do was to get him to see what was going on. You know, see what he was getting himself into."

"That can happen when a guy doesn't want his bubble busted. Did you happen to find out where she might live?"

"No. After Jonathan told me to mind my own business, he wouldn't have anything to do with me. The only time he talked to me was when it involved work. I know he's in trouble. I just hope it's nothing too serious."

"How do you know he's in trouble?"

"His old man was in last week. I could tell by the look on his face that he was mad as hell about something. I don't know why he was so mad, but he was."

"Did he talk to you?"

"No. Hell, he wouldn't talk to me unless it had something to do with selling cars."

"Does he know you and Jonathan are friends?"

"Sure. He thinks Jonathan gave me a job because we're friends. It's not true, of course."

"How are you doing? I mean as a salesman?"

"I'm one of Jonathan's top producers. Before this all happened, Jonathan was going to promote me to Sales Manager."

"And now?"

"I don't know. If I wasn't such a good salesman, I think the old man would fire me. One thing about the old man, he would never fire a good salesman unless he stole from him. He would probably hire the devil himself if he could sell his cars.

"I think since Jonathan and I have been such good friends for so long, the old man thinks I had something to do with Jonathan falling for the woman. I didn't, but that doesn't seem to matter to him."

"He hasn't talked to you at all about it?"

"No, not a word. Like I said, he probably thinks I introduced the woman to Jonathan."

"Did you?"

"Hell, no."

"Have you tried to talk to Mr. Endicott?"

"The old man? No. What would I say? I don't have any idea where Jonathan is, if he is safe or not. If I told him that, it would just confirm what he thinks he already knows. But the truth is I don't know anything about where he is or anything else. He cut me out of his life as soon as he fell for that woman."

I sat and sipped on my coffee as I looked at Nolan over the rim of the cup. The way he acted gave me the impression he might actually be a good friend to Jonathan. It sounded almost like a case of Jonathan not being able to see that Jess was trying to help him.

Yet, there was something else about Nolan that didn't set well with me. He seemed to be telling me more than I would have expected under the circumstances. It was almost as if he was trying to cover his own ass. The only question was why?

As far as Mr. Endicott was concerned, I wasn't so sure he should have dismissed Jess so quickly, if in fact he had.

"Nolan, I think you should get back to work before you're missed."

"Are you going to try and find him?"

The look on Nolan's face gave me the feeling he hoped someone was looking for Jonathan. I found myself wanting to believe he was truly concerned about Jonathan's well being and had been telling me the truth, but I was still leery of him. He seemed to need some reassurance that someone was going to try to find Jonathan, but I wasn't sure what he really wanted to know.

"I don't want you to say anything about our conversation to anyone. You go back to work. If you find out anything or hear anything that might help me find him, I want you to give me a call. Here's my card," I said as I handed him one of my business cards. "If I'm not in, leave a message on the answering machine."

"His old man hired you to find him. Didn't he?"

"Someone did, but I can't say anything more. You make sure you keep your mouth shut. If you have anything to say, you be damn sure you say it to me and only to me. Got it?"

"Yeah."

"If Jonathan should get in touch with you, I want to be the first to know about it. Got it?"

"Yeah, I've got it," he said, the look on his face let me know he seemed to be relieved, about what I wasn't a hundred percent sure.

I watched Nolan as he got up and left the restaurant. I stayed behind and sipped the coffee as I thought about what had transpired. I had learned Jonathan had been gone for two weeks. That fact had been left out of the conversation with Mr. and Mrs. Endicott. They had said he disappeared a "few days ago." Someone was lying to me.

The more I thought about it, the more I was convinced my next move was to get set up at Dillon Lake. It would take me a day to get everything ready.

The one thing I would need to do now was to get hold of a Real Estate agent and rent a condo on Dillon Lake. I knew just the Real Estate agent to contact.

I left the restaurant and headed back to my office. I couldn't help but think Nolan was hiding something from me, but I had nothing to go on but my gut feeling.

AS SOON AS I ARRIVED at my office, I placed a call to Marcy Hillman at her Real Estate office in Centennial. Marcy and I had a history. We knew each other quite well. We had been friends for a good number of years. I was there to give her a shoulder to cry on when she went through a messy divorce.

In the settlement, she got their condo on Dillon Lake. It would be the perfect place for me to operate from and to tie up my boat, if she would let me use it. I was familiar with the condo since I had been there on several occasions. It was nicely furnished and it was in the ideal place for what I needed.

"Marcy, how are you doing?"

"Peter?"

"Sure is."

"It's good to hear your voice. It's been ages."

"It has and I'm sorry about that."

"How are things going for you?" she asked.

"Well, that's why I called."

"What's the matter? Is there something wrong? How can I help?"

"Nothing's wrong," I said smiling to myself.

"You don't call me for nothing. What's up?"

"Marcy, I need a favor."

"You know anything I have is yours. What do you need?"

"Would you consider renting your condo on Dillon Lake to me for a little while?"

"Sure. How long do you need it?"

"I'm not sure. It could be for a month, but hopefully not for more than a week or so."

"Sure, but you don't have to rent it. You're welcome to use it anytime. Can I ask why you need it, or is it a secret?" she asked with a hint of playfulness in her voice.

"It's no secret. I'm working on a case that will take me to Dillon and Frisco. I need to look like I have money to burn and your condo fits the bill nicely."

"Yes it does. You have to admit my ex was good for something," she said with a hint of sarcasm.

"I'd like it by tomorrow evening."

"Sure. I didn't have any plans to use it unless you want me to join you for a couple of days. I'm sure I could get away."

"That's a very tempting offer, but I think under the circumstances I better go alone."

"Oh," she said with a hint of disappointment. "You want me to bring you the key, or would you like to stop by and pick it up?"

"I was thinking more along the lines of dinner tonight, if you're available. My treat, of course."

"Sounds like a great idea and I would love to, but I have an early evening showing."

"We could have a late dinner. Say at eight o'clock at The Broker."

"Oooh, that does sound delicious and the time would be perfect. I'll meet you there?"

"Great. I'll be there."

"See you at eight," she said then hung up.

I took a couple of minutes to call for reservations at The Broker Restaurant. After thumbing though my mail and finding nothing of any real interest, I headed for home.

Once at home, I took a few minutes to listen to the evening news, then took a long warm shower, shaved, then started getting ready to meet Marcy.

WHEN IT WAS TIME to head out to the restaurant, I left my apartment and drove over to The Broker Restaurant. It was located in the downtown area and considered one of the best restaurants in Denver. Once inside, I was shown to a table. I ordered a drink and waited for Marcy, but I didn't have long to wait.

Marcy came strolling across the room toward the table in her usual graceful manner. It had been a long time since I had seen her and she looked great. She took long strides on her long shapely legs. Her brown hair with reddish highlights flowed out behind her and her deep brown eyes sparkled as she smiled at me.

The dress she was wearing didn't look like something she would wear to show a piece of property. It had a deep V-shaped neckline, thin shoulder straps and open back. The soft material clung to her shapely body. She had obviously taken the time to run home and change. I had to admit I was impressed at how nice she looked. From the looks on the other men's faces in the restaurant, I wasn't the only one who took notice of her. I stood up and held a chair for her as she gracefully moved up next to the table.

"You look fantastic," I said as I watched her sit down.

"You don't have to say that. I've already told you that you can use my condo," she said with a smile. "But I like the way it sounds."

"You do look fantastic," I said as I sat down. "Are you hungry?"

"I'm starving, but I would like a drink first."

I motioned to the waiter. After ordering her favorite drink, I leaned my elbows on the table and looked across the table at her.

"How have you been?" I asked hoping she would hear my concern for her.

"I'm fine. My business is going well. The prices of houses are up and they are selling. Life is good."

"You know what I mean."

"Yes. I do. I get a bit lonely from time to time. I really miss having you around. It's been a long time," she said softly, than added, "Too long."

"It has been a long time," I agreed.

"But not too long?" she asked as she looked into my eyes.

"I wouldn't say that."

"I could get to like having you around, you know."

"Maybe for a little while, but you know as well as I do we're not really suited for each other on a long term basis."

"Maybe, you're right. We are great friends," she said with a big smile. "I would hate for a change in our relationship to ruin that."

"So would I. Are you ready for dinner?"

"Good idea since I could eat a steer right now."

I again motioned for the waiter. He came over to our table and took our order. As soon as he left, Marcy leaned forward and looked at me. Her eyes sparkled in the candle light.

"What can you tell me about the case you're working on?" Marcy asked.

"Not much. I can tell you it's about parents who think their son has taken up with the wrong woman."

"That's nothing new. How old is the son?"

"Mid-twenties."

"Don't they know he's old enough to make his own mistakes?" she asked.

"I told them, but there seems to be more to it."

"How so?"

"They think the woman is after his money and possibly some of the old man's."

"Mothers of sons always think that of every woman their sons date."

"Maybe, but in this case there's a chance their son is in danger of giving up more than his money, possibly his life."

"Oh. I guess I don't really want to hear about it after all."

Marcy had never been one who wanted to hear anything even a little bit unpleasant, but I couldn't blame her. She had had enough unpleasantness in her life.

The arrival of our dinners couldn't have been planned any better. Our conversation ended and we immediately began to eat. The way we dove into our meals was a sure sign we were both hungry. After we finished dinner we sat back for after dinner drinks.

"Tomorrow I have to get a SUV in Fort Collins and cash a retainer check. Are you busy in the morning?"

"Not really. You want me to take you to Fort Collins?"

"In your fancy new Cadillac?" I asked. "It tends to make a good impression."

"It does do that," she replied with a smile. "I would be pleased to take you to Fort Collins in my "fancy new Cadillac", if you like."

"Can you pick me up in the morning?"

"Sure, but I have a better I idea. Why don't you just spend the night with me? It's been a long time since we've spent a night together," she said, looking into my eyes hopefully.

The thought of the last time we had spent a night together flashed through my mind. It was right after her divorce and she needed someone to hold her. She spent a lot of time crying, and I spent a lot of time just holding her until she cried herself to sleep. We spent most of the next morning making love.

"I don't think it's a good idea. I have a lot to do before I'm ready to go to Dillon. In fact, I have a lot to do tonight."

"I understand. What time would you like me to come by for you?"

"About eight?"

"In the morning?"

"Yes," I said with a grin.

"I have to get up that early?"

"Too early for you?"

"Not really. I'll pick you up at eight," she said with a grin.

"Thanks. I really appreciate it."

I watched her as she downed the last of her drink.

"You ready to go," I asked.

"I think so. I have a few things to do tonight myself."

I motioned to the waiter for the check. As soon as I paid the check and left a tip on the table, I walked Marcy to her car and opened the door. As I stood back holding the door, she walked up, leaned over the door and kissed me lightly on the lips.

"Thanks for being so understanding. You truly are a good friend, my very best friend," she said softly.

"Thanks, and thanks for being my friend."

She smiled, leaned over again and gave me another light kiss only on the cheek this time, then gracefully lowered herself into the driver's seat. She looked up at me and smiled as she slipped the key into the ignition and started the car.

"I'll see you tomorrow morning," I said.

"At eight o'clock," she said with a smile.

I closed the door and stepped back. She backed out of the parking space and started out of the lot. I watched her as she turned out onto the street and headed toward her high-rise apartment building downtown.

As soon as she was out of sight, I got in my car and headed for my place. The drive to my apartment seemed to be a little more pleasant than usual. Maybe it was because I had done what was right. I can't say I did it to be noble, but it was right.

When I got home I slipped into something comfortable. I spent the rest of the evening packing some of the things I would need in Dillon. After getting everything ready, I went into my bedroom and got ready for bed.

As I slipped in between the sheets, I thought about Marcy and how fantastic she looked. Spending a night with her would have been a pleasure, but the last thing I wanted to do was to spoil what we had as friends. Besides, I had a woman in my life right now who loved me. The last thing I wanted to do was to hurt her.

CHAPTER THREE

Marcy arrived at my place right on time and insisted I drive. I got behind the wheel of her Cadillac and headed for Interstate 25 north to Fort Collins.

Traffic southbound into Denver was pretty heavy and moved slowly in the morning, but the northbound traffic out of the city moved along fairly well. It took a little over an hour to get to Fort Collins and another fifteen to twenty minutes to find the Wells Fargo Bank.

Marcy waited in the car while I went inside. I introduced myself to a woman who looked like she knew her way around the bank. She immediately took me to one of the officers of the bank.

The check Walter Endicott had given me was cashed without comment. I had most of the money wired to my business account in Denver. Thanks to modern electronics, I didn't have to wait very long for confirmation that it had been received and deposited into my account. The balance of the retainer I took in cash.

As soon as I was done at the bank, we drove to Walter Endicott's Chevy Dealership. Driving up in Marcy's new Cadillac and walking into the dealership with such a stunning woman on my arm tended to make the salespeople take notice. I could see the dollar signs in their eyes. Little did they know I was there for a vehicle, but they would never see the commission from the sale of it.

"May I help you, sir," a middle-aged man in a sport coat and tie asked.

"Yes. I would like to talk to Mr. Endicott, please. I believe he is expecting me?"

"Yes sir. Right this way."

The salesman led me to Endicott's office. As we walked in, Walter stood up and looked at Marcy, then at me. I got the impression he was not sure how much he should say in front of her.

"Walter, this is my friend Marcy Hillman. Marcy, this is Walter Endicott."

"Nice to meet you, Ms. Hillman," Walter said as he reached across the desk to shake her hand.

"Nice to meet you, too. You may call me, Marcy," she said with a smile that would melt butter.

"Very well, Marcy," Walter replied, then he looked at me.

"You can speak freely in front of her, Walter. Why don't we take a walk around the lot while we talk? That way your salespeople won't get too suspicious."

"Good idea."

"Marcy, would you mind waiting here for us?" I asked.

"No, not at all."

"I'll have some coffee brought in for you," Walter said.

"Thank you."

On the way out to the lot, Walter stopped by his secretary's desk and asked her to see what Marcy would like in her coffee and to get it for her. She smiled politely and got up while we went on outside.

"Have you decided on what you would like?" Walter asked.

"I think we decided a Tahoe would be a good choice, so let's look at some of those," I said more for the benefit of the salespeople who were standing around.

"Right this way," Walter said with his most professional smile.

Walter guided me out of the showroom. We walked toward a row of Tahoes. He appeared a little nervous as he kept looking around, presumably to make sure there was no one in hearing distance of us.

"Have you heard anything from your son or the woman he is with?"

"Not a word," he replied, disappointment showing in his voice.

"Do you have the pictures for me?"

"Yes."

He looked around again to make sure no one could see him before he reached inside his coat pocket and pulled out the pictures. I took them and slipped them into my coat pocket without looking at them.

"Thank you. If you hear anything, I want you to give me a call at this number," I said as I handed him one of my cards. "It is to the answering machine in my office. I will check it everyday."

"Do you think you will be able to find him?"

It was a good question and I could hear the worry in his voice. There was no guarantee that I would find his son. And if I did find him that he would be alive. I needed to convey that to Walter as gently as possible.

"Frankly, I don't know, Walter."

"You don't know?"

"No. I don't know. I'm sure you would rather I be honest with you than to lie to you. I don't know if I can find him. All I can do is to do my best, and I will certainly do my best. Now if that's not good enough for you, we can call the whole thing off right now. But I want to make it clear, once I start, I finish. Is that clear?"

"Yes. It's clear. I guess I can't ask for anything more than that."

"Good. As long as we understand each other."

"I understand, Mr. Blackstone. I guess I'm worried about my son."

"Like I told you before, I will be in touch with you every couple of days unless I have something important to tell you."

"I remember."

Just at that moment I saw a dark metallic blue Tahoe that looked expensive. It had all the trimmings including a trailer hitch, something I was going to need.

"I think I would like this one, Walter," I said as I pointed to the blue Tahoe.

"That's a nice one. It looks expensive. I'll have it ready for you in an hour. Do you want to wait for it?"

"I'll take Miss Hillman to lunch, then come back for it. It's important this looks like a typical cash deal. Shouldn't we go back to your office and make out some papers?"

"Yes. I guess I'm a little nervous about all this."

"I know this is hard for you, but you have to keep your end together. Don't do anything you wouldn't normally do for someone who pays with a check.

"By the way, I know that you and your wife are worried about your son. I understand. I really do. But it's very important you don't show it. Everything you do has to look as normal as you can possibly make it. Do what you normally do including going home when you normally do, and eating dinner when you normally do."

"Right," he said letting out a long sigh. "We need to return to my office. You give me a check and I'll pretend to call your bank to clear it. Then I'll have them prepare the vehicle while I make out the paperwork."

"Okay. Let's do it."

We walked back to Walter's office and played out our roles. It wasn't long before we walked out of the office. At the front door we stopped and shook hands.

"Thank you for doing business with us," Walter said.

"Thank you for your personal attention. I will be back to pick up my vehicle in about an hour."

"We'll have it ready for you."

I turned around and took Marcy by the arm and led her out of the dealership. We walked directly to her car.

"Now what?" she asked.

"Everything is arranged. So how about we go to lunch?"

"Okay."

After she got in the car and I was walking around to the driver's side, I saw a shop worker walking across the lot toward the blue Tahoe. It looked like everything was working as it should.

I TOOK MARCY TO LUNCH at the Olive Garden on College Avenue. When we were finished, we returned to the dealership where I picked up the Tahoe. I left for Denver with Marcy following behind in her Cadillac.

We returned to Marcy's where I got the keys to her condo. We said brief goodbyes, then I returned to my place to get ready to go to Dillon Lake.

I took part of the afternoon getting my boat out of storage. Since it needed a little work, I gathered up what I would need and put it in the boat. I figured I could get some work done on it while looking for Jonathan. After I packed my binoculars and my camera with its telephoto lens, I also packed an extra gun and ammo. I had no idea what to expect, but I wanted to be prepared for anything.

While getting things ready to leave, I slipped my 9 millimeter automatic in my belt holster. I loaded everything in the Tahoe. As far as I was concerned, I was ready to head for the mountains and Dillon.

THE DRIVE TO DILLON was pleasant and uneventful. It was about dinnertime when I arrived at Marcy's condo in the East Shore Estates. I left the boat trailer hooked on the Tahoe for the night. I figured I could put it in the water first thing in the morning, then spend the rest of the morning messing around with the boat at the marina. It would give me a chance to get some work done on my boat while I looked around. It might also give me an idea of where things were and what the normal activities might be on this side of the lake. In the afternoon, I could go into the town of Dillon and maybe take a trip to the other side of the lake to Frisco.

As I was unloading my suitcases from the vehicle, I noticed a young couple walking out of one of the condos. They seemed to be enjoying each other's company. As they walked past me, the young woman looked me over and smiled. I returned the favor by looking her over and smiling back, but I continued on my way to Marcy's condo.

Once inside, I unpacked my things and put them away. If someone broke into the condo, I wanted it to look like I was living there on a permanent basis. I noticed Marcy must have called someone to get the place ready for me. I was sure of it when I went to the kitchen and opened the refrigerator. It was not only full of food, but there were things she would know I liked. I was glad she knew me so well.

It didn't take much for me to get settled in. Everything I needed except for my personal items were already there. It was now time for me to start the show.

I CHANGED INTO MORE CASUAL attire before getting a steak out of the refrigerator. After firing up the gas grill on the balcony I made a small tossed salad, and poured myself a Heineken. I took it along with the salad and the steak out on the balcony. I tossed the steak on the grill.

"Hi, neighbor," a soft friendly female voice said.

I turned to find a young woman standing on the balcony of the condo next door. She was wearing short shorts and a skimpy halter top, which she filled out very nicely.

"Hi, neighbor," I replied, smiling back at her.

"You just move in?"

"Yes."

"I'm Lora. What's your name?"

"Peter."

"Are you married, Peter?"

"Not that I know of."

"A man with a sense of humor. I like that," she replied with a pleasant smile.

"Well, thank you."

"I noticed a new Tahoe and sailboat in the parking lot. Are they yours?"

"Yes. I just got the Tahoe this morning, but I've had the sailboat for some time."

"Maybe you could take me out on your boat sometime?"

"Maybe."

"I have to go. Maybe I'll see you tomorrow."

"Maybe. I'll be around."

I watched her as she disappeared inside the condo. I turned my attention back to my steak. It was about ready.

As I sat down to eat, I thought about Lora. She was a cute little thing and seemed very friendly. I might find time to take her out on my boat for an afternoon of sailing, but at the moment I had more important things to think about.

The most pressing thing on my list of things to do was to find Jonathan. According to FBI statistics, the chances of finding a missing person diminish rapidly as each day goes by. And in the case of a kidnapping, the longer it takes to find the person kidnapped the less likely he will be found alive. At this time, I had no evidence to support the idea Jonathan had been kidnapped, but I couldn't rule it out, either.

The more I thought about it, the more I was beginning to think it might be a good idea if I paid a visit to the local Sheriff. Showing them the pictures of Bonny Ford, as she called herself, and one of Jonathan Endicott could prove helpful. They might be able to give me an idea where I could find them. Even if nothing came of it, the Sheriff would know I was in the area.

AS I ATE AND THOUGHT about what I needed to do, I watched the marina from the balcony. There didn't seem to be much activity in the evening. It was getting on toward dark and most of the boats had already been tied up in their berths. The lights on the marina were starting to come on lighting up the docks.

Looking out over the lake, I could see a nice sized sailboat with the sails down. It looked as if it was anchored off a point of land. The point looked pretty rocky and steep.

Since I couldn't tell for sure if it was anchored or not, I went inside and got my binoculars. Staying inside the condo so no one could see me and think I was nosey, I looked out at the boat. I could make out the anchor lines from the bow and stern. It was probably anchored for the night.

It had a few lights on, but none of them were inside lights. All the windows and portholes were dark. I could not see anyone on deck. They could have been inside the boat with curtains closed over the windows and portholes. From the angle of the boat, I was unable to make out the name of it.

I set the binoculars on a table and returned to the balcony. I finished my meal while keeping an eye on the boat. When I was done, I took everything inside.

AFTER I HAD CLEANED UP and put things away, I got the pictures Walter had provided me. I sat down at the kitchen table and examined them carefully, using a magnifying glass to see any details that might be important. I actually spent more time looking at the background of the pictures than anything else.

The picture of Bonny Ford was the one I was most interested in. The picture had been taken outdoors. I was hoping the background would give me some clue as to where the picture had been taken. It might help in locating her, or at least in figuring out where she had been. There were no buildings or any other structures in the photo, and certainly nothing in the photo that I was able to recognize.

There was nothing in the foreground of the picture that would tell me where she was standing, either. She could have been on a boat, a dock, or a rock for all I knew. If she had been on a boat, I might be able to find out where on the lake she had been. I wasn't sure how it would help, but it might provide me with a starting point.

As Mrs. Endicott had said, the picture of the woman was not very good. It was of a woman who was standing sideways to the camera. Her shoulder length hair tended to block off most of the features of her face. I had to agree with Mrs. Endicott's comment about the picture. It did look as if she had turned sideways so it would be harder to identify her. Her effort to avoid a good picture almost worked, but not quite.

The woman in the picture had a small dark mark on the side of her face about an inch back from the corner of her left eye. Since it was partially covered by her hair, I couldn't tell how big it was, but it could have been a birthmark. The mark might help to identify her, if I ever found her.

Examining the photo, I noticed her clothes were nothing unusual. It would not be difficult to find any number of women, both young and old who might be wearing jeans and sweatshirts similar to what she had on. There was some kind of writing on the front of the sweatshirt, but I could not make out enough to determine what it said. There was only one letter and part of another visible. There was no logo or emblem that I could see.

I decided to put up the picture for now and take a walk around the condos in an effort to get the lay of the land, so to speak. I put the pictures in the back of a drawer in the kitchen where they were not likely to be found if someone broke in, got nosey and searched the condo.

I LEFT THE CONDO and headed toward the parking lot. While in the parking lot, I checked to make sure my vehicle was locked up. I also checked the cover on my sailboat to make sure it was secure, then headed to the end of the parking lot toward the drive leading to the marina.

The marina was made up of about twenty-five berths with about twenty sailboats tied in them. I walked down on the dock and noticed each berth was numbered. I knew Marcy had two berths, numbers six and seven. They were good sized and my sailboat would fit in well among those already there. I would take my sailboat to the launch area in the morning, then tie it up in one of the berths belonging to Marcy.

The sun had set, but there was still a soft glow in the clear sky off to the west. To the east, the stars were starting to show in the darkening sky. There was a gentle breeze drifting in off the lake and lights were beginning to show up around the lake.

I could hear the soothing sounds as ripples of water splashed gently against the sides of the boats. There was a couple near the end of one of the docks who looked liked they were enjoying the pleasant evening.

When I turned around to head back to Marcy's condo, I looked up at the building. I noticed there were lights in several of the condos, but a number of them were dark. I had no idea how many of them were occupied, but from the looks of the number of boats in the marina I would have to guess most of them.

The quiet of the evening, the soft sounds of the lake and the view across the lake with the flickering lights from the houses and buildings in the distance made for a very pleasant and relaxing evening. The whole picture didn't seem to fit in with the reason I was there. Tomorrow I would start my search for Jonathan and the woman he apparently had run off with.

I returned to Marcy's condo and relaxed for a little while on the balcony. I noticed the lights on the boat anchored off the point had dimmed down as if whoever was there had settled in for the night.

After taking one last look around, I went inside and watched a little television before turning in. The quiet of the area made it very conducive to sleeping. I went to sleep in minutes.

CHAPTER FOUR

I woke fairly early to the sound of some rather pleasant music coming from somewhere outside. After rolling out of bed, I walked over to the open window and drew back the drapes. Out on one of the docks I could see some guy who looked like he was washing down the deck of a small sailboat. There was a radio nearby on the dock. The music was country western which was not my choice, but it wasn't bad.

The sun was up and the sky was clear. The only thing marring the sky was the remains of a vapor trail left by a jet going to some destination in the west. It looked like the beginning of a beautiful day. In fact, it looked so nice I decided to get dressed, have my breakfast, then get my boat in the water. After breakfast I walked out onto the balcony with a cup of coffee in hand to take in the view.

The first order of business was to see if the sailboat was still anchored off the point. It was a little disappointing to discover it was gone. I looked around to see if I could find it, but it was nowhere in sight. I wished I could have gotten the name of it, even if I had no idea why it seemed important.

The time had come to get my boat in the water. It would give me an opportunity to take a look around the marina as well as get a feel for what activities took place around there in the morning.

I drove down to the boat ramp, but quickly realized it was too shallow to put my boat in there. There was a privately owned marina down the road. I had seen ads saying they had the equipment to lift boats into the water, at a price.

It was only a mile or so down the road so it didn't take me long to get there. After talking to the owner of the marina for a few minutes, I towed my boat over to the lift. I watched them as they slung several large web belts under my boat and gently lifted it off the trailer and set it gently in the water. It cost me a few bucks, but they had my boat in the water in less than twenty minutes making it well worth the cost.

After taking my Tahoe back to the condo, I returned to the marina on foot. The walk gave me a chance to see what was on this end of the lake. There were mostly condos and apartment buildings along the shoreline as well as a few small docking areas used by those living there. Although I couldn't see the entire lake, it seemed pretty quiet at this hour. There were only a few boats out on the water.

There was a gentle breeze, which made for a great day to relax while sailing. I untied my boat and started the motor to take it out away from the dock. As soon as I was clear of the dock, I shut off the motor, let out the sail and settled in for a nice leisurely bit of sailing.

It had been a couple of years since I had done any serious sailing. I felt a little rusty at first, but soon got the hang of it again. While my boat had been in storage I had worked on it, but it still needed a good cleaning as well as some minor repairs.

I decided to sail around for a little while and maybe go over near the point. It would be interesting to see what might be on the other side of it.

One of the things I hoped to do was to find out where the picture of Bonny Ford had been taken. It would go a long way in helping me get some idea of where I might find Jonathan and her. I wasn't a hundred percent sure she was even in the area. I only had Walter's information to go on, and it didn't seem to be too reliable.

I didn't have the picture of Bonny Ford with me. Even without the picture I was reasonably sure I would recognize the background from it if I were to see it.

As I sailed past the point, I didn't see anything that would make me think the picture had been taken near there. However, I did see the same large sailboat again. It was now anchored in the cove on the backside of the point. Once again, there didn't appear to be anyone on board.

Sailing on past the stern of the boat, I got a chance to see the name on it. It was the *Crystal Blue*. The name seemed to fit the sailboat as it was painted in bright white with sky blue trim. The name could have been in reference to the crystal blue water it sailed on. No matter why it had that name, it was a very nice and very beautiful boat. It looked as if it might sleep as many as six people comfortably making it considerably larger than my boat, which was only a twenty footer and could sleep four in a pinch, two or three fairly comfortably.

As I glanced back over my shoulder at the boat, I noticed a small white dingy in the distance. It was pulled up on the shore. It was hard to see because of the brush and rocks along the shore, but I guessed that it belonged to the *Crystal Blue* since it was painted in the same colors. I wished I had brought my binoculars with me. The dingy was too far away to get a good look at it without them.

I began to wonder why the boat had been moved from off the point to around behind it. The weather reports had not indicated the weather was about to change making it necessary to move the boat to a more protected area. In fact, it wasn't very far from where it had been. It would have taken a considerable amount of effort to move it such a short distance, then anchor it again. I guess my suspicious nature makes me question why people do what they do.

Unable to answer my own questions, I decided it was probably time for me to head back to the East Shore Estates marina and dock my boat for a while. I hadn't even taken the time to clean up my boat after it had been stored for the past couple of years. Besides, I wanted to outfit it in case I decided to spend a night out on the lake.

I came about and started working my way back toward the condo. It was smooth sailing back to the point. I found I had not lost my touch. Everything I had learned about sailing was coming back quickly.

As I started around the point, I caught a glimpse of a woman coming out of the rocks toward the white dingy. I lost sight of her quickly as I rounded the point. I hadn't gotten a very good look at the woman. I doubted I would be able to recognize her if I saw her again. There didn't seem to be anything special about her, at least that I could tell from such a distance; but I still wondered why the woman would have gone ashore at that location. The shoreline there seemed to be rocky and it didn't look like there would be much of interest in the immediate area. That, along with the fact the woman was in a bathing suit, caused me to wonder what she had been doing in the rocks. It didn't look like a good place to sunbath.

As I approached the East Shore Estates's marina, I took down my sail and secured it, then started the motor and went on into the docks under power. I found the two berths belonging to Marcy and guided my boat into one of them.

After securing the boat to the dock, I began working on cleaning the cabin. It wasn't very dirty, but it hadn't been used for sometime. I also made it a point of observing the other boats while I worked. I took mental notes of where each boat was docked in the marina and who came out to the dock. I got a good idea who owned which boat that way.

It didn't take long for me to get the cabin cleaned up, get the galley squared away, get things stowed in their proper places and make the two main bunks. By the time I was finished, it was getting on toward noon. I felt I could wash down the deck and hull later.

It was time to have some lunch and then pay a visit to the local Sheriff's Office.

I LIKE TO CHECK IN with the local law enforcement when I'm working outside the Denver area. I had found they tend to be a little friendlier if I take the time to let them know I'm in the area and what I'm up to, especially since I carry a gun.

It wasn't very long and I was on my way to Breckenridge, the county seat of Summit County. I found the Sheriff's Office, parked out in front and went in. The Sheriff was in so I asked to talk to him. I waited for the deputy to make sure he had time to visit with me. He apparently did as I was escorted to his office.

I entered his office and found a man in his mid forties with slightly graying hair sitting behind a large oak desk. He was a little overweight, but looked like he was capable of taking care of himself if he had to. He stood as I entered.

"I'm Sheriff Tom Stillwell. How may I help you?" he asked in a pleasant voice.

"My name's Peter Blackstone. I'm a private investigator from Denver."

"Are you here on business, Mr. Blackstone," he asked as he pointed at a chair in front of his desk.

Before I sat down, I handed him my PI license and my concealed weapons permit. He took a moment to look at them before giving them back.

"To answer your question, yes," I said as I sat down. "I'm here on business. However, I would like the fact I'm a private investigator kept quiet if you don't mind. I have no idea who might be involved in my investigation. Until I do, I would like it kept between us."

"Before I agree to that, I would like to know what you are working on."

"That seems fair enough. I'm looking for a man by the name of Jonathan Endicott."

"Walter Endicott's kid?" he asked with a hint of surprise.

"You know him?"

"I know Walter, not the kid. Has the kid done something that should concern me?"

"Not that I'm aware of."

"Then why the interest in him?"

"I can't get into the details, but it seems he disappeared with a woman and his folks are worried about him."

"Isn't this something for Missing Persons to handle?"

"Probably. It's a little hard to explain, but they want as few people involved as possible. Publicity and all. They don't want the public exposure because of his business."

"I see. What do you want me to do for you?"

"At the moment I don't think there is anything. I like to check in with the local law enforcement agency. However, if you should see him, you might let me know. At this point, all I want to do is talk to him."

"Okay, I'll keep it quiet, for now. But you have to let me know if there's anything going on that concerns this office."

"No problem. I will keep you posted on any developments. If I find proof of anything illegal going on, I will inform you immediately."

"Okay. Is there anything else?"

"I have a picture of the woman he ran off with, and a picture of Jonathan," I said as I reached inside my sport coat and pulled out the pictures. "Have you seen either of them in the last week to ten days?"

I handed him the pictures and waited while he looked them over. He shook his head as he studied each photo.

"I'm not familiar with either of them. The one of the woman isn't a very good photo."

"I know. It could be intentional. I did notice one thing that might help identify her though. There's a small birthmark just behind the corner of her left eye."

"I see it," he said then looked up at me. "Can I take copies of these? I'd like to give them to the deputies working in Frisco and Dillon areas. I'll tell them to just watch for them and notify me if they see them. That's all."

"Sure. That would be great, but I don't want your officers making them nervous. I could lose them forever if they think the cops are looking for them."

"I understand. We'll be discreet."

"Thanks. I'll give you my card. You can get hold of me at this number in Dillon, or through my answering machine in Denver. I will be checking my answering machine usually twice a day."

"Okay."

I thanked him for his time and left his office after he had made copies of the pictures.

I DECIDED TO DRIVE over to Frisco to look around a bit. Near the edge of town was the Smooth Water Marina. It was a privately owned marina with docking and boat storage. It handled repairs to boats as well. There was also a boat supply office.

I saw the *Crystal Blue* moored near the end of the dock so I pulled into the parking lot. I wasn't sure what difference it made, but I sat behind the wheel of my vehicle looking at the boat for several minutes.

I wondered if it might be of interest to find out who owned the boat. A boat as big and as nice as it was would certainly catch someone's eye. Since it was docked there, I figured the owner of the marina would probably know the name of the owner.

I got out of my vehicle and walked down to the boat shop and went inside. There were two men in the shop. The men looked like they might be father and son. Since I needed a couple of things for my boat, I started looking around.

"Good afternoon. May I help you?" the older man asked.

"Yes. I need two four inch cleats and two one and a half inch single pulleys for my sailboat."

"Brass, chrome or plain cast?"

"Chrome, please."

"Be right back," he said and walked over to another area of the shop.

While he was getting the items I had requested, I took the opportunity to look out the window at the *Crystal Blue*. When he returned with the items, I glanced at him and smiled.

"Pretty nice sailboat."

"Yeah, it sure is," he replied as he looked out at the sailboat.

"Do you know who owns it?"

"It was owned by Parker Henry Jones of Denver."

"I've heard of him," I said, but didn't give any indication that I knew him fairly well. "He died a few months ago, didn't he?"

"Yeah."

"Who owns it now?"

"His wife, but she ain't the one using it. I think the ones using it are just rentin' it. They got a letter from Mrs. Jones sayin' they can use it."

"I don't know about you, but I don't think I would let anyone use it if it was mine," I said, wondering if Mrs. Jones would feel the same about it.

"Me, neither. Too nice a boat to be rentin' out to strangers."

"Maybe they're not strangers. Maybe their family," I suggested.

"They ain't family. I know the Joneses, all of them."

"Oh. How much do I owe you?" I asked as I thought about what he had said.

I paid for the parts and started out the door. As I was about to turn toward the parking lot, I noticed a woman come out of the cabin. She stood on deck for a minute or two just looking around before she turned back toward the cabin.

When she turned back around, she looked toward me. I wasn't one hundred percent sure she was looking at me, but I acknowledged that I had seen her with a slight nod. There was no change of expression on her face as she stared in my direction. She did nothing to indicate she didn't like me looking her way. In fact, she did nothing to indicate that she even saw me.

I returned to my vehicle. As I was about to get in, I glanced back toward the boat again. She was still standing on deck looking in my direction. I had been too far away to get a real good idea of how old a woman she was, but I did notice she had a very nice figure. She could have been forty or eighteen for all I could tell from my vehicle.

As I got in my vehicle, I remembered what Nolan had told me. He had said the woman Jonathan ran off with was maybe forty years old, but she had the body of an eighteen year old. Except for the fact that the woman had dark brown hair, not blond, she could have fit Nolan's description.

The problem was how was I going to get close enough to be sure she was the woman I was looking for? I didn't think walking up to the boat and talking to her was a very good idea. Besides, what would I say to her? The best thing for me to do now was to return to the East Shore Estates.

AS I DROVE BACK to the East Shore Estates, I began to think about the dingy from the *Crystal Blue*. I had to wonder why it had been beached below the steep rocky hillside on the back side of the point. The more I thought about it, the more I wondered if the road in front of the condos went around to the point. If not, there might be a road that would go out on the point where I could get a better view. It certainly wouldn't hurt any to take a little drive and find out if there was somewhere I could turn off and get a little closer to the point.

I continued on past the East Shore Estates for about three miles. As I came around a slight curve, I saw a dirt road. It looked like it might go out toward the point. Since I was driving a four wheel drive Tahoe I could certainly make it.

As I turned off the paved road, I hesitated for a moment. I had no idea whose land I would be driving on. I stopped for a minute while I considered my options.

I began to think about what would happen if I was trespassing. If someone stopped me and told me I was trespassing, I could turn around and leave. My desire, or better put, my need to see what was on that side of the lake and on the top of the point was enough to get me to move forward. I figured the worst that could happen was someone would make me leave. I could see no reason not to try.

The road twisted and turned, went up and down hills, through gullies and ravines and in and out of wooded areas for several miles. I didn't seem to be getting any closer to the point, but then with all the turns I couldn't be too sure.

As I came out of a draw with my engine working pretty hard to get me up a short steep grade, I noticed a small shack a hundred yards or so off to my right. Since the road didn't seem to head over toward it, I stopped to study the area for a minute or so. The shack looked a little out of place setting out there in the open.

I was wishing I had brought my binoculars with me, but remembered my camera was on the floor behind the seat. My camera had a high powered telephoto lens. It would be as good as binoculars.

I got out, opened the back door and took my camera out of the box. After putting it together, I aimed it over the hood of my vehicle toward the shack and looked around. All was quiet. There didn't seem to be anyone around. The shack looked as if it had been deserted for a good number of years.

I zoomed in on it with my camera and snapped a couple of pictures for future reference, then set the camera on the seat.

I got back in and drove up the road a little further, but didn't see any indication it went much closer. I decided against driving across the open grassy field toward the shack. Instead, I got out of my vehicle and stood with the Tahoe between the shack and me while I reached under my sport coat for my gun. I checked it before I slipped it back under my coat then started walking toward the shack. I had no reason to believe there was anything dangerous about this place; but it was my nature to be careful, especially since I had no idea what my current investigation might involve and who might be involved.

When I was still a good twenty to twenty-five feet away, I was surprised by a man stepping out from behind the shack. I instantly stopped and looked at him.

He was a tall man in his mid-to-late forties with weathered skin and a thick handlebar mustache like those worn in the late eighteen hundreds. He was wearing a cowboy hat, western style work shirt, jeans and cowboy boots that had seen better days. The thing that impressed me the most was the lever action saddle rifle he held loosely in his hands. He showed no signs of wanting to threaten me with it while still making sure I saw it.

"You lookin' for somethin', Mister?"

"No, not really," I replied calmly.

"Do you know whose land you're on?"

"No. I'm afraid I don't," I replied.

"You know you're trespassin'?"

"As a matter of fact, I didn't. I didn't see any signs when I turned off the road."

"Well, that might be 'cause there ain't none. What do you want? I seen you takin' pictures of this old shack."

"I found the old shack kind of interesting, that's all."

"This old place?" he asked as if I were not too bright.

"I guess if you see it all the time it's not very interesting, but for us from the city it's fascinating."

"You some kind of photographer or somethin'?"

"Not really. Well, I'm sort of an amateur photographer. Can you tell me something about the old shack?"

"Not much to tell. It was an old miner's cabin, so I've been told. Ain't been used for, I don't know, a heck of a long time."

"Oh. Mind if I take a few more pictures of it?"

"No, I guess not," he said after thinking on it for a minute.

I let him know I appreciated his cooperation then turned and went back to my Tahoe. Before I retrieved my camera from the back seat, I quickly removed the telephoto lens and replaced it with a wide angel lens.

As I approached the shack, I noticed he had moved away from it, but he still kept an eye on me. He apparently didn't like the idea of having his picture taken. I had half expected him to move even further away, but he didn't. By putting the wide angel lens on my camera, I hoped to get a picture of him off to the side without him realizing it.

I focused my camera on the shack and took a couple of pictures. With the wide angel lens I was able to get a couple of good pictures of him.

"Would you mind moving over in front of the cabin? I'd like to get you in the picture so it will give some reference as to the size of the cabin. It seems kind of small for a miner's cabin."

"Nay. I don't like my picture taken none. You got your pictures of the cabin?"

"Yes, I believe so."

"Then I'd appreciate it if you'd leave."

"Sure. Can you answer a question for me?"

"I guess." He replied reluctantly.

"How can I get to the point that sticks out into the lake from here? I'd really like to get a couple of pictures of the sunset from there."

"My boss don't like people up here. But if you go back to the road, go about five and half miles maybe six miles on around, you'll come to a dirt road. Take that road to the gate and park there. Then you can hoof it on out to the point. Just go along the ridge. It'll take you out there."

"Is it on your boss's property?"

"Nay. I think it belongs to the Feds. Government land, I think."

"You mean its U.S. Forest Service land?"

"Yeah. A lot of people go out to the point that way. It's a bit of a walk, but it's nice. You could get there from here easier, but my boss don't like strangers on his land."

"I understand. Thanks for your help."

He just nodded, then stood there while I turned and headed back to my Tahoe. As soon as I got in the vehicle, I looked toward him. He was still standing there watching me. It was obvious he was making sure I was leaving.

I started the Tahoe, turned around and headed back the way I had come. When I came up on the other side of the draw, I could see the cowboy in my rearview mirror only now he was on a horse. He must have had the horse hidden in the draw behind the cabin as I had not seen or heard it.

As I drove back toward the road, I had to wonder what constituted a 'lot of people' to him. I got the feeling he didn't see a lot of people back in there.

When I got to the road, I stopped and looked both ways. I was trying to decide which way I should go. I wanted to go out on the point where the dingy had been beached, but doubted I had time before it got dark if it was "a bit of a walk", as he so carefully put it. I decided to go back to the East Shore Estates, develop my film, and get some dinner.

It only took me a few minutes to get back to East Shore Estates. After parking the vehicle, I took my camera and my photo case inside. The photo case contained everything I would need to develop the pictures. I didn't have the equipment with me to make enlargements, but with the help of a magnifying glass I would be able to pick out a lot of the details from the finished photos. If I needed enlargements, I could go back to my apartment in Denver and make them.

I had set up a dark room in the second bathroom. After developing the photos, I hung them on a line strung between the shower stall and the top of the medicine cabinet. While they were drying, I went to the kitchen and made dinner.

IT WAS SUCH A NICE evening I decided to eat on the balcony. It would be a little while before the sun would set over the mountains to the west.

As I took a bite of my dinner, I heard two voices coming from the dock below. The deeper voice sounded very angry while the higher pitched voice sounded scared.

I moved over to the railing and looked down. Standing on the dock near the edge of the lake was the tall blond muscleman I had seen with Lora earlier in the day. He had hold of Lora's arms and was shaking her like a rag doll. When he stopped shaking her, Lora was cowering as if she was expecting to get hit at any moment. He raised his hand and threatened to hit her.

"You better not be lying to me," he said angrily.

"Hey! Why don't you pick on someone your own size," I yelled down at him.

"Mind your own damn business," he yelled back as he looked up.

"You hit her and I'll make it my business."

"Oh, yeah. Well, get your ass down here and we'll see about that."

It was not my nature to butt in where I wasn't welcome, but this was different. If he was going to strike a woman half his size, I wasn't about to stand by and do nothing.

I didn't bother to answer his challenge. I turned away from the railing and headed for the door. On my way, I grabbed my gun from my coat and slipped it in my belt behind my back.

When I came round the corner of the building toward the dock, he had his large muscular arms crossed in front of him in a gesture of defiance, and to make sure I could see how big and muscular his arms were. I'd met muscle bound apes like him before, as far as I could see this guy was nothing special.

Lora was cowering behind him with no place for her to go unless she wanted to get wet. I could see the fear on her face as she looked around him.

"Well, it's too bad you're not as smart as you are brave. Since you want to stick your nose in where it doesn't belong, then I guess I'll just have to rip it off your face," he said with a nasty grin.

"Let her go," I insisted calmly.

"Let her go?" he asked. "Okay. I'll let her go."

Before I could react, he turned around and pushed Lora off the dock into the water.

"Now it's your turn, asshole," he said as he quickly turned back toward me.

I didn't say a word. As he stepped toward me, I reached behind my back, pulled my gun and swung it up in front of his face. He suddenly froze in place. From the look on his face, it had to have been a hell of a surprise to be suddenly looking down the barrel of a gun. It must have looked liked a cannon to him.

"Checkmate, asshole. In case you don't know what that means, it means you lose."

Keeping one eye on him, I took a second to make sure Lora was okay. She was dripping wet, but she had made it safely to shore. Other than the fact she was wet, she appeared to be unhurt.

"Now it's your turn. Back up," I ordered.

I could see the sweat start to run down his face as I stepped toward him. He began to back away, not taking his eyes off my gun for even a second.

"What are you going to do?" Lora screamed from the shore.

"That depends on him. Does he live around here?"

"No. He lives in Frisco."

"I'm going to say this just once," I said softly to him. "If I see you around here again, you will not like the results. Do I make myself clear?"

The big ape didn't answer. I didn't think he could with his heart stuck in his throat, but he did nod.

"If I hear of you even threatening a woman again, any woman, I'll have the Sheriff knocking on your door so fast you won't know what the hell happened. Do you understand?"

Again he nodded.

We had reached the end of the dock and he had no place to go. He looked back over his shoulder then looked down at the water. I didn't say a word. I didn't have to. He knew what was expected of him. He glanced back at me then jumped in. I watched him as he swam off toward one of the other docks.

As soon as he was getting out of the lake at the other dock, I turned around and went back to where Lora was standing.

"Are you all right?"

"Yes," she replied as she looked at me.

Her face was pale and her eyes big. The look on her face led me to believe that she was afraid of me. It didn't make sense.

"You should pick your boyfriends a little better."

My comment seemed to make her regain her composure. She went from calm to being almost hysterical in a matter of seconds.

"You think I should find someone else. Someone who carries a gun? Someone who waves it around to frighten people half to death? You're more dangerous than he is," she screamed.

"Only to the likes of him," I assured her.

I couldn't believe her. I looked at her as if she had gone over the edge. I had saved her from a beating and she was upset with me? Didn't make any sense. As far as I was concerned, the woman was nuts.

I shook my head, turned around and started toward the corner of the building. When I got to the corner, I stopped, turned around and looked at her for a moment before speaking.

"The next time your boyfriend wants to slap you around or beat the hell out of you, you can bet I'll not do anything to stop him. And one day he just might kill you," I said, then turned and continued around the corner.

The old adage of "No good deed goes unpunished" ran through my head.

I RETURNED TO THE CONDO. My dinner had gotten cold. I heated my dinner in the microwave and sat down at the kitchen table to finish it, still unable to understand the woman's reaction.

After I finished eating, I gathered up the pictures I had taken earlier. I spread them out on the kitchen table and began looking through them. One thing I noticed in the pictures I had not noticed when I was at the shack was the lock on the shack's door. The hasp and lock looked almost new. It was shiny, not rusty, like I would have expected based on what I had been told by the cowboy. I was sure I had been lied to, but didn't know why.

Another trip to the shack was in order, but it would have to wait. Right now it was time to get some rest.

I needed to do one more thing before I went to bed. I needed to check and see if the *Crystal Blue* was anchored off the point again.

After getting ready for bed and turning off all the lights in the condo, I went out to the living room. I found my binoculars then went to the balcony window. While in the darkness of the room so I could not be seen by anyone outside, I scanned the lake looking for the *Crystal Blue*, but didn't find it. I knew it could be on the backside of the point, but I had also seen it at the other end of the lake earlier.

During the evening, I had sort of watched out for it but didn't see it again. I put my binoculars on the table, took one last look out over the lake, then turned in for the night.

CHAPTER FIVE

I woke thinking about the old miner's shack and the new hasp and lock on the door. There had to be a reason for a new lock and I wanted to know what it was. There was little doubt in my mind that the cowboy had lied to me about the shack not being used for a long time. He seemed too aware of what was going on in his little corner of the world not to have noticed it.

His boss, if he had a boss, may not have wanted anyone on his property, but I felt there was more to it. Something was being hidden in the shack and I would have bet money he knew what it was.

There was something about the cowboy that made me think he was playing a part. He may have acted like a simple uneducated cowboy, but I didn't buy it. He had to know a lot about what was going on at the shack, and probably had something to do with it. He was there to make sure no one got too close to the shack, and I wanted to know why.

As I sat down to eat my breakfast, I began to think about more than the old shack. There had been the woman and the dingy around on the backside of the point. What had the woman been doing there? Was it possible the woman and the cowboy were in on something together? Had the woman been to the shack?

They all seemed like good questions, but I had no idea who to ask. I also wondered how far the shack was from the beach where the dingy had been beached. I didn't think it was very far, maybe less than a mile.

MY THOUGHTS WERE SUDDENLY disturbed by a soft knock on the door. I had no idea who it could be since there were so few people who knew I was there. I got up from the table and walked to the door, but stopped just as I was reaching for the doorknob. I thought it might be the muscle bound ape I had the run-in with last night. The last thing I wanted to do was to meet him on his terms, especially if he was thinking about getting even for humiliating him.

I retrieved my gun from the closet near the door then walked back to the door. With my gun in one hand, I reached out and quickly jerked the door open with the other. I was ready for almost anything, but I was not ready for what I saw.

Standing in front of the door was Lora, my cute little neighbor, only she wasn't looking so cute. She had a fat cut lip, what looked like a fairly deep cut above her left eye and her right eye was almost swollen shut. I also noticed she was holding herself around the middle as if it hurt her to breathe.

It didn't take much for me to figure out what had happened to her. I took a quick look around before I slipped my gun into my belt and reached out for her. I grabbed her just as she started to fall. I slipped my arm around her and led her inside, kicking the door shut before gently guiding her into the kitchen. She moaned with pain as I helped her sit down on a chair next to the kitchen table.

"Did your boyfriend do this to you?" I asked as I grabbed a towel and dampened the corner of it.

I didn't wait for an answer because I already knew the answer. I knelt down next to her and started cleaning the blood off her face. The look in her eyes told me all I needed to know. He had beaten her and she was remembering my warning. She had come to me because I would understand, and because she knew I could protect her.

She didn't say anything as I cleaned her face except to moan a little and flinch when I touched a tender spot. The big ape had done a real number on her face, but it would heal except for maybe a couple of small almost unnoticeable scars. It was her breathing that worried me the most. It seemed painful for her to breath.

"I think I better take you to the hospital."

"No. Please," she pleaded.

"You could be seriously hurt. You might have some broken ribs, maybe some internal injuries."

"No. Don't take - - me to the - - hospital," she said as tears filled her eyes and she gasped for breath.

"You have a choice, Lora. Either I take you to the hospital, or I call for an ambulance and the cops."

She looked at me with those beautiful blue eyes. I wanted to give in to her, but she was hurting and there was little I could do to help her.

She coughed and the pain it caused showed in her face. It was clear she probably had some broken ribs. She needed more help than I could give her and she needed it now. I didn't wait for her to respond. I reached over, picked up the phone and dialed 9-1-1.

"9-1-1 emergency. What is your emergency?"

"I need an ambulance and the police," I began.

I quickly gave the emergency operator the address to the East Shore Estates and a brief report on Lora's injuries. As soon as she advised me that help was on the way, I explained what had happened. I was instructed to stay on the phone until help arrived, which I did.

The only thing I refused to give the emergency operator was my name. I wasn't ready to let Lora know my last name, not just yet. All she knew was I was Peter.

As soon as I heard the sound of sirens, I hung up and went to the door. The first on the scene a Deputy Sheriff. I let him in and directed him to the kitchen. He looked at Lora, then at me. From the look on his face I got the impression he was wondering if I had been the one to beat her.

"You're looking in the wrong place," I told the officer.

Before I could say anything more, I heard the ambulance come to a stop out in front. I watched them as they got their equipment out of the ambulance. As the two EMT's came in the condo, I pointed toward the kitchen.

I stood back while they went to work on Lora. The officer stood next to me. While I was watching the EMT's, the deputy was watching me. Suddenly, he stepped back as he drew his gun and pointed it at me.

"Hands on top of your head," he ordered nervously.

It took me a second to realize what was going on. I hadn't even thought about the gun in my belt. Since I had no desire to be shot by a nervous cop, I did as I was told. He leaned over toward me. While watching my face, he pulled the gun from my belt and stepped back.

"I have a permit for that," I said calmly.

"Turn around."

I didn't hesitate. After all, he had the gun and I hadn't done anything wrong. I didn't want to give him any reason to shoot me.

The next thing I knew, he was putting cuffs on me. I didn't resist, which gave him no reason to get rough with me.

Once I was cuffed, he turned me around and pointed to the sofa. I moved over to the sofa, sat down and waited for him to decide what to do next.

"Officer, if you ask the young lady if I beat her, she'll tell you I didn't do it. As for the gun, I have a permit to carry a concealed weapon. It's in my wallet."

"You sit there and shut up. I'll get to you later," the tone of his voice showing how angry he was.

He had obviously decided I had done it and that was all there was to it. As for me, I decided I would simply wait until I could call my attorney and let him do my talking.

THE EMT'S HAD FINALLY GOTTEN LORA ready to transport to the hospital when Sheriff Tom Stillwell came in the door. He looked at me, then at his deputy.

"What's going on here?"

"He had a gun in his belt when I arrived. I think he worked the girl over," the deputy said.

"What makes you think he did it?"

"Most the time it's the boyfriend," the deputy said, suddenly not so sure he had made the right decision.

"He is right about one thing, Sheriff, it was her boyfriend that beat her up. I just don't happen to be her boyfriend, but he didn't bother to ask either of us about it."

"What do you know about this, Blackstone?"

The look on the deputy's face when the Sheriff called me by name was priceless. I noticed he had swallowed rather hard as he realized he might have made a really big mistake.

"You mind taking these cuffs off and giving me back my gun," I said. "Then I will answer any questions you have.

The Sheriff looked at his deputy and nodded his head. The deputy immediately took the cuffs off then glanced at the Sheriff. It was obvious he didn't want to give me back my gun.

"Give him his gun," Stillwell ordered.

The Deputy gave me my gun, and I set it on the table at the end of the sofa. I sat down and motioned for the Sheriff to sit down, too.

"Go get a statement from the girl as soon as you can," he instructed his deputy before sitting down. "We'll talk about this later."

The deputy didn't say anything. He simply glanced at me, then turned and left the condo. The Sheriff would probably have a long hard talk with him when they got back to the office.

"Well?"

"I had a bit of a run-in last night with a big blond, muscle bound ape out on the dock," I started out.

I spent the next few minutes telling him about what had happened last evening. He seemed very interested in what I had to say. I also noted he didn't seem too surprised when I described the ape. I got the feeling he had had run-ins with him before, too.

"You know who the guy is?" I asked.

"He's a local bully. His name is Butler, Max Butler. He likes to beat up on women and smaller men."

"What's been keeping him out of jail?"

"It seems everyone's afraid of him and will not press charges."

"I can't press charges against him because I waded in after I told him that he better not hit Lora. However, I would be glad to be a witness as to the threats he made to her last night, but I have a problem."

"What's that?" he asked.

From the look on Stillwell's face, I got the impression he thought I wouldn't want to testify on Lora's behalf. There was nothing further from the truth.

"My problem is with my current investigation I can't risk letting anyone know who I am, at least at this point."

"I understand. I can keep him away from her for awhile."

"I think it would be a good idea. Do what you can. I'll let you know when I can help put him away."

"Good."

"I STILL WANT YOU to keep me posted on your current investigation. Are you making any progress?" Stillwell asked.

"I'm not sure. I ran into some cowboy yesterday. Maybe you can tell me who he is and who he works for?

"Maybe. What's he look like?"

"I've got a picture of him," I said as I stood up and went into the bedroom.

When I returned from the bedroom, I handed the picture of the cowboy standing near the old shack to Stillwell. He looked at it for a moment or two, then looked up at me and smiled.

"This is Henry "Hank" Martin. He doesn't work for anyone I know of. What makes you think he works for someone?

"He told me he was guarding his boss's property when I took the picture. You know who owns that place?"

"That old shack is on federal land. The government owns it."

"Well, isn't that interesting," I said as I thought about what the Sheriff had to say.

"What about the old miner's shack?" I asked.

"What about it?"

"Why would someone put a new lock on it if it was an old shack on federal land?"

"The last time I was out that way, there wasn't any lock on it. There isn't anything to lock up. The building is just about to fall down. The timbers are rotten, the wood floor inside is falling apart and the roof leaks like a sieve. No one in their right mind would store anything in there," Stillwell said.

"I'm beginning to think I should take another look at the shack, only this time I want to see what's inside. Would I have any trouble breaking the lock?"

"Not from me as long as it is not a lock belonging to the Feds. If they locked it up, it should have a warning sign on the building and the lock should be brass with the letters U S stamped on it. You'll have no trouble knowing if it is a federal lock. From what I can see in this picture, it's not a brass lock so it's probably not a federal lock."

"Great. I think I'll go back up there."

"When you planning on going?"

"Soon."

"I have to go check and see if I can get Lora to file a complaint against Butler, or I would go with you."

"I wish you could come along."

"I could meet you there later," Stillwell suggested.

"Good idea."

"I'll see if I can get Lora to file a complaint then come out to the shack."

"Okay. I'll take my time before going."

"I best get going. See you in a little while. You be careful around Hank. He can be down right nasty if he puts his mind to it," Stillwell said as he handed the picture back.

I nodded as I took the picture. I stood there thinking about the cowboy while Sheriff Stillwell left the condo. There was no doubt in my mind I would not only be careful, I would be prepared to meet him next time.

AS SOON AS SHERIFF STILLWELL left, I went back out to the kitchen. My half eaten bowl of Cheerios had turned a bit soggy and my coffee was cold. I took a deep breath, then put my coffee in the microwave and zapped it for a few seconds. As soon as it was hot, I sat down and finished the Cheerios.

I had a lot of questions running around in my head. Why the lock on the shack? What was in there? I had to wonder if there would be anything in the old shack of interest to me. There was only one way to find out.

My thoughts turned to Hank, the cowboy with the rifle. There was no way for me to know if Hank bought my story yesterday or not. If the shack had anything to do with what I was looking into and he didn't buy my story, I'd be willing to bet there was nothing left in the shack by now. If he was smart, he would have cleaned out the whole place, torched it and got the hell out of there.

If he had cleared out of the shack but didn't burn the place down, there was a good chance there would be some evidence left behind. Overlooking a small detail often ends up getting the criminal caught. There was a good chance what was left behind might tell me what he had used the shack for. It might even tell me if someone else had used it.

With my breakfast finally finished, I figured it was time to take a little trip out to the miner's shack. I took my gun off the end table and put it in my belt holster. After gathering my binoculars and my camera and case, I headed out the door to my vehicle.

ON THE WAY TO MY TAHOE, I took a quick look toward the marina. I didn't see anyone out there except for the guy who had been working on a boat for the last couple of days. It didn't seem like he had made very much progress on the deck, but then maybe he wasn't in much of a hurry to get it done. If he was hired to do the job, my guess was he was working by the hour.

I drove out to the road and headed around the lake like I had yesterday. When I got to the dirt road leading back into where the shack was located, I turned in. This time I caught a glimpse of a sign lying on the ground in the weeds near the gate. I hadn't noticed it yesterday, but then it wasn't easy to see and I hadn't been paying as close attention as I should have. The sun was also in a different position in the sky and reflected off the sign.

I stopped to get a better look at the sign. It was an official looking sign stating I was entering U.S. Forest Service land. There was nothing on the sign to indicate that I couldn't continue on.

I stayed on the narrow dirt road as I had yesterday following the twists and turns, and the ups and downs. When I came up out of the deep draw, I could see the shack off to the right. I was relieved to see it was still there.

I stopped and stepped out of my vehicle. The first thing I did was check my gun to make sure it was ready to use. I wasn't about to let Hank get the drop on me again.

The second thing was to get my binoculars out and scan the area. I had no intentions of being surprised again. I saw no one around, but I remembered Hank had come up from a gully behind the shack.

Since I was in the same place I had been when I took the first pictures of the shack, I got out my camera with its telephoto lens and took a couple of pictures of the shack. I immediately noticed the new hasp was still on the door, but the new lock was gone. It was my first clue Hank might have cleared out of the shack. The real question was, is he still around?

I took a couple of minutes to scan the area with both my binoculars and my camera with its high power lens. The only thing I saw was a couple of rabbits running toward the back of the shack. I figured if they were running round back of the shack, it was highly unlikely there was anyone behind the shack.

Since there was no cover between the shack and my vehicle, I decided I would drive a little closer to it rather than risk being out in the open by walking. I got back in and set my things on the passenger's seat and laid my gun in my lap. I wanted it in easy reach just in case.

I drove closer to the shack, keeping my eyes moving. The last thing I wanted was to be surprised.

Driving very slowly, I moved to within twenty yards or so of the shack and stopped. I sat there for a few minutes just looking around before I slowly opened the vehicle door. Keeping the vehicle between the shack and me, I stepped out. As I did, I held my gun in my hand. It was safer if I moved around behind my vehicle using it for cover. I moved out from behind the vehicle and closer to the shack.

Once I was close to the shack, I moved around behind it so I could check the gully. There was no horse. In fact, there was no sign of life at all in the gully.

I turned and continued on around the shack. When I got to the door, I reached out with one hand and took hold of it.

I jerked open the door as I ducked back against the wall in case someone started firing at me. There was nothing. Not a sound.

AFTER WAITING A MOMENT OR TWO, I peered around the door and looked inside. From the doorway I could see the entire inside of the shack. There was only one room and it was empty except for an old rusty metal bed frame against one wall.

Stepping just inside the cabin, I took a few minutes to look around. There were several small cabinets on one wall above a short counter top with a rusty pot sitting on one end. The floor was made of old wooden planks that had rotted through in several places.

The only things out of place were the dark colored pieces of cloth nailed over the two small windows. It was obvious they were rags and that they were not very old. If they had been old, they would have been nothing but a few pieces of faded, rotten cloth hanging in shreds on the nails. There was also the fact that the heads of the nails didn't appear to be rusty as I would have expected.

Before rummaging around the shack, I started looking at the floor. With the door open and the morning sunlight shining in, I was able to see the floor pretty well. The first thing I noticed was the dust and dirt off to the sides of the room and out of any major traffic was relatively undisturbed. Yet, where most people would walk, it was disturbed a great deal.

The new lock yesterday and the absence of it today suggested that someone had been inside recently and probably as recent as yesterday or early this morning. The only questions were who and why?

I needed to examine the shack very closely for something that would tell me what it had been used for. I returned to my vehicle to retrieve my flashlight. While I was there, I changed the lens on my camera so I could take closer pictures.

Once I had gotten my flashlight and the lens changed, I began going over the inside of the shack very carefully looking for clues as to what went on there. I began at the door and carefully worked my way around the floor gradually working my way across the room. I took pictures of every little detail of the inside of the shack including some footprints in the dirt.

There was a post that supported the center beam of the shack. I noticed the floor on one side of the post looked as if it had been cleaned or wiped. More accurately put, it looked like the dust and dirt had been sort of pushed around and away from the post. I knelt down and began studying the pattern of dirt on the floor as well as taking pictures of it. It soon became apparent someone had been sitting on the floor very close to the post. He probably moved the dirt around when he moved in an effort to change his position, probably to get comfortable.

There appeared to be fresh marks on the post just a few inches above the floor. Upon examining the post it became clear someone, or something, had been tied to the post.

I sat back on my heels and looked over the area around the post. The way the dust and dirt had been moved around along with the rope marks on the post, it became obvious that someone had been tied to the post and had tried to get loose.

It was then I noticed a small piece of cloth caught on a rusty nail in a floor board. I bent down for a closer look. I couldn't be sure, but it looked like it was from a shirt. It didn't look like it belonged there. It didn't match the cloth over the windows and looked as if it was new. It certainly was not what I would have expected to find in a shack this old. It was not faded or worn, either. It was torn as if someone had caught it on the nail while struggling.

Someone had been held there against his or her will. I had to wonder if it was Jonathan.

JUST AS I WAS ABOUT to continue my search, I heard a vehicle. I drew my gun and moved close to the door. I let out a sigh of relief when I saw Sheriff Stillwell's car come up out of the draw and turn toward the shack. I stepped out to meet him while putting my gun back in the holster. I watched him as he got out of his car and walked toward me.

"I see you got in okay," he said.

"It was easy. There wasn't a lock on the door when I got here."

"Really? You said there was a new lock on the door."

"There was, but not now. Whoever had been using this place has cleared out."

"Find anything interesting?"

"Oh yeah. I think someone was held hostage here."

"Any idea who?"

"Not that I can prove right now. Come on in and let me show you what I found. Maybe you have some different ideas of what might have gone on here," I said.

I led Stillwell into the shack and showed him what I had found. He seemed very interested in everything I showed him. He even agreed with me that someone had been held there.

We spent the next half hour or so going over the place looking for any additional evidence. Other than the footprints of cowboy boots in the dirt inside and outside the shack, the only other footprints appeared to have been made by tennis shoes of some kind.

I took pictures of the footprints, plus several more of the inside of the shack. I especially wanted pictures of the post and the area around it. A few pictures of the small piece of cloth caught on the floor nail were also taken. I figured the more pictures I took; the less chance there would be we missed something important.

I decided I would take the pictures to my friend, John Farrell, who worked in the State Crime Lab in Lakewood. He might be able to make some sense out of them. I also took the piece of cloth from the nail and put it in an evidence envelope provided by Stillwell.

While I was collecting the small piece of cloth, I noticed what looked like a few drops of dried blood on the corner of the post and at the base of the post. I took my pocket knife and cut a sliver from the post with blood on it and added it to the evidence I would take to John for testing. I also scraped a little of what I thought was probably blood off the floor. I had no idea if what we found was human blood, animal blood, or not blood at all. But I wanted to know one way or the other.

WHEN SHERIFF STILLWELL and I were finished gathering what we thought might prove to be evidence, we went outside. I stopped a few steps from the front of the shack and looked around. Stillwell stopped and looked at me.

"What's on your mind, Blackstone?" Stillwell asked.

"How far are we from the lake?"

"About half to three quarters of a mile, maybe. Why?"

"Which way?"

"Down that gully," he said as he pointed toward the back of the shack. "You going down there?"

"If I follow the gully which side of the point will I be on?"

"Actually, you'll end up at the cove on the back side of the point. The west side," he added.

"I think I'll take a walk down that way."

"Okay, but just before you get to the lake, it gets kind of steep and rocky. It's pretty rough the last two to three hundred feet and along the shore."

I looked at him, then looked toward the gully.

"You got a few minutes?" I asked.

"Sure. Why?"

"You game on going along?"

"Sure, but what are you looking for?"

"Tracks."

"Okay. I'm game, but why?"

"I didn't see any tracks indicating there have been any vehicles around here except for yours and mine. Whatever was in the shack was most likely taken out and down to the lake."

"Makes sense. You think whatever was in the shack might have been dumped in the lake?"

"God, I hope not."

"You think this guy you're looking for, Jonathan Endicott, might have been dumped in the lake?"

"I hope not."

After locking all the evidence we had gathered in my vehicle, we started out. We walked along the trail carefully looking for tracks as we went. It didn't take us long to find footprints in the bottom of the gully where the ground was soft. We actually found three sets of tracks.

One set of tracks were made by cowboy boots which we figured belonged to Hank. They appeared to be going down toward the lake. There was also a set of tracks made by a horse which I believed were made by Hank's horse. Since the horse tracks were over the boot tracks, it was clear the horse had been led down toward the lake.

The third set of tracks were made by soft sole shoes, probably deck shoes from the looks of them, the kind of shoes worn on sailboats. The third set appeared to be small, most likely made by a woman. The tracks showed the deck shoes had gone both ways, but in this case they had come up from the lake and returned back toward the lake. I took time to take a couple of pictures of each set of tracks with a one dollar bill laid beside the tracks. The bill would help make it easier to determine the shoe size. After taking the pictures we continued on down the gully.

It wasn't long before we found a second set of tracks made by the horse. Those tracks showed where the horse had come back up the trail and turned off. They went up the side of the gully. The tracks coming up from the direction of the lake were on top of the ones going down meaning that the horse was returning from the lake. There were no tracks from the cowboy boots returning from the lake. The obvious reason for no boot tracks coming back up from the lake was that Hank had been riding his horse back.

The question that came to mind was why had he walked his horse down and rode him back? The gully was not steep enough that he couldn't have ridden his horse both ways. The answer was easy. There was something on the horse on the way down that was not on the horse on the way back. It could have been any number of things, but I couldn't help think it was a person either sitting in the saddle or slung over it. There were other possibilities, of course, but my nature caused me to think the worst.

Just as the trail started to twist and turn down among the rocks, I found a place where the horse had been tied to a small tree. It was where the trail to the lake got very rocky and became much steeper.

From that point on, it was too rocky to find any kind of tracks. There was no way to follow.

"Looks like we lost them," Stillwell said.

"Yes. We lost them right out there," I said as I pointed out at the cove. "That was where the *Crystal Blue* was anchored the other night."

Stillwell looked around. I had to wonder what he was thinking.

"Pretty good place to anchor," he said thoughtfully. "It's hard to see from anywhere except from out on the lake. From the lake they could see anyone approaching for some distance."

"I was thinking the same thing."

"You thinking this might have something to do with your investigation?"

"My gut says, yes. But I've got no solid evidence to prove it."

"Maybe the evidence we gathered will provide the proof. If you can come up with anything I can use, I'll jump in with both feet and help you any way I can," Stillwell said.

"Thanks. I appreciate it, but right now I'm pretty much on my own. Let's head back."

Sheriff Stillwell simply nodded as we turned and headed back toward the shack. When we got back to our vehicles we parted company. I followed him back to the paved road. He turned right and I turned left. He headed on around the lake while I headed back to the East Shore Estates.

On the way back, I decided I would return to Denver. I could drop off the film and the evidence at the crime lab in Lakewood on my way home. I could also call Walter Endicott from there and tell him what I had so far, which was nothing.

CHAPTER SIX

AS I DROVE ALONG INTERSTATE 70 toward the Denver area, I began to think about what I was going to tell Walter and Mrs. Endicott. At this point in my investigation I had nothing solid to tell them. I still had no idea where their son was, or what condition he was in. The only things I had were assumptions, speculations and a hell of a lot of questions I couldn't answer. Until I had more to say, there was nothing I could tell them except that I'm working on it.

I turned off the interstate at Lakewood and drove directly to the State Crime Lab. When I arrived there, I found John Farrell was busy so I had to wait for a little while.

As I sat in the waiting room with my evidence neatly concealed in the brown paper bag on my lap, I had to wonder what it would prove or disprove. I could think of any number of things from proving Jonathan had been held prisoner to it being animal blood and proving nothing at all. So far my investigation didn't seem to be going anywhere.

My thoughts were disturbed when a door swung open and John came out into the waiting room. I stood up and moved toward him.

"Hi, Pete. What's up?"

"Hi, John. I'm hoping you can help me with a case I'm working on. It just might become a criminal case."

"I take it you have something for me?" he asked as he looked at the bag.

"I do, but I'm not sure what."

"Come on back to my office."

I followed him through the doors and down the long almost sterile looking hall to his office. Once inside his office, he stepped around behind his desk while I sat down in front of it.

"What have you got?" he asked.

"I have a roll of film that needs to be developed. It contains photos of footprints and photos of a possible crime scene. I say "possible crime scene" because we are not sure a crime was committed there. I also have what we believe to be blood evidence and – -,"

"Hold it a minute," he said interrupting me. "What do you mean when you say "we"?"

"Oh. I gathered the evidence in the presence and with the help of Sheriff Tom Stillwell of Summit County. You will find his initials are on the evidence bags along with mine," I said as I handed him the brown paper bag.

"I know Tom. He's a good man. Blood evidence? What kind of blood evidence?"

"I scraped what I believe to be blood from the floor of an old miner's shack near Dillon Lake. I also cut a sliver of wood that looked like it had blood on it from a post inside the shack. It looked like someone might have been tied to the post. I took photos of each area both before and after I removed the samples."

"I take it you have no idea how old the blood is?"

"I'm not even sure that it is blood. If it is, whether it is human or animal," I admitted.

"Tell me what you do know?"

"Damn little at this point, John."

"What are you working on?"

"All I can tell you is a young man is missing, and he could be in real danger if he isn't dead already."

"Do you think he might be dead?"

"At this point, I don't know. I sure hope not."

"Okay. If, and I say IF, your evidence proves to be human blood I can do DNA testing on it. It would be a great deal of help if you can get me a sample of your missing guy's DNA to compare it with. Do you think you can do that?"

"I can probably do that. What do you need? Would his tooth brush, hair brush or comb do?"

"Probably. Can you get those things?"

"I would think so," I replied. "Do you want all of them?"

"It would be best if you could."

"Okay. I'll see what I can do."

"Good. I want you to get them for me as soon as possible. Where can I get in touch with you?" John asked.

"You can call me at this number," I said as I gave him one of my cards.

"Since I have no idea who's involved in what I'm working on, or if anyone knows what I'm working on, don't leave any messages at that number. If you don't get me, call my home number and leave a message on the answering machine. Don't mention who you are or why you're calling. Simply say something like you want to get together to take in a basketball game or some other event that will give me a clue as to when you called. Then I'll call you."

"Okay. I can do that."

"I should be able to get what you need by morning. I'll stop by with it on my way back to Summit County."

"Okay. It will take me a couple of days or so to get this done. It's been a zoo around here."

"I understand, but the sooner the better."

"Sure," he replied as I stood up.

I shook John's hand and left his office. As I got into my vehicle, I realized I had no idea where Jonathan lived. I knew it would not be difficult for me to find out.

It occurred to me that Jess Nolan would not only know where Jonathan lived, but since they had been such close friends he might have a key to get in. My next order of business was to get hold of Nolan.

I WENT DIRECTLY TO MY OFFICE in the downtown area and placed a call to the Toyota dealership where Nolan worked. I got hold of the secretary and she paged him. It didn't take long before he was on the phone.

"Hello, this is Jess Nolan."

"This is Peter Blackstone."

"Hi. Do you have any news about Jonathan?"

"Not yet. I need a favor."

"Sure. What can I do?"

"I take it you know where Jonathan lives?"

"Sure."

"I need to know where he lives and if you can get me in his place? Do you have a key to his place?"

"No, but unless he changed things, he has a key hidden under a turtle next to one of the shrubs in front of his house."

"Good. Can you get away for a little while?"

"I'm out of here in about fifteen minutes. Will that be okay?"

"That'll be good. Give me his address and I'll meet you there."

Nolan gave me the address of Jonathan's house. I was a little surprised to hear it was in a fairly nice family type neighborhood. I left my office and drove to the address Nolan had given me. I pulled up across the street from Jonathan's house.

Since I didn't see Nolan anywhere around, I simply sat in my vehicle and waited for him. I didn't know who I could trust so I decided it would be better if I just waited. The last thing I needed was to have the cops catch me rummaging around in Jonathan's house. At least with Nolan having the key, it would put him in as much trouble. I just hoped he was smart enough to realize that.

The houses along the street were mostly ranch type with attached two car garages. The lawns of most of the houses were well groomed as were the shrubs. It was what I would consider a nice middle to upper middle class neighborhood.

There were basketball hoops on a couple of the garages, and I noticed a few bicycles indicating there were some pre-teens to young teens in the neighborhood.

It was pretty quiet this time of day. I guessed most of his neighbors were in having their evening meal. Traffic on the street was almost non-existent and there were only a few children playing in the drives.

I couldn't help but think that a bachelor would seem a little out of place in the neighborhood. I had to wonder why a young single guy who had money would live there. From what Nolan had told me, Jonathan didn't seem to be the type of guy who would settle down in a family type neighborhood, especially since he could live almost anywhere he wanted. Given the information I had on Jonathan, I would have thought he was more the LoDo condo type. Living in an area where the action and girls could be found, so to speak.

My thoughts were interrupted when I saw a new red Toyota Camry come around the corner. If my memory served me right, it was the same car I had seen Nolan driving when he met me at the Perkins Restaurant. I watched as the car turned into Jonathan's driveway.

NOLAN STEPPED OUT OF THE CAR and stood next to it as he looked around. As soon as he spotted me, I got out and walked across the street toward him. I noticed that he looked around as if he was looking for someone. I had to wonder what he was looking for, or if he was expecting someone.

"Glad you could get away."

"No problem. I was due to get off anyway. I figured if I waited until it was time, no one would think a thing about me leaving," he said.

"Good thinking. Can you get me in?"

"Sure."

I followed him as he walked up to the porch. Instead of going onto the porch, he side-stepped it and bent down next to a bush. I watched him as he lifted a cast iron turtle and took the key out from under it. He smiled as he showed me the key, then stepped up onto the porch. I waited as he put the key in the lock and turned it.

As soon as the door was unlocked, I reached out and took hold of his arm. He turned and looked at me. When I shook my head, he stepped back and made room for me to move past him. I reached under my coat and put my hand on my gun as I pushed the door open. I had no idea what I could expect, but I was not about to take any chances.

The door opened without a sound. I slowly pushed on it until it was wide-open. I could see most of the living room from the doorway. Seeing nothing I should be worried about, I stepped into the living room, stopped and looked around. At first glance there didn't seem to be anything out of place. In fact, the furniture, fixtures, and other small items tended to make the house look like a decorator had gotten it ready to put on the market to sell. I had to wonder if Jonathan was planning on moving.

It wasn't until I looked at the wall where the fireplace was that I noticed something that didn't seem right. On either side of the fireplace were tall wide bookshelves from floor to ceiling. The interesting thing was there were two fairly large areas on the book shelves that were completely empty. The rest of the shelves had a few books, knick-knacks, photographs, and assorted memorabilia. Except for the open spaces on the shelves, the house was clean and orderly.

"Oh God," I heard Nolan say behind me.

The "Oh God" didn't sound as spontaneous as I would have expected if something was really wrong. It seemed a little too smooth, too not surprised, almost as if it had been rehearsed.

"What's the matter?" I asked as I turned and looked at him.

"Jonathan's stereo set is missing. It was top of the line and very expensive."

Nolan started off toward another room, but I stopped him. I didn't want him out of my sight. His reaction was not what I would have expected. I felt it was reason enough not to trust him completely.

"Where are you going?" I demanded.

"To see if any of his other electronics are gone."

"Wait. You stay with me. I don't want you touching anything. You understand?"

"Yes."

"We're going to make a list of what is missing. What other electronics did he have?"

"A fancy computer, a flat screen TV, and another stereo system in his den. All of them very expensive. He has a TV in his bedroom as well."

"Okay. We're going to go from room to room and record everything you can remember that is now missing."

"Okay," he agreed, but seemed a little reluctant to do it.

We started with the living room. He told me what he thought was missing and I wrote it down. I had to wonder what was going through Nolan's mind. He didn't seem like he really wanted to make a list of items that were missing. If he was such a good friend, it would make sense for him to want to be as helpful as possible.

As we were going through the house, I noticed what looked like a heavy duty power cord like those used to hook up a computer, printer, or scanner to a power source. Nolan acted as if he hadn't even seen it. There was little doubt in my mind he had seen it, but chose to ignore it. I wondered why? It got me to thinking he might know more than he's telling me, a lot more. I made a note of the cord, but said nothing about it.

We continued on until we had been through the entire house. I decided it was time to see what might be in the garage. I found the garage to be neat and clean. There was a new Toyota Camry parked on one side of the garage. It didn't strike me as the type of car a young single man would drive. It had dealer tags on it which would indicate he used the Camry for work.

"Anything missing in here?" I asked Jess.

It appeared he was just acting as if he was looking around the garage, and that he already knew what his answer was going to be. I took a minute to look around as well.

"Not that I can see," he finally said.

I didn't believe him. It was a little too obvious that there had been a second vehicle in the garage and it had been there recently. In the dust on the garage floor I noticed tire tracks. The tracks were wide as was the tread pattern, indicating fairly wide tires, tires like those found on some of the larger SUV's.

It was time for me to get him out of there. It was also time for me to find out a little more about Jess Nolan. He had started out trying to convince me that he was really concerned about his friend, but his actions were somewhat suspicious, at least to me.

"I think it's time we get out of here."

"We're just going to leave it?"

"What did you think we were going to do?"

"I don't know. Maybe call the cops."

"Why? We don't know if Jonathan took the missing items with him, or if he was robbed. In fact, we don't know anything."

"I guess you're right."

"Besides, how are you going to explain the fact that you and I are in his house? Remember, we don't have his permission and we sure as hell don't have a warrant. If I recall, you and Jonathan are on the outs. I don't think his father would take it very well that you are in his son's house."

"I see your point," he replied.

Nolan's body language seemed to indicate he was relieved that I was not going to call the police. Why? What was he hiding from me?

We locked up the house then left the way we came in. I watched Nolan get into his car. Although his back was to me, he seemed pleased with himself for some reason. As far as I was concerned it was a good enough reason for me to want to know more about him. I waited for Nolan to leave, then drove around the block.

AS I DROVE BACK TOWARD Jonathan's house, I decided it would be best if I didn't park too close. I drove on down the street past the corner, turned around in a driveway and parked behind a pickup. From where I was sitting, I could see the front of Jonathan's house through the pickup's windows. I could see it well enough to see anyone coming or going, but it would be difficult for anyone to see me from the house. All I had to do was to wait and see if anyone came by.

There was little doubt in my mind that Nolan would return, the only question was when. I had watched him pocket the key to Jonathan's house after unlocking the door, but he didn't put it back when we left. I wasn't sure if it was intentional or not, but I decided to hang around for a little while in the hope of finding out.

I waited for at least an hour before a red Camry came around the corner at the other end of the block where Jonathan's house was located. It was the same Camry Nolan had been driving earlier. As he came toward me, I half expected him to pull into the driveway like he had before, but he didn't. Instead, he drove past the house and turned at the corner.

His actions surprised me. I had to wonder what he was doing. He was either looking to see if I was still hanging around, or he was making sure I had gone giving him clear access to Jonathan's house without anyone watching him.

There was also the possibility he was leaving the area after making sure I was gone. It was then that I remembered there was an alley behind Jonathan's house.

I gave Nolan plenty of time to go around the block at least one more time. When Nolan didn't come back around I decided to check out the alley. It made some sense. Going in the back way would give him a better chance of getting into the house without being seen by anyone.

I started my vehicle and drove to the corner. After making sure he was not parked along the side street, I turned the corner and drove to the alley. As I started to turn into the alley running behind Jonathan's house, I caught sight of Nolan's car. I slammed on the brakes and quickly backed out of the alley. The last thing I wanted was for him to know I was there.

Nolan's red Camry was parked in the alley partially hidden by a dumpster. I parked my vehicle where it could not be seen by anyone in the alley, then began working my way down the alley on foot. I stayed close to the board fences alongside of the alley. I kept the dumpster between Nolan's car and me.

When I got close to his car, I took a quick look around the dumpster and found he was still inside the car. He was sitting behind the wheel. I waited and watched him for a minute, but he never moved. I began to think that there might be something wrong.

It was time for me to make a decision. Was I going to confront him, or leave him there? I decided to confront him. I wanted to know why he had circled around, and why he was parked in the alley.

I approached the car carefully, not sure of what to expect. As I moved alongside his car, I could see his face in the outside rearview mirror. His head was cocked slightly to one side and his eyes were open, but it looked like he was not seeing me. He still didn't move. By all rights I was close enough he should have seen me.

I stepped up alongside the car and looked in. The first thing I noticed was blood on the side of his head. It didn't take a Medical Examiner to understand he had been shot in the head. Being careful not to leave any fingerprints where the police might find them, I reached in and checked his neck for a pulse. There was no pulse. He was dead.

I looked around but didn't see anyone. Whoever had shot him had used a gun with a silencer, otherwise I would have heard it, but I had heard nothing.

There was no way I could ignore what had happened. I didn't have a choice. It was time to get the police involved, like it or not.

I RETURNED TO MY VEHICLE and placed a call to Captain MacDonald of the Homicide Division. Fortunately, I was able to get hold of Mac within a minute or two.

"Detective MacDonald, how can I help you?"

"Mac, this is Peter Blackstone."

"What do you want now?"

I took a few minutes to tell Mac that I had found a guy in a car in an alley and that someone had shot him in the side of the head. I gave him the address. I tried to make it sound like I had just stumbled onto the body while working on something else, but I don't think he bought it. Mac was too smart for that. Besides, we only half trusted each other. Mac told me to wait at the scene.

While I waited at my vehicle for Mac to show up, I thought about our relationship. It was rather rocky at best. Mac had threatened several times to toss me in jail for various reasons like withholding evidence and keeping a witness from him, but he never did it. I think he realized I could be more help to him out of jail. I had helped him a few times over the years and it carried a lot of weight with him.

My thoughts quickly turned back to Nolan. My mind was full of questions. The first one was why was Nolan shot? I had a few quick thoughts on that, but none with any kind of evidence to back them up. If he was involved in the disappearance of Jonathan, then maybe someone thought he was going to talk. That might explain why he was shot, but talk about what?

Other questions came to mind as well. Questions like how did anyone know Nolan was there? If he was followed, they would have seen both of us leave. Nolan had driven off and hadn't returned for an hour or so. Where did he go, and did he talk to anyone? Had he planned to meet someone behind Jonathan's house?

The time between when Nolan pulled into the alley and I pulled up where I could see him couldn't have been more than five or six minutes at the most. That led me to believe someone had set him up during the hour when he left and when he returned. Someone had to have been in the alley waiting for him, but who? I had not seen any other vehicles in the area, but someone could have gotten in and out of the alley without me seeing them.

MY THOUGHTS WERE DISTURBED by the sound of sirens coming my way. A quick look at my watch showed me it hadn't taken long for the police to get there. I no more than got out of my vehicle when two patrol cars came around the corner. One of them pulled across the end of the alley while the other pulled up in front of my vehicle. From where I was standing I could see a third patrol car block the alley at the other end of the block.

An officer got out of the car in front of mine. The look on his face didn't seem too friendly.

"You Blackstone?"

"Yes."

"You called in a shooting?"

"Yes."

"What happened here?"

"If you don't mind, officer, I'll wait and give my statement to Captain MacDonald. I've already talked to him. He's on his way here."

"Okay, but we need information fast if we are going to catch the guy that did this."

"I understand, but I don't know what happened except the young man in the red Camry was shot in the side of the head and he is dead."

"Do you know him?"

"Like I said, I'll give my statement to Captain MacDonald."

"I'll take that as a yes," the officer said looking at me through squinted eyes.

There was no doubt in my mind that he didn't like my answer, but there was little he could do without breaking the law. He knew it and I knew it. I moved over to my vehicle and leaned against the front of it while I waited for Mac.

While I waited I couldn't help but wonder what Nolan had gotten himself involved in. Did it have anything to do with Jonathan's disappearance? I felt a look into Nolan's background was not only a good idea, it was now essential. I needed to know everything there was to know about him, who his friends were, if he had a criminal history, everything.

As I jotted down a note to check on him as soon as possible, a dark colored sedan came around the corner. It had a flashing light on the dash. It was Captain MacDonald. He pulled to a stop next to the curb and got out of his car.

Mac was greeted by the officer I had talked to. As they talked for a moment, Mac glanced over at me. I was sure the officer had reported to him that I would not give a statement to anyone other than Mac.

Mac walked on down the alley toward the Camry while the officer walked toward me. The officer didn't say anything to me. He just stood there watching me. I had a pretty good idea what was going on. Mac was going to check out the murder scene, and the officer was going to make sure I didn't go anywhere.

I watched as Mac looked inside the car. From where I was I couldn't see if he found anything. He also spent a few minutes looking at the ground around the car. I figured he found tracks from another vehicle. He bent down and looked at the ground then looked down the alley.

Before long, a van from the Criminal Investigation Unit pulled up. Two men and a woman got out and walked down the alley toward the car. It was their job to find any evidence left behind.

As soon as they came on the scene, Mac talked to them briefly, then walked back toward me. I knew it was my turn to get questioned about what I knew.

"WELL, PETE. WHAT DO YOU know about this?"

"Damn little, I'm afraid."

"Tell me anyway. Does this guy have anything to do with what you're working on?"

"At this point, I'm not sure. It's possible."

"Do you know this guy?"

"His name is Jess Nolan. He works, or I should say, worked as a car salesman for Endicott Corporation. He worked at the Toyota Lexis dealership on Broadway."

"You seem to know a lot about him."

"That's about it. I met him at the dealership."

I noticed Mac took a look at the new Tahoe I was leaning against. I got the impression he bought at least part of my story.

"Did you talk to him about the case you're working on?"

"Yes, but nothing came of it."

Mac looked at me for a minute. I was not sure if he believed me.

After he glanced back down the alley, he turned back to me.

"He's found shot to death in his car behind Jonathan Endicott's home. Do you think this had anything to do with Jonathan Endicott?"

"Could have, but I don't see any connection at this time."

"You going to let me in on what you're working on and why you're in this neighborhood?"

"I'd like to, but I've got a problem with that. I'm not sure my clients would be very happy with me if I filled you in on what I was investigating. As for why I'm in this neighborhood, I'm simply following up a lead."

"Did your lead have anything to do with the guy in the car?"

"No."

"Did it have anything to do with Jonathan Endicott?"

I didn't really want to lie to Mac, but I couldn't really tell him what I was doing, either.

"No."

"If that changes you will let me know, won't you?"

"If what I'm looking into has any connection to Nolan's death or anything else of a criminal nature, I will let you know," I said lying threw my teeth.

"Immediately?"

"Immediately."

He just stood there and looked at me. I had no idea what was going on in his mind, but if I were him I'm not sure I would have believed me, either. The only thing keeping me from telling Mac what I was working on was protecting the confidentiality of my clients. I wouldn't do anything illegal, but I might bend the rules a little if I felt it was necessary to my case.

I also had something else to consider. If Jonathan was not already dead, letting what little bit of information I had leak out might very well change that. If I found out he was dead, I would tell Mac everything I knew and would change the focus of my investigative efforts to finding the killer or killers.

Mac turned and looked down the alley. He seemed to be watching the Criminal Investigators, but I knew him well enough to know he was thinking very hard about my part in Nolan's death.

"Are you done with me, Mac," I asked, a little reluctant to disturb his thoughts.

"I'm through with you - - - for now. I want to know where I can find you if I want to talk to you again," he said without turning around to look at me.

"Call my office. If I'm not in, leave a message. I'll get back to you."

"Okay."

I waited for a moment to see if he was going to turn around. When he didn't, I walked back to my vehicle. As I was reaching to turn the ignition key, I glanced toward Mac. He was looking over his shoulder at me. I doubted he had believed very much of what I had told him.

I started my vehicle and drove away. There were a lot of things running around in my head. One thing was what had happened to all the electronics taken from Jonathan's house? It occurred to me that Nolan might have had something to do with it. My next move was to find out where Nolan lived and pay a quick visit to his place.

CHAPTER SEVEN

Since I knew Nolan lived somewhere in or near the downtown area of Denver, I made a brief stop at my office to find his address. I quickly checked for any messages on my answering machine, then checked the phone book for Jess Nolan's address.

It didn't take me long to find out where Nolan lived. He had a place in one of the refurbished and remodeled warehouses only a few blocks from Coors Field, the home of the Colorado Rockies. The area was known as LoDo which stood for Lower Downtown. Some of the old warehouses in the area had been made into condos while some were made into fashionable loft type apartments. The old warehouse Nolan lived in had been converted into loft apartments. Since I was familiar with the area, I knew right where his apartment was located.

Nolan lived in just the place I would have expected a single up and coming hotshot salesman would live. It seems those elaborate loft apartments were intended to impress the girls, which was probably the reason why Nolan liked living there. There was also the fact it was only a few blocks from Larimer Square Historic District. Larimer Square was well known for its micro breweries, sports bars and partying, especially after basketball, baseball, hockey or football games.

LoDo was only a short distance from my office. It only took me a few minutes to get there. However, finding a place to park was another matter. It took me longer to find a parking place then it did to drive there, but I finally found a parking space on a side street only a block from the building where Nolan had lived.

Once in the building, I checked the mail boxes to find out which loft belonged to Nolan. I figured I didn't have a great deal of time to nose around. Once the police got things straightened out where Nolan's body had been found, they would go to his apartment to search for leads to his killer.

As I walked up to the door to his loft, I checked the hall to make sure there was no one around. I didn't see anyone so I tried the door to his loft and found it locked. I took my lock picks out of my coat pocket and picked the lock. For all the expense of one of the lofts, the locks were cheap and I had no trouble picking it. I was in the loft in seconds.

Once inside, I quickly closed the door and stood there for a minute looking around. I wasn't looking for anything specific. I wanted to get a feel for the man who had lived there. How the room was decorated and what was in the room could often tell me more about the man than the man himself.

The main room was large and contained the living area, the kitchen and a dining area. It was clean, orderly and neat. There didn't seem to be anything out of place. The furniture was modern, functional and fit the décor. It was not to my taste, but then it wasn't my loft.

There was a very large bookshelf with a rather large stereo system including speakers big enough to be used in a theater. There was also a large flat screen TV. They appeared to be like the ones Nolan had described as missing from Jonathan's house.

I began to wonder if the stereo system and the TV had been stolen from Jonathan by Nolan. I hadn't overlooked the possibility they were just like Jonathan's, either. After all, if Jonathan and Nolan had really been such close friends and for as long as Nolan had said they were, they probably had similar tastes in things, except for living areas.

As much as I would have liked to stand around and take a better look at things, it was time to check out the other rooms. There were four doors off the living area. The first one turned out to be a very large closet. It could have been a small room, but it had storage shelves and a place to hang coats. It, too, was neat and orderly like the living area.

The second door was to a bedroom with a bathroom off one side. It was a large room and had a king size bed. I couldn't help but think it would make for a lot of fun with the right person. I was sure that was why Nolan had it. Again, the room was neat and tidy with no signs of the bed having been used. The sheets appeared to be clean and crisp, and the pillow cases were unwrinkled as if they had been changed sometime earlier today, which was a possibility. A quick look into the bathroom gave me no surprises. It was orderly, as well as clean. Towels were perfectly matched in color and style and neatly placed on the towel racks. The bathroom looked almost as if it had never been used.

The third door was also to a bedroom with a bathroom. However the room was nothing like the other bedroom. It was not as big as the other bedroom and it looked like someone had just crawled out of bed and hadn't bothered to make it. There were clothes tossed over a chair in the corner and some dirty sox on the floor. A small amount of change had been loosely tossed on the dresser along with other personal items. The room looked like it had been used.

I went into the bathroom. It looked like it could use a good cleaning. A shaving cream can and razor had been left out. The sink looked like it hadn't been cleaned in weeks.

The more I thought about it, the more it became clear to me what was going on. Nolan used the smaller bedroom everyday. The larger bedroom he was keeping for the purpose of impressing the girls when he scored with some chick at one of the bars in Larimer Square. I got the feeling his loft was all for show, except for the small bedroom and bath.

I had to wonder how much he made. This was a pretty expensive place to live. Not likely a car salesman could afford a place like it without some extra income from somewhere.

A quick glance at my watch told me I had been here about as long as I dared stay. The last thing I needed was to get caught by the police in Nolan's loft.

As I turned around to leave, I saw a computer table in the corner behind the door. There was a large monitor and a very nice printer, but there was no PC unit. A closer look at the desk revealed an area about the size of a PC unit where the dust seemed heavier. That led me to believe the PC unit had been removed recently. I wondered why. Was it in for repairs, or did someone steal it to get information from it?

I didn't have the time to search for it. Even if I did, I seriously doubted I would find it anywhere in the loft. I didn't have time to look for much of anything if I planned to be gone before the police arrived. It was time to get out.

I quickly moved to the front door and listened carefully. All was quiet out in the hall. I opened the door, peered out, then quickly stepped into the hall and closed the door behind me. After making sure the door had locked and I had wiped off my fingerprints from the door knob, I left the building.

As I stepped around the corner of the building, I saw Mac drive up in front of the warehouse. I let out a sigh of relief. The last thing I wanted was to get caught by him snooping around Nolan's loft.

I got in my vehicle and headed away from LoDo. I remembered I still didn't have what I needed for John to do the DNA comparison to the blood samples. It was getting late and to stop by Jonathan's parents' house at this late hour would not be a good idea. It occurred to me it might be best if I stopped by in the morning when Walter was not likely to be home.

Even with the lateness of the hour, I knew Jennifer would probably still be up. I knew she liked to read before going to bed.

IT DIDN'T TAKE ME VERY LONG to get to Jennifer's apartment. There were still lights on so I walked to the door and knocked. She answered the door in her red robe. I always liked that robe because it showed off the nice curves of her body. She was ready for bed.

"Hi," I said as I took a second to look her over.

"Hi. What are you doing here at this hour?"

"If it's too late, I can go."

"No. Come in," she said as she stepped back.

"I could say I was in the neighborhood, but it wouldn't be the truth. I wanted to stop and see you."

"That's nice," she said with a big smile. "Where have you been the past few days? I haven't heard from you."

"I've been in Dillon working on a case."

"Are you finished with it, or did you miss me so much you had to come and see me?" she asked playfully.

"To say I missed you so much I had to come and see you would not be a total lie. I have missed you."

"But?"

"I could use a little help."

"What kind of help?"

"Can you find out if someone has a criminal record for me?" I asked.

"I suppose I could. Is it important?"

"It could be."

"Who do you want to find out about?"

"Jess Nolan. I would guess his name is Jesse Nolan. He was a car salesman for Endicott Corporation."

"You said 'was'. I take it he no longer works for Endicott Corporation?"

"No. He's dead."

"Then why do you need to know anything about him?"

"He might be connected with the investigation I'm working on. I don't know how. In fact, I'm grabbing at straws."

"Okay. I can do it for you."

"Thanks, honey. I owe you."

"You certainly do," she said with a devilish grin.

"I guess I best be going."

"You're not going to stay?"

"As much as I would like to, I need a clear head for tomorrow. I wouldn't mind a rain check when I'm done with this case."

"Okay. You've got it. Will you be going back to Dillon?"

"Yes."

"When?"

"Probably tomorrow morning, or early afternoon."

"I'll call you on your cell phone when I get the information you want."

"Thanks, honey."

"Do I at least get a goodnight kiss?"

"Sure," I said as I stepped closer to her.

I reached out and put my hands on her narrow waist and drew her to me. I leaned down as she put her arms around my neck. Our lips touched in a light kiss that soon turned into a passionate kiss. I could feel the firmness of her body as she pressed against me.

I pulled back a little and looked down into those Irish green eyes of hers. She was all woman, from her long red hair to her long slender legs. The feel of her body against me was not an unfamiliar feeling, but it was a feeling I had come to know and love. Over the years I had had the chance to enjoy the feel of her body on several occasions. I was enjoying the feel of her body pressing against me now.

"I'm sorry, honey, but I have to go," I said reluctant to let go of her.

"I understand. You will be careful, won't you?"

"Yes. I will."

I gave her another long, passionate kiss. It was one to let her know I really cared about her. I then turned and left.

Just the thought of her and the feel of her lips against mine would stay with me for some time.

I walked to my vehicle thinking of her. In fact, I thought of her all the way to my apartment on the other side of town.

Jennifer and I had a long relationship. We were the best of friends, which meant we shared our lives with each other. We also comforted each other when things were not going very well. We asked nothing of each other except to be there when we were needed.

ONCE I ARRIVED AT MY apartment, I parked my vehicle in front of the garage. I entered my empty apartment. It was so quiet there and so lonely I almost wished I had stayed with Jennifer.

I stopped by my desk to see if there were any messages on the answering machine. There were two. I reached over and pressed the button.

The first message had come in early that morning. It was from Walter Endicott. He wanted to know if I had found his son. I wasn't at all surprised. Walter was a very impatient man. He was probably used to getting what he wanted immediately, if not sooner.

The second message was from Mrs. Endicott. The tone of her voice made me listen very carefully to what she had to say.

"Mr. Blackstone, I would like you to call as soon as you can. Please don't call before eight in the morning or after six in the evening. What I have to say to you, I would prefer Walter didn't hear. Thank you."

I had to wonder what was so important she didn't want her husband to know about it. Although it caused me to worry a little and made me very curious, I decided I would respect her wishes. I found it interesting that she told me what time to call and when I would be able to visit her without Walter around, something I had planned to do anyway.

It was getting late and I needed to get some rest. I set my alarm, then crawled into bed. I was tired and found it easy to doze off.

I WOKE FAIRLY EARLY. There were a number of things I had to do, but the first was to take a shower. I got right in the shower. As the warm water ran over me, I began to think about the message Mrs. Endicott had left on my answering machine. It was hard to imagine what information she had that she didn't want Walter to know. She was a very smart woman and knew what was important and what was not. She also knew Walter better than anyone, and probably knew he had failed to tell me something I really needed to know.

Once I was out of the shower I sat down to my usual breakfast, a bowl of Cheerios with fruit, a glass of orange juice and a cup of coffee "brewed" in the microwave. When I was finished, I cleared away the dirty dishes, rinsed them off before putting them in the dishwasher. I don't usually rinse my dishes before putting them in the dishwasher, but since I didn't know when I would get back to run the dishwasher, I decided rinsing them was a good idea.

The next order of business was to pay a visit to Mrs. Endicott to find out what information she had that was so important. It would also be a good time to get a sample of Jonathan's DNA for John to test at the State Crime Lab. I was sure Mrs. Endicott would have something around that would have Jonathan's DNA on it.

AS SOON AS I WAS READY, I got in my vehicle and drove to the home of Mr. and Mrs. Endicott. It was in one of the very fashionable neighborhoods in Cherry Creek. The houses were in the price range of a million dollars and up. From the looks of their home, it appeared to be in the upper range. The home was a very large two story brick home with large windows and a three car garage with servant's quarters over it. The lawn was well kept as were the shrubs around the house.

I turned into the driveway and drove up to the house. As I got out of my vehicle, I took a second to look around. The neighborhood appeared to be a quiet place with little activity in the morning. I walked up to the door and rang the doorbell. A young Hispanic woman answered the door. She was wearing a clean and neatly pressed white dress.

"May I help you," the woman said with only a hint of an accent.

"My name is Peter Blackstone. I would like to speak with Mrs. Endicott, please."

The young woman held the door and motioned for me to enter into the foyer. I stepped inside.

"Would you wait here, please? I'll see if she is available."

"Certainly."

I watched the young woman as she turned and left the foyer. While I waited, I took a moment to look around. From what I could see, the Endicotts lived very well. The house had the look of one decorated by a professional. There were a number of paintings I believed might be originals. Some of what I saw didn't seem to be the sort of things I would have expected Walter to like. I seriously doubted they were from the world he had grown up in. In short, I found it hard to picture Walter in the house.

"Good morning, Mr. Blackstone," Mrs. Endicott said as she disturbed my thoughts. "I didn't really expect you to come by. A phone call would have been adequate."

"I was in the area so I decided to drop by. Your message sounded urgent."

"Please come with me to the study. It will provide us with more privacy."

She didn't wait for me to respond. She simply turned and walked down the hall. I followed her.

Once inside the study, she told the young woman to get us coffee. She motioned for me to have a seat in a high back chair across a large coffee table from a matching sofa. She sat down on the sofa.

Nothing much was said while we waited. I had a feeling she didn't want anyone hearing us, or interrupting her once she started.

It wasn't long before the young woman brought in a silver serving tray with matching silver creamer, sugar bowl, and coffee pot. There were also two china cups and saucers on the tray with silver spoons. The young woman set the tray on the coffee table then poured two cups of coffee. After handing one to me and one to Mrs. Endicott, the young woman left the room closing the door behind her.

"The reason I wished to talk to you was - - -, well, - - ah - my husband was, shall we say, not completely honest with you when we met in your office," she said, apparently not too sure how to tell me.

I took a sip of the coffee and looked at her over the rim of the cup. It came as no real surprise, but I did want to know what it was he had failed to tell me.

"To be perfectly honest with you, Mrs. Endicott, I'm not surprised."

"You mean you knew he wasn't telling you everything?" she asked.

"Mrs. Endicott, often people don't tell me everything I need to know. It makes it much more difficult for me, but I usually find out sooner or later. Sometimes I find out too late."

"I'm sorry I didn't say something sooner," she said.

"I take it you have something you feel is important for me to know. What is it?"

"Well, you see, - - Jonathan didn't take all the money Walter said he took."

I just sat there looking at her without any change of expression as I took another sip of coffee.

"Jonathan took only fifty thousand of it from the business."

"Are you saying that Walter exaggerated a bit?"

"I wouldn't say that," she said nervously.

"Then what would you say, Mrs. Endicott?"

"You have to remember Walter thinks a great deal of Jonathan. He would do anything for him. You understand that, don't you?"

"I'm sure Walter thinks the world of his son, but what I need to know is what he did?" I asked growing impatient with her.

"Walter took one hundred thousand out of the same account Jonathan had taken the fifty thousand from and gave it to the woman to let our son go."

"When did this happen? When did he give her the money?"

"Five days before we came to see you," she replied, her voice soft and restrained.

"Has he talked to the woman since he gave her the money?"

"Yes. A couple of days after he gave her the money she demanded more."

"That's when Walter decided he needed help?" I asked.

"Yes, but it took him a couple of days to actually contact you."

"How much is she demanding now?"

"Five hundred thousand dollars."

"Can Walter come up with the money?"

"Yes, but he thinks if he gives it to her, she will simply ask for more. That's why he wanted your help."

"How did Walter get the money to her?"

"It was in cash," she replied.

"No. How did he get it to her? Did he deliver it himself or was there a go-between? Maybe a drop off somewhere?"

"Oh. I'm sorry. I'm just so worried about Jonathan."

"I understand."

"He gave it to Jesse Nolan to drop off."

Now that didn't make a lot of sense to me. I had been led to believe Walter didn't like Nolan. It got me to thinking about Nolan's part in this. It was clear Nolan was involved in Jonathan's disappearance after all.

It also gave me something to think about when it came to the killing of Nolan. If he had been killed so he couldn't talk, that would explain a lot. I also began to wonder if Nolan was involved in helping with the planning of Jonathan's abduction. It was certainly a possibility. The thought came to mind that possibly Walter had killed Nolan believing he didn't give the money to the woman when she demanded five hundred thousand.

"Do you know why the money was given to Nolan to deliver?"

"I'm not sure, but Walter said he was to give the money to someone who knew Jonathan well and could report back that Jonathan was okay."

"And who knew Jonathan better than Nolan. Your husband knew that," I said, mostly thinking out loud.

"Yes. Jonathan and Jesse have been close friends for years."

"So I've been told. Did Jess report back to Walter that Jonathan was okay?"

"I'm not sure, but I don't believe he did."

"Mrs. Endicott, I need something of Jonathan's that would have his DNA on it."

Her mouth fell open and she put her hands over her mouth. Her eyes got big and she held her breath as she looked at me.

"Mrs. Endicott, I have nothing to indicate Jonathan is dead. As far as I know he is still alive. I simply need it in case I come upon some evidence and need to rule him out. I have a friend in the State Crime Lab who wants to run some tests to establish Jonathan's DNA; so if we come up with something, he can eliminate Jonathan."

"You already have something, don't you? You already have something to compare it to, don't you?" she asked, her face showing she was sure I did.

"Yes," I replied reluctantly. "But there's no reason to believe the evidence we have is from Jonathan. We simply need to rule it out. Even if it is, there was so little it may not mean anything."

"You have some blood, don't you?"

"Yes, but there is no reason to think it is Jonathan's."

"There must be, or you wouldn't be asking for something with his DNA on it."

"We do have a sample of blood, but it is not anywhere near enough to convince me that he is dead. It's only a couple of drops."

She sat there and looked at me for several minutes. I was wondering what I could say to make this easier for her. Suddenly, she looked down at the floor and took a deep breath. After a moment or so, she looked back up at me. The expression on her face seemed to show she believed me, and she had regained her composure.

"Mr. Blackstone, my husband and I have kept too much from you already. I think it would be best if you took a look in Jonathan's bedroom. You might be able to find something that would give you what you need. You may also find something that will help you know our son better and help you in your investigation."

"Thank you. It could prove to be very helpful."

"Right this way, please," she said as she stood up.

I FOLLOWED MRS. ENDICOTT up the spiral staircase to the second floor and down the long hallway of their large home. She stopped at a door and looked at me.

"This is Jonathan's bedroom. He stayed here a few days a month, sometimes more. He always said he got lonely in the house he had in Denver."

"Have you been to his house in Denver?"

"Yes, just once when he first moved in."

"Tell me. Why did he buy a house in what would be considered a family oriented neighborhood instead of, say, a loft in LoDo like his friend Nolan?"

"He always said that some day he would get married and have a family. When that day came he would want to live around people with kids. He liked kids. With the price of houses going up so fast, he felt it was a good investment, too."

"I see," I replied, then looked at the door to Jonathan's room.

"Well, I will leave you to do what you have to do. I'll wait for you in the study," she said.

"I shouldn't be too long."

I watched her as she turned and walked back toward the stairs. As soon as she was out of sight, I reached out and opened the door to the bedroom. I stepped inside and closed the door.

THE ROOM WAS VERY LARGE for a bedroom. Everything was neat and clean. I was sure the maid had kept the room in good order, probably changing the bed after each time Jonathan had stayed.

I went into the bathroom and looked around. I noticed a toothbrush hanging on a bracket with a glass. The glass appeared to be clean, but the toothbrush had been used. I reached in my pocket, took out a small plastic bag, put the toothbrush in the bag and set it on the edge of the sink.

Opening the medicine cabinet, I found a brush and comb. They had hair follicles on them. I bagged them as well.

There were the usual things one expects to find in a medicine cabinet such as shaving cream, razors, skin conditioner and deodorant. The one thing I didn't find was medications of any kind. There were no aspirins, antacids or any other over-the-counter meds, and certainly no prescription drugs. I wasn't sure if he was on any kind of medication or not. I made a mental note to ask Mrs. Endicott before I left.

I returned to the bedroom and began looking around. The closet was full of clothes. His dresser and chest of drawers were full. Everything indicated someone lived there or was there a lot. With a house of his own only a twenty minute drive away, I wondered why he had so many clothes at his parent's home.

As I was about to leave the room, I noticed a big armoire in the corner. It seemed strange he would have one with such a large walk-in closet. I decided to take a look inside.

I opened the armoire and discovered it was not for clothes. It was a computer cabinet. There was a computer and monitor, a scanner and a printer with a fax. There were also a couple of file drawers and places for other things such as paper, printer cartridges and disks or CDs.

On the inside of the doors were pictures of several different cars. I wondered if this was his office away from the dealership. I had nothing to lose by turning on the computer and maybe everything to gain. I reached over and turned on the switch. The computer started, but soon asked for a password. Not being any kind of an expert on computers, in fact knowing very little about them other than the few simple programs I used, I had no idea what to do.

I quickly felt I needed help if I was going to break into his computer. I knew where I could find such a person, but it would have to wait. I had spent about as much time in his bedroom as I thought was justifiable. I could always come back with my friend and break into the computer if I thought it became necessary, and if they would allow it.

After I shut off the computer, I closed the cabinet and gathered the evidence I needed for John, then left the room and returned to the study. I found Mrs. Endicott sitting on the sofa. As I walked into the room, the look on her face seemed to be pleading with me to give her answers about her son, but I didn't have any.

"Is this Jonathan's toothbrush, hair brush and comb?" I asked as I held them out for her to see.

"Yes," she replied.

"I'll get them back to you as soon as I can."

"Thank you. I appreciate all you're doing."

"Did Jonathan take any kind of medication, prescription medication or otherwise?"

"No. He was in good health. He took good care of himself. He never used drugs like a lot of young people do these days."

"I may need to come back with a friend of mine and break into his computer. There may be something in there that will help me find him. Would it be okay?"

"Yes. Anything that will help you find him."

"I'll be in touch. I can find my way out."

She nodded and forced a slight smile. At that moment I wished I could have said something to make her feel better, but I had nothing to tell her.

I left the house and immediately headed for the State Crime Lab to give my evidence to John.

CHAPTER EIGHT

I ARRIVED AT THE STATE CRIME LAB about thirty minutes or so after leaving the Endicott home. My first order of business was to give John the items I had removed from Jonathan's bedroom at his parents' home.

Entering the lab building, I went directly to the reception desk and told the young woman behind the counter who I wanted to see. The receptionist notified John that I was there. She told me it would be a little while before he would be available. I walked over to a chair and sat down to wait. As it turned out, it was only a matter of a few minutes before he showed up.

"Come with me," John said, then turned and started down the hall to his office.

I followed John back to his office. He seemed to be a little impatient with me. I had to wonder what was bothering him. I hoped he had not gotten into any trouble because he was helping me. As soon as we got to his office, I went in and sat down while he closed the door.

"Did you get what I need," he asked. "I don't have a lot of time. I have a meeting in fifteen minutes."

"I'll be brief. I think I have what you need."

I held out the bag to him. He took it and looked inside.

"This should do nicely. Are you sure these belonged to the young man that is missing?"

"As sure as I can be. His mother identified those items as belonging to him."

"Good. I did a quick test on one of the samples you brought in yesterday. It is blood, and it is human."

"I was afraid of that."

"We still don't know if it is blood from the young man you're looking for. I won't know for a couple of days. Can you tell me who it is you're looking for?"

"I'm sorry, John, but as much as I would like to, I can't, yet."

"It might help if you could. I could run a check of his DNA with those in our data bank. If I do, I might be able to find out anyway."

"I doubt he is in your DNA data base, but I would really appreciate it if you didn't do that just yet."

"Why not?"

"I'm afraid if it gets out he is missing, it could result in his death. If whoever has him finds out we know about him, they might kill him and run."

"So you think he might still be alive?"

"John, at this point, I'm not sure. I do know there was not enough blood in the shack for me to assume he is dead."

"If he is dead, then you don't think he was killed at the shack?"

"No. If he is already dead, I seriously doubt he was killed there. I do think he was held there for a while, but for how long I have no idea."

John nodded that he understood and looked as if he was thinking about something. I was thinking, too.

"John, if it turns out the blood is not the young man's I'm searching for, you should probably run it against the DNA in your data base," I said.

"I'll do that, but not until I let you know what the outcome is. Is that fair?"

"Very fair. And thanks, John," I said as I stood up to leave.

"I'll give you a call in a couple of days."

"Good. I best get going. I still have a lot to do."

"See you later," John said.

I nodded then left the lab.

AS I APPROACHED MY VEHICLE, I noticed a pickup with someone sitting in it. My first thought was Mac had put someone on my tail, but there was something wrong with the picture I was seeing. It was not the type of vehicle the police usually used. It was a dark green Chevy pickup with dark tinted windows and chrome steel wheels. It looked like it was about five or six years old.

I got in my vehicle and drove out of the parking lot. I didn't think much about the pickup until I noticed it seemed to be following me. Since I had no idea who it was, or if they were tailing me for sure, I decided to do a little lane changing to see what would happen. When I changed lanes, he changed lanes. That, along with the fact he stayed back a bit, left me with no doubt it was a tail. I didn't want him following me to my next destination. It was time to ditch him.

I led my tail onto the interstate and headed west along I-70. He followed like he was on a leash. Traffic was not bad for this time of day, but there was enough it would not be too difficult for me to lose him in it. I began by slowly changing lanes more or less forcing him to move toward the center of the interstate away from the exit ramp side of the road.

He didn't seem to be very well trained in tailing someone so I doubted it was a cop. I waited until I found a place where he would be pretty well boxed in by the other cars and unable to make any sudden lane changes. However, I was far enough ahead of the group of cars that I could make my move. It was my opportunity to leave him on the interstate with no chance to follow me.

As I came upon an exit, I darted off across several lanes of traffic and pulled off on the exit ramp. It was not the safest thing for me to do, but I made sure I had plenty of room before doing it. There was nothing he could do without causing an accident except to continue on down the interstate. The next exit was about a mile down the road. By the time he could get back, I would be long gone.

After exiting the interstate, I headed back across town using mostly side streets and secondary streets. It was probably best if I stayed off the main streets as I had no idea if he had any friends that might pick up on me. I had to wonder who had been following me.

Since I had not noticed him before, I began to wonder how long he had been following me. It could have been for some time as I had not been too worried about being tailed before I found the evidence was human blood. The more important question at the moment was why? I would be keeping a closer look out for anyone tailing me from now on.

I HEADED FOR THE HOME of Mrs. Parker Henry Jones. I knew where she lived. I had been there before when Parker was alive. It was in a very exclusive neighborhood with expensive houses. On the way over, I kept a close eye out for the Chevy pickup, but didn't see it again. I also watched to make sure there was no one else following me.

I turned onto the street where the Jones house was located. It didn't take me but a few minutes to find it. I pulled into the curved driveway that circled in front of the house and parked in front of the large porch.

As I got out of my vehicle, a rather tall, well built man stepped out on the front porch. He had the look of a bodyguard; well built, strong and alert. From the look on his face, he was there to make sure Mrs. Jones was not bothered.

"Can I help you?" the man asked politely while sizing me up at the same time.

"Yes. I would like to speak to Mrs. Jones."

"Do you have an appointment?"

"No, but I think she would like to talk to me anyway."

"And what makes you think that?"

"First of all, I was a friend of her late husband and had worked for him on several occasions. Secondly, I think she would like to know someone is using her boat, the *Crystal*

Blue, without her knowledge. Give her my card, please," I said as I handed it to him.

The big guy took my card and looked at it, then looked at me. He was thinking about what he should do. There was also the possibility that he was trying to remember if he had met me before. I remembered seeing him a little over a year ago, but just once.

"Come in," he finally said.

"Thank you," I replied and followed him into the entryway.

"Wait here. I will tell her you're here."

I nodded and watched him as he disappeared into a room down the hall. Within a few minutes, he returned.

"Come with me, please," he said.

I followed him down the long hall and into a large room. The first thing I noticed was Mrs. Jones sitting in a chair with a quilt over her lap. She was either sick, or she was still in mourning for her husband.

"Come in, Peter," she said with a smile.

"How are you getting along," I said as I walked over to her, bent down and kissed her lightly on the cheek.

"As well as can be expected, I think the saying is," she said as she pointed to a chair.

"I'm sure. I was so sorry to hear about Parker," I said as I sat down. "He was a good man. I was out of town on a case and didn't hear about it until after the funeral."

"I understand. I want to thank you for the nice card you sent. It was very thoughtful of you."

"I'm sorry I didn't get here sooner to visit you."

"It's okay, Peter. I haven't been receiving guests lately. Now what is this David tells me about my boat?"

"First of all, I didn't know the *Crystal Blue* was your boat until I talked to the man at the marina where it was docked. I knew you had a boat, but didn't know where you kept it. Parker had told me how much you love your boat; and when I heard somebody was renting it from you, I had my doubts. I thought I would come and see you to find out if you had actually rented it out."

"Heavens, no. I would never rent my boat out to anyone. I'll call the police and have them arrested," she said.

"Margaret, I know how much the boat means to you, but maybe you could hold off for just a bit, please."

"Why, Peter?" she asked, the expression on her face showing her surprise at my request.

"I think the people on your boat may be of interest to me."

"What do you mean 'of interest' to you?"

"At this point, I'm not sure. All I really know is they are on your boat without your permission. That could get them put in jail for trespass or possibly for theft, but nothing more. I would like a little time to find out if they have anything to do with my investigation. If they do, they could be put away for kidnapping or possibly murder."

"Oh, my heavens," she said looking at me. "Did they murder someone on my boat?"

"Not that I know of. I suspect them of only kidnapping so far," I said with a tone of confidence I didn't really feel.

"If they are the kidnappers and you have them arrested for being on your boat illegally; they would be arrested, post bail and then run before I have a chance to find out more about them. So you can see why I would like you to wait for a little while before you contact the police?"

"Yes, I see," she said thoughtfully.

"I would certainly understand it if you want to have them arrested now and that is your right."

"No. Ah, no. I can wait for awhile if you think it will help you."

"I do. Thank you so much. I'll do what I can to find out if they are involved with my investigation as quickly as possible. If I find they are not, I'll have Sheriff Stillwell arrest them right away. Would that be okay with you?"

"That would be fine, Peter. Parker trusted you with his life, I can certainly trust you with my boat. You do what you think is best. You can represent me when it comes to my boat. I'll put it in writing if you wish," she said with a grin.

"I don't think it will be necessary. However, if it becomes necessary, I'll let you know. But thank you for the offer, Margaret."

"David, would you be so kind as to get Peter a cup of coffee? He likes it black."

"Yes, Ma'am," he replied.

"Never mind, David," I said as I stood up. "I really must be getting on back to Dillon. I'll stop in to see you when I get back in town."

"Promise?"

"I promise, Margaret. There is one other thing I should mention. I don't want you to say anything about where I am. I was followed earlier today."

"Really? Do you know who it was?"

"No. I lost him on the interstate."

"Oh. We won't tell anyone you were here, will we David?"

"No, Ma'am," he replied with a slight smile.

"I'll talk to you later," I said, then leaned down and kissed her lightly on the cheek again.

"Be careful, Peter. And don't be a stranger," she said as I was walking out of the room.

I stopped and looked back at her and smiled.

"I'll be careful, and I will come by to see you when I get done with the case I'm working on. Maybe by then you will feel like going out to dinner with me?"

"I'd like that, Peter."

I turned back around and followed David to the door. He opened it for me. I stepped out onto the porch, then turned and looked at David.

"David, is Margaret doing okay?"

"She is doing fairly well, sir. She has had some trouble adjusting to the loss of Mr. Jones. They were very close, you know."

"Yes, I know. Excuse me for asking, but what is your job here?"

"I was Mr. Jones's bodyguard and I guess you could say his butler. Mrs. Jones has kept me on. I sort of look out for her."

"You still have my card?"

"Yes, sir."

"Call me if she needs me."

"I will, sir."

"Thanks, and you can call me Peter or Pete."

"Okay, Peter," he said with a smile. "You can call me David."

I nodded and smiled, then turned and headed for my vehicle. I glanced over the hood of the vehicle at David before I got in and drove away. He was still standing on the porch watching me as I turned out on the street.

I thought it was nice of Margaret to keep David on. He seemed like a nice enough man as well as very capable. If he was trusted by Parker, it had probably been a good decision on Margaret's part to keep him around. I know it made me feel better knowing he was there, and she had someone to look after her.

I DROVE BACK TO MY OFFICE and checked my answering machine. It didn't take that long to get there. I parked in the building's parking garage. Since I had been followed earlier, I was careful to notice the cars in the garage. I didn't see any vehicles that didn't belong there.

There was just one message on my answering machine. It was from Jennifer. She reported that Nolan had a criminal record, but he had not been convicted of anything, and none of the cases had been solved. He had been questioned for extortion twice, assault three times, and theft once.

It was a pretty lengthy record for someone so young. I had to wonder if that was why Walter didn't like having Nolan working for him. Walter would have done a background check and would know about Nolan's criminal record. I was sure Walter didn't like the fact his son had hired him anyway.

The only reason I could think of for Nolan being hired was his long time friendship with Jonathan. And the only reason Walter would have let Jonathan keep him on was because Walter was the kind of father who gave his son the space to do what he wanted.

I made a few notes, then left my office. The drive back to Dillon was uneventful. I didn't see anyone following me, but at this point I really didn't care. I had nothing to hide at the moment.

The drive back gave me time to think. I had to wonder who had killed Nolan and why. Was it possible he was in on Jonathan's disappearance? Was he blackmailing someone who didn't take kindly to it? Or had he pissed someone off who didn't like the fact he got away with something? There was little doubt in my mind Nolan had made a few enemies, and not just those who were not happy with the deals they got on cars he had sold them.

I ARRIVED BACK at East Shore Estates shortly before dinnertime. There was music coming from one of the balconies. It was country western music. I didn't really mind, but I expected more rock music since there seemed to be a lot of young people around. But then I remembered the guy working on the boat in one of the berths played country western music.

Dinner for me was simple. I wasn't very hungry so I fixed myself a steak on the grill and a salad to go with it. I had sat down to enjoy my dinner and watch a little television when I heard a loud scream. It sounded like it was coming from below the balcony somewhere around the marina.

I pushed back from the table and ran out on the balcony. Looking down, I could see several people running out onto the dock. There was a woman standing several berths from the end of the dock. She had her hands over her mouth as she stared at something.

It took a couple of seconds for it to soak in that she seemed to be staring at the berth where my boat was tied. I wondered what she had seen that was so shocking to her. It was then I realized there was someone lying on the deck of a boat, my boat.

I heard someone yell, "Somebody call 9-1-1."

I already had my cell phone in my hand and was calling 9-1-1 as I headed out the door and down to the marina. By the time I got there several people had gathered around, but no one had stepped onto my boat.

"Excuse me. Let me through, please," I said as I made my way toward my boat.

"9-1-1 emergency. What is your emergency?"

"This is Peter Blackstone. I live at the East Shore Estates on Dillon Lake. There's a man down on my boat in the marina," I said.

While I was still trying to get past the last big guy on my way to the boat, I described the situation to the operator. Just as I stepped by him and had a clear view of my boat, I heard someone say, "It's the guy you forced into the water at gun point."

That comment caused me to stop and look for the person who said it. I recognized several of the people from the complex, but didn't see who had made the comment.

"Please stay on the line. I'm dispatching emergency assistance now," the operator said.

I looked at the deck of my boat and sure as hell, it was the guy I forced into the lake at gun point. It was the same guy who beat up Lora. Sheriff Stillwell had told me his name was Max Butler.

"Send the police, too," I said then hung up.

"Everybody stand back," I said as I stepped onto my boat. "I've called for the police and an ambulance."

"I don't think he needs an ambulance," someone said, but again I didn't see who said it.

Max Butler was lying on the deck of my boat on his side. His head was twisted so he was looking up at me. His eyes were open, but he was not seeing anything. He was dead. The last thing he needed was an ambulance.

I noticed a large bloody area on the front of his shirt right over the heart. As I stepped over him, I also noticed there was a smaller spot on his back. I'd seen enough shootings to know he had been shot in the back and the slug exited out the front probably ripping right through his heart. It had to be a pretty good size caliber gun to do so much damage.

The most interesting thing was there didn't appear to be as much blood on the deck of my boat as I would have expected. I looked around the deck and outside the cabin near the body. There was no blood splatter on my boat or any of the boats nearby that I could see. Everything so far indicated he had not been shot on my boat. I wondered who had shot him and then went to the trouble of dumping his body there. It had to be someone with a need to discredit me, or someone who wanted me out of the way for some reason. I didn't know of anyone other than Sheriff Stillwell who knew why I was there.

I turned and looked back toward the dock to see who was standing around. Most of the people standing around lived in the complex of condos. I knew some of them had boats in the marina.

The man who had been working on the boat the past few mornings was standing on the dock looking directly at me. It wasn't the fact he was looking at me that concerned me as much as the way he looked at me. It was almost as if he knew me and maybe thought I should know him. If I did know him, I didn't recognize him; but there wasn't a great deal of light out on the docks. I only wished I could have seen into his mind so I would know what he was thinking.

I stood up and was about to go ask him if he had seen anything when I heard sirens coming up the road. It sort of reminded me that it was the job of the police to question any potential witnesses, not mine. I would leave him to them, at least for now.

IT WOULD HAVE BEEN NICE if Sheriff Stillwell had been the first on the scene, but I wasn't that lucky. The patrol car pulled up at the end of the dock driven by the same deputy I had dealt with yesterday. He was not the sharpest tool in the shed, but I felt with a little direction he had potential of becoming a good cop. He was at least trying to be a good cop. The only consolation was Sheriff Stillwell would most likely be along very soon.

"Okay, everybody move down to the end of the dock and wait there," he announced. "I'll get to you in a minute."

When the crowd moved off the dock and out of the way, it left me facing the deputy. The look on his face seemed to tell me that our late evening encounter wasn't going to be a very pleasant one.

"You again," he said with a disgusted look on his face. "I suppose this is your boat?"

"Yes, it is."

"It seems you just can't stay out of trouble."

"I'm not in trouble."

"What do you call it when there's a dead body on your boat?"

"Coincidence?"

"Don't get smart with me. You may have Sheriff Stillwell fooled, but you're not fooling me. Hand over your gun," he said as he reached out to take my gun while sliding his other hand over his own gun.

"Sorry, but I don't have one on me tonight. It's in my condo."

"Got rid of it so it can't connect you to this murder?"

"No. It's in my condo.

"I'll bet," he said sarcastically.

"You'd lose."

"Watch your mouth."

"Listen deputy, the only thing you've gotten right so far is Max Butler was murdered," I said with a hint of frustration.

"You know I can arrest you for murder."

"Do it. But I don't think Sheriff Stillwell will like it very much. You've already proven to him you're not much of a cop."

From the expression on his face, my comment obviously didn't set well with him, but then it wasn't supposed to. However, it seemed to get his attention. I suspected the talking to he got yesterday from his boss helped him think a little before he made a fool of himself, again.

The expression on his face started to change, and then he looked at the body lying on the deck of my boat. I let him look at it for a minute or so before saying anything.

"If you look closely, you will see he was probably shot with a large caliber pistol or possibly a rifle. Only a high powered gun would blow a hole threw a man like that. It would be my guess a rifle was used."

What I said seemed to get his attention. He glanced over his shoulder at me and looked at me as if he were waiting for me to tell him more. I decided not to disappoint him.

"Take careful note at how little blood there is on the deck of my boat. You might also notice there isn't any blood splatter when the shot that killed him was obviously a through and through. If he was killed where he lies, there would be a lot more blood on the deck and it would be all over everything, which means he was killed somewhere else. In police lingo, my boat is not the primary crime scene," I said as I watched him to see what he would do next.

The deputy walked over closer to the body and took a look at it and the area around him. He was thinking about what I had told him. Since he didn't say anything, I felt I should.

"Might I suggest you start interviewing your witnesses before they all drift off and you lose them?"

He turned and looked at me as if I had suggested something completely foreign to him. He suddenly seemed to come awake and looked toward the end of the dock.

"Yes. That's a good idea. Wait here. I'll want to talk to you again in a little bit," he said, his voice changing to a more pleasant tone.

"I'll be right here," I assured him.

The deputy stepped off my boat and walked along the dock toward where everyone was standing. I stepped off my boat and sat down on a large deck box on the dock only a few feet from my boat. I watched as the deputy started talking to some of the witnesses.

I began looking at those who had been on the dock. Most of them seemed willing to tell the deputy what they had seen, which I doubted was much of anything. It was about that time I realized the guy who was always working on his boat was not among those who were hanging around. I wasn't sure if he had just gotten tired of waiting, or if there was some other reason he had left. Whatever the reason, he was not there.

While I waited for the Sheriff to show up, I found myself thinking about the guy I had seen on the docks and how he looked at me. There was something about him that didn't set well with me, but I couldn't get a handle on what it was at the moment. The only place I could remember seeing him was on the dock working on his boat. I remembered thinking he was taking a long time to refinish the deck.

The thought of his boat caused me to look over at the berth where it had been moored. The boat was gone. The last time I saw the boat he wasn't anywhere near being done with it. I looked out toward the lake. There was no sign of him sailing away from the marina, but it was dark out over the lake making it almost impossible to see anything outside the area of the docks.

It was about that time I saw Sheriff Stillwell coming down the grassy hill toward the dock.

CHAPTER NINE

Sheriff Stillwell looked over at his deputy, then came out on the dock to where I was sitting.

"What happened here?"

"Got me."

"You shoot him?" he asked as he looked at the body.

"No. Someone with a real serious weapon did. Blew a hole clean threw him. About all I can tell you is he was not killed here, and he probably never knew what hit him."

"Oh. You sure about that?"

"The canon used on him would have made a hell of a mess of my boat if he had been killed where his is. The only blood is beside and under the body."

"I'll take a look," he said, then moved on by me.

Sheriff Stillwell was a serious law officer. He was methodical and paid attention to detail. He looked over the scene with a great deal of care. When he was done, he came over and sat down on the box next to me.

"You called it right. He was shot once, but not here."

"That's all it takes if you do it right."

"Any ideas on how the body got there?"

"Not at the moment. I haven't given it much thought, but I'll probably figure it out."

"Here comes the ambulance," he said as he stood up. "If you come up with anything, let me know."

"Sure enough. Let me know when I can have my boat back."

"Sure."

"I guess it doesn't matter if Lora signs a complaint against Max now," I said.

Sheriff Stillwell glanced over at the body then said, "Not any more."

I STOOD UP THEN LOOKED toward the end of the dock to where the deputy was still interviewing witnesses. I then turned around and looked down the dock toward the berth where the guy had been working on his boat. There was a reason the boat was gone and I wanted to know what it was. Even though I hadn't seen where he went when the deputy told everyone to move to the end of the dock, I was pretty sure he had left in the boat. Since I had other things on my mind when I came running down to the dock, I couldn't say for sure if it had been there when all the commotion started.

Maybe if I walked down the dock to his berth I might be able to find out what the guy's name was. I turned and walked to the berth. I checked the number. Now all I had to do was check with the maintenance man to find out who the berth was assigned to.

Since the maintenance man was not around in the evenings, it would have to wait until tomorrow. There was nothing more I could do tonight so I decided I would return to my condo and finish eating my dinner.

When I got to the condo, I put my steak in the microwave to heat it up a little. While it was heating, I ate the salad. I guess I hadn't realized how hungry I was.

While I ate, my thoughts again returned to the guy fixing up his boat. I had to wonder why I hadn't said anything about him to the Sheriff. It was probably because I wanted to talk to him first.

I reviewed in my mind all the times I had seen him. Every time had been out there, on the docks. He had always been playing country western music on his boom box, and he had always been working on the boat. I couldn't recall seeing him anywhere else. Yet, this evening, there was no boat in the berth where it had been.

It suddenly occurred to me that maybe he had moved his boat to another berth. Marcy had two berths, it only seemed logical that he could have two, also. That thought caused me to stand up and go out on the balcony. On the way out, I grabbed my binoculars.

I began scanning the marina starting with my boat. My boat had people crawling all over it and there were some standing around on the dock next to it. There was, of course, Stillwell, a couple of ambulance attendants waiting for the Coroner to release the body to them, and a couple of deputies milling around on the dock. There was the County Coroner and his assistant examining the body on the boat.

The marina was lit by only a few lights on the docks. The lighting was not bright on the dock except for on my boat and the berth where it was tied. A couple of bright lights had been set up to help the Coroner with his examination. They would also be needed for the Crime Scene Investigators.

I began to look at the other boats in the marina. I counted sixteen in all. I knew who owned most of them from just being observant. Two of the larger sailboats had lights on inside them, but I didn't see any activity on either of them.

The one thing I didn't see was the boat I was looking for. When was it moved? More importantly where was it now? And where was the owner of it?

The lake seemed so calm tonight, not the way I was feeling at the moment. My thoughts had turned to what had taken place there. Why was Butler's body dumped on my boat? Who had found it necessary to kill him and why? There was no doubt in my mind Lora had good reason to see him dead, but I couldn't see her shooting him. Besides, she would not have had the strength to move him, plus, as far as I knew she was still in the hospital.

There was also the question of what did this have to do with my investigation? Did it have anything at all to do with it? I had nothing to indicate that it did.

There were just too many questions to get them answered tonight. It was getting late and it had been a very long day. Tomorrow I would get back on track to finding Jonathan, but right now it was time to get some much needed sleep.

I WOKE UP TO THE SOUND of country western music once again. At first it didn't register in my sleep induced brain. I simply laid there and listened to it for a few minutes. When it finally registered that the guy I wanted to talk to had been playing county music while working on his boat, I jumped out of bed and ran to the window. Looking down on the marina, I saw the same guy working on his boat in the same berth it had been in since I arrived. This was not the time to think, it was the time for action.

My need to talk to him was so strong I didn't waste time having breakfast. It could wait. I dressed quickly, grabbed my gun and headed out the door while sticking it in my belt.

He was still working on his boat as if nothing had happened when I came around the corner. As I walked out onto the dock, the first thing I noticed was the yellow police tape around the berth where my boat was moored. It was a little soon for the forensic people to have finished their search for evidence. They had been over it with a fine tooth comb last night, but would probably like to take another look at it in the daylight to make sure they hadn't missed anything.

I walked past my berth and continued on down the dock. Caution was the word for the day as far as I was concerned. I had no idea what I was getting into, or how this guy fit into my investigation, if at all. I didn't take my eyes off him as I approached. He turned his head, looked up at me and smiled.

"Well, good morning, Mr. Blackstone."

"Good morning to you, whoever you are."

"I take it that means you don't recognize me," he said with a smile.

"That would be correct," I replied, trying to place him while still being cautious of him.

"I recognized you the first time I saw you, but then I'm not likely to forget someone who was instrumental in getting me put in jail."

I looked into his eyes. Then it came to me. I had not been the one to put him in jail, the justice system had done that. All I had done was point the police in his direction. I had only seen him twice, once was at his trial when he had a beard, mustache and long brown hair. He was also wearing a suit.

The man in front of me was clean shaven and his hair was neatly trimmed with a hint of gray in it. He was wearing jeans, a red T-shirt and deck shoes with paint and varnish stains on them.

"Phillip Hudson. I thought you were in jail."

"I got out a couple of months ago for good behavior."

"You staying clean?"

"Sure have and plan to stay that way," he said. "By the way, I've always wondered how you figured out it was me that stole the car and robbed the store."

"It was by accident, actually. I didn't know you robbed the store. As for the car you stole, it belonged to a friend of mine. I saw you driving it down the street the day you stole it. I thought I recognized the car and called my friend. When he told me his car was stolen, I called the cops and gave them your description along with where I had seen you. As for robbing the store, the cops were the ones who told me about that. If you hadn't been watching me so closely these past few days, I would never have paid a bit of attention to you."

"At first I didn't want you to know I was here, but then I changed my mind."

"Why did you change your mind?" I asked.

"Because I was sure if you saw me enough times you would figure out who I was, sooner or later."

"You're right. I probably would have."

"Listen, I don't know why you're here, but whatever the reason I had nothing to do with it, and I don't want to get dragged into it. I've got a good job working on boats around here. If people found out I'm an ex-con, they wouldn't let me near their boats. You understand?"

"Sure. I'm not interested in having a lot of people know who I am, either," I said.

"I'll make a deal with you. You don't tell anyone about me, and I won't tell anyone about you."

"You stay clean and that will be the way it goes. Fair enough?"

"Yeah, sure," he said with a smile.

"You mind answering a few questions for me?"

"No. Hell, if I don't answer them you'll just sic the cops on me, and I'll end up having to answer them anyway."

"Maybe, maybe not. Did you see who put the body on my boat?"

"No. I've been minding my own business working on this boat."

"Have you seen anyone hanging around my boat?"

"No. Wait. I saw a guy in a cowboy hat and cowboy boots talking to someone on the dock yesterday, - ah - sometime around noon. I don't know what was said, but the person he was talking to pointed at your boat. He could have been asking which boat was yours, but I can't be sure. I couldn't hear them."

"What did he look like?"

"Like I said, he was wearing a cowboy hat and boots. He had on a western shirt and jeans that looked well used. He had a pretty good sized hunting knife on his belt, I remember that. Oh, he had a large silver belt buckle. He had a thick black mustache and long dark hair that hung out from under his hat."

"Do you know who he was talking to?"

"No, but I've seen her around here."

"It was a woman?"

"Yeah. Tall, blond hair, not too bad looking. I don't think she knew him though. She kind of stepped back away from him when he stopped her to ask her questions."

I thought about what he had said. From his description of the woman, it could have been any of about three women I'd seen around the complex.

The description of the man was a dead ringer for the cowboy I had seen at the old shack, Hank Martin. It made me think he was the one who shot Butler. I knew him to carry a rifle.

"One more thing. Where did you go last evening when the cops arrived?"

"By the time they got here, it was getting pretty dark. I took this boat and moved out into the lake and on down past the next marina. I stayed there until everyone cleared out then came back. I didn't want the cops looking at me too closely. You understand?"

"Yes. They could make it difficult for you," I agreed.

"They sure could. If I get into any trouble, I could lose my job and end up back in prison. I'm on probation. I really like working on these fancy boats. No one bothers me, I work by myself, and the pays pretty good. It's a great life. Better than what I had before I went to prison."

I looked at him wondering if he was telling me the truth. The one thing that made me want to believe him was the fact he was still there. He had not cut and run. The fact he was a two-time loser might have had something to do with it, too. One more time and he would be put away for a very long time even if it was for something relatively minor. He could have disappeared without any difficulty at all, but he hadn't.

"I want you to do something for me."

"Sure. What is it?"

"I want you to keep an eye on my boat. Let me know if anyone comes snooping around it. It might be worth something to you."

"Okay."

"I'll talk to you later."

He simply nodded and returned to his work of refinishing the deck of the boat. From what I could see, he was doing an excellent job. I stood there for a minute or so thinking before I turned around and walked back toward the condo. I wasn't sure if he would be of any help to me, but at least he would know I was keeping an eye on him as much as he was watching me.

I RETURNED TO THE CONDO and fixed my breakfast. Once it was ready, I sat down to eat. I mentally reviewed what Hudson had told me.

Hudson's comment about the cowboy intrigued me. He had described Hank Martin perfectly. I wondered what Martin's interest in me was. He was probably working with the girl Jonathan had run off with. It may have been Martin who had followed me. I didn't know what kind of vehicle Martin drove, but he struck me as the pickup truck type of guy.

It began to look more and more like Jonathan didn't run off with the woman, but had been kidnapped. It wasn't the first time I thought that, but at least I now had some reason to believe it was not a bad theory.

The longer I thought about it, the more it seemed there were too many people involved in the disappearance of Jonathan. The fewer involved meant the less the chance of someone talking and the less chance of getting caught.

The longer a person was missing, the less the chance of finding him alive. In this case, it had already gone on way too long. If I were to find Jonathan alive, it would have to be very soon; or I would most likely find him dead, if I found him at all.

There was no doubt in my mind Jonathan would be disposed of as soon as those involved came to the realization Walter was not going to fork over any more money without some proof of life. If Jonathan was still alive, it was only because they needed him to prove it to Walter. Once he had served their purpose, they would kill him and dispose of his body as quickly as possible.

Jonathan might also be killed if his kidnappers felt someone was getting too close to finding out who had kidnapped him. There was no question that the longer they kept Jonathan alive, the greater the chances they would be caught.

MY THOUGHTS WERE SUDDENLY disturbed by the phone ringing. I got up, walked over to the phone and picked it up.

"Hello."

"Pete?"

"Yes."

"This is John."

"Hi, John. Do you have something for me?"

"Yes. The blood you found in the shack belonged to the man you're looking for."

"Are you sure?"

"There's no question about it. The DNA from the brush, comb and toothbrush were all perfect matches to both samples you brought in, the one from the floor and the one from the post. I also found a small strand of rope in the piece of wood you gave me. It had his blood on it, too. It tells me the guy you're looking for had been tied to the post. There's no doubt he was in the shack. I would say he had been there for several days at least."

"Great. That tells me the cowboy is involved in this somehow," I said more to myself than to John.

"What cowboy?" John asked, his voice showing a bit of excitement.

"The one I saw at the old shack the day before Sheriff Stillwell and I searched it. He ran me off, but not before I got a picture of him."

"Do you know his name?"

"The Sheriff identified him as Henry Martin, also known as Hank. Why?"

"I remember a few years back there was a kidnapping case here in Denver involving a guy who was referred to as "The Cowboy"."

"You think there might be a connection?" I asked.

"I don't know, but it wouldn't hurt to check into it. I'll see what I can find out about the old case. Maybe it will give you something to go on."

"Let me know what you find."

"Will do. Talk to you later."

"Okay, and thanks," I said then hung up.

That bit of information put a whole new slant on the situation. Finding the cowboy might help lead me to Jonathan. It was a bit of a stretch, but it was better than anything else I had at the moment.

The more I thought about it, the more I was beginning to think it might be time to pay another visit to the marina where I saw the *Crystal Blue* docked. I might be able to get a little more information out of the owner of the store.

IT DIDN'T TAKE ME LONG to get ready to go. Just as I was about to pull the door on the condo shut and leave, the phone began to ring again. I almost didn't answer it, but I thought it might be important.

"Hello."

"Peter Blackstone?"

"Yes."

"Sheriff Stillwell. The forensic team tells me Max Butler was not killed on your boat."

"I think I told your deputy that last night."

"Yes. You did, but we found that someone had rummaged through your boat. Did you know that?"

"As a matter of fact, I didn't. I had not had a chance to go below and check out the cabin. Did you find any evidence that he was killed in the cabin?"

"No. There was no indication he was killed on your boat, either on the deck or in the cabin. We didn't find any fingerprints to indicate he had been on your boat at all. There was a strong indication that someone was looking for something on your boat, but they must have been wearing gloves. The only prints we found were yours. You got any idea what they were looking for?"

"None at all. I didn't have anything on board except what I might need if I decided to spend a night on board."

"No papers or files or anything like that?"

"Nothing. I don't keep things like that on board. It's too hard to keep them secured. Besides, I just took my boat out of storage earlier on the day I arrived here. I hadn't had time to do much with it except to clean it up a little and put in a few supplies. I haven't even had a chance to change out a couple of pulleys and a couple of cleats that need to be replaced," I replied.

"Did you have any guns hidden aboard?"

"No. Like I said, it's too hard to secure things aboard the boat."

"Well, someone must have thought you had something they wanted. But we did find something else."

"What was that?"

"Remember the deck box on the dock next to your boat?"

"Yeah. What about it?"

"It looks like Butler's body had been put in there for awhile. We figure it was hidden in there, then put on your boat shortly before it was discovered."

"You and I had been sitting on the box."

"Yeah. Ain't life strange?"

"It sure is. Don't take this wrong, but when will I be able to get my boat back?"

"I would think you could have it back by late this afternoon. I'll ask the forensic people to finish up and get it back to you."

"Thanks. By the way, the evidence I took to the State Crime Lab turned out to be very helpful."

"How's that?"

"The blood evidence shows Jonathan was most likely tied up to the post in the shack and was probably there for several days. It looks like Martin had something to hide in the shack after all."

"I'll put out an APB on Hank Martin. I think he has something to do with this, too. I want to know what it is."

"Okay, but my guess is he has gone into hiding and he might be hard to find. He probably knows the back country pretty well. That will make it easier for him to hide."

"You're probably right, but I'm still going to look."

"Okay. I'll talk to you later."

"Okay."

After I hung up the phone, I sat and looked at it for a moment or two. I wasn't interested in the phone, it was what Stillwell had told me. I couldn't figure out what anybody expected to find on my boat. All I had put on the boat was some food and general supplies.

I turned and looked at the door. My mind was full of unanswered questions, and I didn't see how any of them were going to get answered sitting there. I got up and again started out the door.

I went to the parking lot and got in my vehicle. I took a minute to make sure I had my binoculars and my camera before I started the vehicle. I also took a minute to look around before leaving. It seemed to be the prudent thing to do since I had been followed in Denver. Seeing nothing of interest, I put the vehicle in gear and headed for the other side of Dillon Lake.

THE TIME IT TOOK TO GET to the other side of the lake gave me time to think about what was happening. Very little was making any sense. As I approached the Smooth Sailing Marina, I remembered there was an area near the office where I could park with little chance of being seen. If the *Crystal Blue* was still docked at the marina, I would be able to watch it for a bit. If it was not there, I would go in the office and talk to the owner. I needed to know who was on the boat and as much as I could about them.

As I pulled around the corner near the Smooth Sailing Marina, I saw the *Crystal Blue* still docked there. It took me a few minutes, but I found a parking place that would make it difficult for anyone on or near the dock to see my vehicle. Yet, it would allow me the opportunity to watch the boat with little chance of being seen by anyone on the boat.

I sat in my vehicle and kept an eye on the boat through my binoculars. There was no one on deck for about the first thirty minutes or so. I was beginning to wonder if anyone was on board at all. Finally, the woman I had seen on the boat earlier in the week came up on deck. The woman seemed to be rather busy.

After a little while, the woman left the boat and disappeared behind one of the buildings. Since I didn't see her come out onto the road, I got curious as to what she was doing. In a few minutes she returned carrying a couple of grocery bags. It was clear she was taking supplies aboard the boat.

She boarded the boat and immediately went below deck with the packages. I got the impression she was getting the boat ready to set sail.

Nothing else happened for the next hour. No one appeared on deck and no one went aboard or got off the boat.

It wasn't until I saw the woman come back on deck that I sat up and took notice.

She had no more than stepped out on deck when she stopped and looked back over her shoulder toward the cabin. I could see her lips move. She was talking to someone, but I couldn't see who it was. She looked a little upset. Maybe she had a spat with her boyfriend, or maybe something had gone wrong and she was unhappy about it. The best I could do at the moment was to speculate, but I needed facts, not speculation.

The woman headed aft and began untying the tether lines. She worked her way forward along the deck untying each line as she came to it. It quickly became clear she was untying the boat in preparation to leave.

I got my camera out and watched her through the high power lens. I snapped a couple of shots in the hope of getting a better picture of her. If nothing else I would have pictures of her stealing the boat which would get her some jail time if it turned out that I couldn't get her for anything more serious.

She was untying the last rope when she hesitated for a second and looked around. Her actions indicated she was making sure no one was watching. I managed to get a couple of good shots of her face, one showing the small birthmark on the side of her face. It confirmed she was the woman in the picture Walter Endicott had given me. If it was the same woman Nolan had told me about, then there was at least a chance her name was Bonny Ford.

I seriously doubted Bonny Ford was her real name and that Nolan had told me the truth. If he had had a part in all this, I was sure he would not have given me her real name.

As soon as the *Crystal Blue* was untied from the dock, the boat slowly moved away under power, I continued to watch it in the hope of getting a picture of whoever else was on board. I wasn't that lucky. It wasn't long before the boat was turned and was put under sail. It was moving away and

I had seen no one but the woman. As far as I was concerned, it was time to have a little talk with the owner of the Smooth Sailing Marina. Maybe he could shed some light on what was going on.

CHAPTER TEN

I MOVED MY VEHICLE closer to the marina's office building and got out. I could see the *Crystal Blue* off in the distance. If it continued on its present course, it was headed in the general direction of the cove behind the point where it had been anchored before.

I turned and walked into the marina's office building. The owner was talking with a customer so I walked over to a rack of books and began browsing through them. I was suddenly startled by the voice of someone behind me.

"May I help you?"

I turned and saw the man I had assumed was the owner's son. He was smiling at me and waiting to find out if I needed help with anything.

"I would like to talk to your father."

"Oh, he's not my father. He's my uncle."

"Sorry about that."

"It's okay. A lot of people make that mistake. My name's Bill Harden. My uncle is busy with a customer. Is there anything I can help you with?"

"I'm interested in any information you can provide on the people who just left here aboard the *Crystal Blue*."

"I'm sorry, but that information would be confidential."

"It is my understanding you let them take the boat based on a letter from the owner. Can you tell me if that is a correct assessment of what happened?"

He suddenly looked a little confused. He thought about what I had asked and must have decided it would be okay to answer me.

"Yes, that is correct," he replied.

The smile was gone from his face now. He looked as if he had no idea what I was getting at; but I could see from the look on his face, he was concerned why I wanted to know.

"Well, the owner of the *Crystal Blue* claims she never gave anyone such a letter, nor would she ever rent or loan her boat to anyone. What do you have to say about that?"

"Ah - - I - -, are you the police?" he asked.

"No. I'm Mrs. Parker Henry Jones's representative, and as you well know the *Crystal Blue* belongs to her."

"I think you better talk to my uncle."

"I think that would be a good idea. While I'm waiting, I would like to see the letter your uncle claims he got from Mrs. Jones allowing whoever it was to take her boat."

"Yes, sir," he replied nervously.

I watched him as he quickly headed for the office. On his way, he stopped and whispered something in his uncle's ear. His uncle looked at me for a second, then turned and nodded to his nephew. He returned to his customer while his nephew went on into the office.

It wasn't long before Bill Harden returned with a letter. He handed it to me and I took it over to the window where the light was a little better. I examined it and immediately noticed the name of the person who had supposedly rented the boat was Bonny Johns.

On the surface the rental letter looked legal enough, I guess, but the signature on the bottom was not what I would have expected to see. It had been signed with a cheap ballpoint pen. The lines made by the pen were not smooth and even, but blurred and the ink was blue. I had reason to believe it was not signed by Mrs. Jones.

I knew the Joneses well enough to know they would never sign any kind of legal document or letter in blue ink. Parker was a stickler for signing all things legal, or papers that might be construed as being legal, in black ink. I knew that for a fact because I had seen Parker toss a rather expensive pen in a trash can because it had blue ink. I had no reason to believe that Mrs. Jones would do anything differently.

I looked up at Bill. He seemed a little nervous. I expected that reaction from someone if he was guilty of something. His reaction led me to believe he knew darn well the letter had not been signed by Mrs. Jones and they were in deep trouble.

"Did you accept this letter?" I asked.

"No. My uncle did."

"I'll need to talk to him."

"He will be done in a minute," Bill assured me.

"I'll wait."

I didn't give the letter back to Bill. He glanced at it as if he expected me to return it to him, but must have decided he shouldn't press his luck by bothering to ask for it back. He turned and walked back toward the office, but didn't go inside. He stood next to the office door behind a counter and watched me.

It was about ten minutes before Bill's uncle was done with the customer and came over to me. I was sure he recognized me from the other day, but the expression on his face was not a pleasant one. In fact, he looked a little angry.

"What's this all about and who are you?" he asked sharply.

"I'm Mrs. Parker Henry Jones's representative. Who are you?"

"I'm Tom Harden. I own this marina. Now what's this all about?"

"It seems you let someone take Mrs. Jones's boat, the *Crystal Blue*, without proper authorization."

"I did no such thing. I have a letter allowing me to let Miss Bonny Johns take the boat out anytime she wants," he insisted.

"This letter?" I asked as I showed it to him.

"Yes," he replied after glancing at it.

"Do you have a contract to moor the *Crystal Blue* here at your marina?"

"Yes, of course, not that it's any of your business."

"That's where you are mistaken. It is my business since I am Mrs. Jones's representative in matters concerning her sailboat. Might I suggest you take a close look at the contract? I think you will find Mrs. Jones's signature is not the same as the one on this letter."

"I'm not a writing expert."

I found it interesting he didn't even get the contract to compare the signatures. That told me he probably already knew they wouldn't match. That meant one of two things to me. Either he was in on what was going on on the boat, or he figured he could make a few extra bucks renting out a boat he knew was not likely to be used for sometime by the owner.

"I sure as hell hope you are not planning to use that as your defense at your trial? It sounds a little lame to me."

"I don't need a defense. I've done nothing wrong," he insisted.

"Nothing except to let someone use a very expensive sailboat without the owner's permission. How long do you think it would be before the owners of the other boats moored or stored here would pull their contracts with you once they find out what you have been doing?"

"You trying to blackmail me?"

"No. Blackmail is such an ugly word."

"I should toss you out on your head," he said angrily.

"Maybe you could try, but you won't. You won't because I'll have the cops all over you before you know what happened. How long do you think you'll be in business when you're charged with theft of a sailboat?"

"I didn't steal it."

"Maybe not, but you didn't do a very good job of protecting the *Crystal Blue* while it was in your care. All it would have taken was a phone call to verify the letter. Isn't that right?"

He just stood there looking at me for a moment or two. He knew I was right, and he should have called about the letter. He undoubtedly knew Mrs. Jones would not rent out her boat. Anyone in his business would have known enough to check it out before letting some stranger take her boat.

"You're right. I screwed up," he said realizing he was in real deep trouble.

"You sure as hell did. Now you're going to tell me all you can about whose on the boat."

"There's the woman. Her name is Bonny Johns."

"Are you sure about that?"

"Yes. She had ID. A driver's license and a couple of credit cards with her name on them. Her name was the same as the one on the letter."

"Well you can forget the letter. It's not worth the paper it's written on."

I had to wonder if her real name was Bonny Johns. It wouldn't take me long to find out.

"Who else is on the boat?"

"There was a young man, but I don't remember what his name was. I'm not sure she told me."

"Describe him."

"He was about six foot tall, hundred and seventy pounds or so, and he had medium brown hair. He was well dressed, not fancy, but his clothes looked like they were expensive."

"How did he appear?"

"What do you mean?"

"Was he happy, sad, angry, calm, what?"

"I didn't get a good look at him because the woman handled everything. But I did see him briefly when he went aboard the boat. He had to have a little help getting on board, of course."

"What do you mean he needed help?"

"The poor guy is dying of cancer. He was weak from the chemotherapy he had been getting," he said as if I should have known it.

"Who told you that?"

"The woman, Bonny Johns."

"Did the young man ever come off the boat?"

"No. I don't think so."

That answered a lot of questions as far as I was concerned. If Bonny Johns was the woman Jonathan had run off with, it was becoming clear what was going on. Jonathan may have run off with her, but it had turned into a kidnapping very quickly. It had more than likely been a planned kidnapping from the very beginning.

Jonathan had obviously been drugged, probably sometime after they got to Frisco, in order to keep him under control. I was convinced he was being kept sedated on the boat. He had been held for a while at the shack, but my visit to the shack had probably caused them some concern over keeping him there. After my visit to the shack, they moved him back to the boat for fear of discovery before they were done fleecing Walter for all they could get. The only thing keeping them from killing him and disappearing was their greed.

"Thanks for your help. You can be expecting a call from the local Sheriff in the next couple of days," I said, then turned and started toward the door.

"Wait. Is it necessary to get the cops involved?"

"I think so."

"I can get the boat back by - - ah - - ah - - tonight."

It was clear he was trying hard to save his business and his own skin. I guess I couldn't blame him. I didn't really think he did anything all that illegal, he had just been damn stupid.

"You don't do anything," I instructed him firmly. "You don't go near that boat or mention I was here to anyone; and I'll put in a good word for you to Mrs. Jones, and maybe she won't press charges. Don't try and get the boat back, either. I'll take care of that."

"All right. I'll do what you say, but I don't want to lose my business."

"You do as I say and you might stay out of jail. If you're really lucky, you might not lose your business."

"Okay," he replied as he let out a sigh of relief.

As I left the office, I remembered the woman had gone behind the building and returned with a couple of grocery bags. I decided it would be a good idea to take a look back there.

I went around behind the building and found a new GMC SUV. It was probably the same vehicle that was missing from the garage at Jonathan's home in Denver. I looked it over, but I didn't see anything that could be considered criminal. I thought it might be a good idea if the Sheriff went over it with his forensic team, but he couldn't do that without a warrant. At this point, I couldn't see there was enough evidence to get a judge to issue one.

I left Smooth Sailing Marina, returned to my vehicle, and headed back to the East Shore Estates on the other side of the lake. The one thing I had to do was to get aboard the *Crystal Blue*. If Jonathan was still alive, I needed to get him to safety, then the law could deal with Bonny Johns and whoever else was involved.

ONCE I WAS BACK AT East Shore Estates, I took my binoculars and camera inside. I set my camera with its long range lens on a tripod just inside the doors to the balcony. The last thing I wanted was for one of my neighbors to see me spying on the sailboat. I didn't want to get accused of being a Peeping Tom.

From the living room I could make out only about the back one third or so of the *Crystal Blue*. It wasn't an ideal place to view it from, but it was the best I could do under the circumstances.

Looking through the camera, I couldn't make out any activity onboard the sailboat. It looked quiet out there and appeared to have been anchored for the night. If Jonathan was being held on the boat, it only made sense that those onboard would not be spending very much time on deck where they could be seen.

My best guess was they were spending their time watching for anybody that might be snooping around. A close watch would be important. The last thing they would want would be for someone to discover what was going on aboard the boat.

Waiting was always the hardest thing for me to do. Since I had some time on my hands there was one important thing for me to do. I needed to call Jennifer and have her check on a Bonny Johns for me. It wouldn't take her long to find out if Bonny Johns really existed. I picked up my cell phone and called Jennifer at work hoping she had not left yet.

"Department of Motor Vehicles, how may I direct you call?"

"Jennifer Taylor in licensing, please."

"One moment."

The one moment turned out to be almost ten minutes, but I had little choice but to wait. I was beginning to think she had gone home when she finally answered.

"Licensing, Jennifer speaking."

"Hi, Jennifer."

"Hi, Peter. How's the investigation going?"

"I'm not sure. I need your help, again. Could you do me a big favor and run a name for me?"

"Sure. Who is it?"

"I would like everything you can find on a Bonny Johns. That's J-o-h-n-s. By the way, I won't be surprised if she doesn't exist under that name."

"I can certainly find out. Is this important?"

"It really is, Honey."

"Okay. Just a minute."

I could hear the clicking of the keys of her computer keyboard in the background. It would take her awhile to find out everything.

While I waited my mind drifted off to Jennifer. With all that had happened, it was easy for me to think of her and how nice it would be to spend time with her right now rather than sitting here all by myself staring at a sailboat through a camera.

Jennifer and I had our moments in the sun over the years, so to speak. We were not only the best of friends, but we had been lovers from time to time. We were always there for each other, yet, we gave each other room to be ourselves.

Jennifer was everything a man could want in a woman. She was one of the smartest women I've had the privilege of knowing. She was also very beautiful with her long brownish red hair, cute freckles on her nose and a body any eighteen year old girl would kill for. She was tall, carried herself with confidence and was one of the nicest people I had ever met. On top of all that she was sexy.

"There's no Bonny Johns listed anywhere," Jennifer said, interrupting my thoughts. "No driver's license, no criminal record, no nothing."

She sounded a little bit disappointed that she couldn't help me. I had to admit that I was a little disappointed too, but I really had expected nothing different.

"I had a feeling that would be the case. Would you be kind enough to try Bonny Ford and see what that does?" I asked, then waited for a reply.

"No Bonny Ford, either. I'm sorry."

"That's okay. I expected as much. I sure wish I knew who this woman was, but I guess I will have to find out some other way. Thanks a lot, Honey. I appreciate all you do for me."

"I appreciate what you do for me, too. Anything else I can do for you?"

"Not right now, but maybe later."

"Will I be seeing you soon?"

"I don't know, but I sure hope so. I miss you."

"You do?" she said, her voice sounding like she was really pleased to hear it.

"Yes. I do. I'll call you as soon as I get back in town."

"I'll hold you to it. Be careful, Peter. I love you."

"I will, and I love you, too," I said, then hung up.

Other than the pleasure of talking to Jennifer, I had gotten nowhere with the inquiry. I still had no idea who I was dealing with, and no idea what to expect. There was nothing else for me to do but to plan my next move.

I LOOKED BACK OUT AT the *Crystal Blue* for a minute or two while I thought about what to do next. I didn't really come up with a plan on how I was going to get Jonathan off the boat, just few ideas. I didn't know if Jonathan was even on the boat.

If Jonathan was already dead, they would have disposed of his body. I couldn't help but think that the lake would be the most likely place to dump the body. If they weighted his body down it could take months before his remains were found, if ever.

The more I thought about it, the more I was convinced Jonathan was probably alive. If he was dead, they would be stupid to hang around any longer than necessary.

Since I had seen the boat anchored off the point several times, it seemed like the logical place to keep him. Anyone approaching the boat could be seen coming from some distance and from any direction making it easier for them to hide him.

I doubted they would have taken Jonathan back to the shack. The shack was too hard to protect if anyone like the Sheriff got interested in it. It would be too difficult to keep the Sheriff out of the shack if he insisted on seeing the inside.

I had to figure out a way to find out if he was on the *Crystal Blue*. And if he was, how to get him off it to safety. It would not be easy to get him off the boat if they had drugged him, which was probably the case.

If he was drugged, he would be hard to handle and he would most likely need a lot of help. Helping him would put me at a big disadvantage, especially if I had to defend myself and protect him at the same time. However, I could see no choice in the matter. It had to be done, and done as soon as possible.

I began to plan how I was going to get on board the *Crystal Blue* without being seen. It would have to be after it was dark enough to get close to the boat without being seen.

Time passed by slowly. Every minute that passed meant the less my chances of finding Jonathan alive. I also knew there was nothing I could do until it was dark.

It was getting on toward dusk when I first noticed some movement on the *Crystal Blue*. I hadn't seen any movement for so long that it came as a bit of a surprise. It took me a minute to realize what I was seeing. The woman I had seen on the boat earlier was walking toward the stern. It appeared as if she was talking to someone behind her as she kept looking over her shoulder as she talked. I began to wonder who she was talking to and what she was planning on doing.

A couple of seconds later I saw Hank Martin, "The Cowboy", come into view. That answered a couple of my questions. It told me where the guy had been hiding, and that Hank and the woman were in it together. It was no surprise, but it did confirm what I already suspected.

I watched as Hank reached down off the back of the boat and pulled the white and blue dingy up close. He climbed over the side onto a platform at the waterline on the stern of the boat and got into the dingy. I could see him looking up as he talked to the woman. He was either giving or getting instructions, I couldn't tell which. Based on my earlier encounter with him, I would be willing to bet it was the woman giving the instructions.

It was getting darker by the minute and it would soon be dark enough that I would not be able to see anything but the night lights on the *Crystal Blue*. It was time to put my plan into action.

I caught a glimpse of Hank Martin as he began to row the dingy toward the shore. As he disappeared from sight, I closed the doors to the balcony and put my things away. I fixed a light dinner and ate it, then changed into a long sleeved black T-shirt and black jeans. As soon as I was ready, I went down to the berth where my boat was moored.

I WAS JUST GETTING READY to untie my boat when I heard a voice call to me. I looked up and saw Hudson walking along the dock toward me.

"You headed out?" Hudson asked.

"Yes."

"You might like to know there was a cop nosing around your boat earlier."

"I'm sure there was. It was probably one of the crime scene investigators, remember?

"No. It wasn't them. I'd never seen this cop before."

I was sure he knew all the local cops and sheriff deputies.

"Did you get a name?" I asked.

"Sure did. He gave me his card and told me to tell you to call him," he said as he handed me the card. "He said he had to get back to Denver, but would be around his office tomorrow."

I took the card. It was from Mac. I had to wonder why he had driven all the way up here to talk to me. The only thing I could think of was he found out something about Nolan's murder and wanted to know if it had anything to do with my investigation, but he could have done that by phone.

Another thought crossed my mind. Mac already knew it had a lot to do with my investigation and he wanted to know everything I knew. Either way, it would have to wait until tomorrow.

"What time was he here?"

"While you were gone. I'd say around noon."

"Thanks. I'll talk to you again later. I'm in kind of a hurry."

"Sure," Hudson said, then turned and went back the way he came.

I UNTIED MY BOAT, started the motor and left the marina under power. I didn't stay under power very long. The boat moved through the water much quieter under sail.

It was dark now and although it was against the law, I sailed toward the point with all lights off. The last thing I wanted was to have someone on the *Crystal Blue* see me coming. I also didn't want Hank to see me if he had gone ashore to keep a lookout from the point. It was one time when I wished I had night vision goggles and hoped Hank or the woman didn't.

Most of the way to the point I could hardly see anything. I was doing good to make out the outline of the rocky point. It was nice of them to leave a few night lights on for me. It made it easier to find the *Crystal Blue* in the dark. It wasn't until I got to about a hundred yards from the *Crystal Blue* that I was able to make out any of its details.

I dropped anchor as quietly as I could. As soon as my boat was secured, I sat there looking over the *Crystal Blue* for any signs of movement. I didn't see any. The only thing I could see was a dim light coming from one of the cabin windows. The deck was too dark to see anyone. The only other lights on the boat were the night lights, but they gave off little light on the deck. They were designed to be seen by boats approaching while it was anchored, not to light up the deck.

It was time to make my move. In the darkness, I pulled the cord to blow up my small one man life raft. When it was ready, I lowered it over the stern of my boat into the water. Before I went over the back, I took a second to check my gun. It was ready, but I wasn't so sure I was. I slipped it into my holster and climbed down into the life raft.

I began rowing as quietly as possible toward the *Crystal Blue*. I kept my eyes moving as I didn't want any surprises. It took me awhile to get to the stern of the *Crystal Blue*. I tied my raft to the boat while being careful to watch for anyone who might want to do me harm. It was all clear so I silently stood up and got in a position where I could look over the railing.

As I pulled myself up, I peeked over the railing to make sure the deck was clear. I didn't see anyone. I climbed over the railing. Once I was on the deck, I pulled my gun from the holster and moved closer to the cabin door. I listened but didn't hear anything.

I snuck around and peeked in the first cabin window I could see in. I couldn't see anything inside. There wasn't very much light inside the next window, but I could see Jonathan. He looked as if he was asleep. He was sitting at the end of the bunk with his hands behind him. I was sure he was tied and had probably been drugged as well. It was not going to be easy getting him out of there.

There wasn't anyone else in the cabin. That caused me some concern. I had seen Hank leave, but where was the woman? I hadn't seen her leave the boat, but that didn't mean she was still on board. I seriously doubted she would leave Jonathan alone. I wondered if there was anyone else involved. If I went charging into the cabin I might be running into a trap, not something I really wanted to do.

I quickly realized I had little choice in the matter. It was get him off now or lose him forever. I was about to straighten up when I felt something cold and hard at the back of my neck. No one had to tell me what it was. I'd felt the cold steel of a gun barrel before.

"Stand up very slowly, Mr. Blackstone. I would hate to get your blood all over this beautiful boat."

I wasn't stupid. I did as I was told. As I stood without saying a word, I put my hands in the air then slowly turned my head to look over my shoulder. It was the woman I'd seen earlier on the deck. She was wearing black from head to toe, including the gun in her hand. I hadn't seen her when I boarded the boat. She must have been hiding in the dark on the forward part of the deck waiting for me, or for someone to come after Jonathan.

"Let's go inside," she said softly.

"It's too nice a - - -."

"Shut up," she said as she jabbed me in the back with her gun.

I did as she requested, not that I had a choice in the matter. A gun tends to reduce the number of options available, at least for me.

As I moved into the cabin, I could see her behind me in a small mirror on the cabin wall. I watched her closely for any chance to turn the tables on her. It came in just a brief moment when she looked at the counter where a cell phone was located.

When she reached for it, I swung around. I knocked the gun from her hand with my left hand while I hit her with a hard right to the jaw. Her head snapped back and she went flying on her butt. She ended up in a heap on the floor.

I retrieved my gun and picked up the one she had stuck in my back. As soon as I was sure she was out, I went into the other room to get Jonathan and hopefully get him off the boat before Hank got back.

"JONATHAN. JONATHAN," I called as I patted his face in an effort to wake him.

He opened his eyes, but I doubted he was seeing me very clearly. His eyes were dilated and he didn't seem to understand what was happening around him.

"Jonathan, we have to get out of here."

He simply groaned. I rolled him over and untied his hands. Reaching around behind him, I pulled him to his feet. He could hardly take a step on his own, he certainly couldn't walk.

I began dragging him out of the cabin. Just as I stepped up on the deck with Jonathan in tow, I caught a glimpse of something coming at me from the side. In an effort to protect myself, I turned away sharply. I took a glancing blow to my shoulder knocking me to the deck.

A dark figure came at me, but I was able to push Jonathan at him which caused the figure to stumble. I jumped to my feet and placed a hard right to his chin. He staggered back. I didn't hesitate and continued to press the attack. I hit him again and again, giving him no time to recover from the blows. First a right and then a left, another right and then another left.

He was bigger, taller and outweighed me by twenty to thirty pounds. I wasn't about to give him a chance to recover, not even for a second. When I finally had him back against the boat's rail, I took one last hard shot to his nose. I could feel his nose break and flatten under the force of my fist. It was enough to cause him to fall backwards over the railing and into the lake.

I moved up and looked over the side to make sure he wasn't drowning. The last thing I wanted to do was kill him, but I would have if it came to a choice between him or me. I could see him reach out and grab a line hanging off the stern of the boat. He was breathing hard and didn't have any fight left in him, but he wasn't drowning.

I was about to turn around to get Jonathan when I heard something move behind me. I never got the chance to turn around. I felt a sharp blow to the back of my head, then the lights went out.

CHAPTER ELEVEN

I don't know how long I was out, but when I started to come around and opened my eyes I could see a hint of light in the eastern sky. I had one of the worst splitting headaches that I could remember, not that I was able to remember very much at the moment. My headache seemed to dull the rest of my senses to the point I didn't know exactly where I was. When I tried to move, I quickly found I didn't really want to move because it hurt more than just lying there. All I knew for the first couple of minutes of consciousness was that I was lying down on something cold and hard.

I slowly raised my head up in an effort to look around, but as soon as I did my head began to pound like someone was hitting me with a big hammer. I settled back down, closed my eyes and took a few deep breaths in the hope of relieving some of the pain.

After a few moments of relaxing and trying to get myself oriented, I seemed to be able to function a little better. I was starting to remember what happened and why I was lying on the deck of the *Crystal Blue*.

Suddenly, I remembered I had come aboard the boat to find and hopefully save Jonathan. I had had him in tow at one point and had brought him up on deck from the cabin, then moments later I was having a slugfest with "The Cowboy". I didn't remember anything after that until I woke up on the deck.

My concern soon became one of wanting to know where Jonathan was now. In spite of the throbbing headache, I had to get up. The longer I waited, the better the chance the woman and Martin had of escaping.

I pushed myself up on my hands and knees. It had required a good deal of effort, but I knew it wasn't far enough. I had to get on my feet.

As I stood up, I became rather dizzy. I had to reach out and grab a side rail to keep from falling. I took a couple of deep breaths in the hope of not passing out.

As my head cleared a bit, I started looking around. I didn't see Jonathan on the deck. My first thought was they got away with him. But before I could fully believe it, I needed to check out the boat's cabin.

I worked my way to the cabin door. Feeling as weak as I was, I had to hang on to the rails and doors to keep from falling. When I looked into the cabin, my worst fears had been confirmed.

Jonathan was lying on the floor at the bottom of the stairs inside the cabin. The way his body laid suggested that he might have fallen down the stairs. It was not hard for me to believe since Jonathan had been drugged. He had not been very stable on his feet earlier. However, the amount of blood on the cabin floor next to his body indicated he had probably not simply fallen.

As I worked my way down the stairs, I slipped and fell. My light headedness had caused me to slip and I ended up in a sitting position on the next to the last step.

After taking a moment to regain my composure and shake off the light headedness, I looked at Jonathan. His eyes were open and his head was turned so he was looking off to the side. There was no doubt in my mind he was dead.

I stood up and looked down at him for a minute. There was nothing I could do for him now. I slowly worked my way around Jonathan. I was being careful not to step in the blood and to avoid ruining any evidence that might be there.

When I bent down to get a better look at him, it was clear he had been shot twice at very close range. Both bullet holes were neatly placed in his chest, one of them in the heart.

The fact there were powder burns indicated he had either been shot twice with both shots fired very quickly at the top of the stairs, or he had been shot after he fell down the stairs. There was also the possibility he had been shot at the top of the stairs, then shot a second time after he fell to make sure he was dead.

I also noticed something else. My gun was lying on the floor next to him. It wasn't going to take a forensic expert to know whose gun had been used to shoot him. I thought about picking it up, but it was evidence. To take it from the scene would amount to concealing evidence. There was also the slight possibility my gun would prove I didn't shoot him, although there was a slim chance of that happening.

There was one thing I did see that seemed a little strange to me. His hands were tied behind his back. Even with the splitting headache, I remembered untying him before I took him up on deck. The only reason I could think of for someone retying his hands behind his back was to make it look like it was an execution. And the use of my gun to kill him was to make it look like I had executed him.

There was no doubt this was going to be difficult to explain to the authorities. It was also something I couldn't hide from the authorities. The best thing for me to do was to get hold of Sheriff Stillwell and get him on the scene as quickly as possible. I really needed him to get the state forensic team out here, too.

It was at about that time I heard the sound of a motorboat. It sounded as if it was coming closer. I peeked out one of the cabin windows and saw a motorboat coming toward me. It had a red and blue light bar on it and a Sheriff's Office logo in the center of the windshield. I could also see Sheriff Stillwell in the boat along with a couple of deputies.

I took a deep breath, made my way up onto the deck and sat down on one of the benches along the side to wait.

THE SHERIFF'S MOTORBOAT pulled up alongside the *Crystal Blue*. Stillwell was looking up at me.

"You all right?" Stillwell called out as he reached out and took hold of the railing on the *Crystal Blue*.

"I doubt it," I replied almost under my breath.

I don't think Stillwell heard me, but then I wasn't in any hurry to face him, especially when he saw Jonathan's body in the cabin.

"We got a call there had been a shooting on this sailboat. We thought we better come out and check it out."

"I'd be willing to bet it was an anonymous caller?"

"You're right. What made you think that?"

"Just a guess. And you're right about the shooting. Come aboard," I said without getting up.

Sheriff Stillwell climbed aboard and walked over to me. The look on his face seemed to convey some concern. I hoped it was for me, but I was sure it had more to do with my comment than with how I looked.

"What the hell happened to you? You look like you've been in a fight."

"You're partly correct. I was in a fight, then I got my head cracked open from behind, and now someone is trying to frame me for murder."

"For murder? Who are you supposed to have murdered?"

"Jonathan Endicott."

"The guy you were looking for?"

"It was and I found him. Only when I found him he was still alive."

"I take it, he's not alive now?" Stillwell asked sounding almost as if he didn't want to hear the answer.

"That would be correct. You can see for yourself. He's at the bottom of the stairs in the cabin. I haven't touched anything. By the way, he was probably shot with my gun."

"Your gun?"

"Yeah. You'll find it next to the body, but I didn't shoot him."

Stillwell looked at me for a moment or two, than walked over to the cabin door. I watched him over my shoulder. From the look on his face, I got the feeling he was wondering what had happened. As a matter of fact, so was I.

"You might want to get the state forensic team out here. There has to be something in the cabin or on the boat to clear me, or at least prove someone else might have killed him," I said.

Stillwell looked at me, then back into the cabin again. He then turned around and walked up to me.

"First I'm going to take you to the hospital so you can get your head looked at. Then I'll take you over to the office and get a complete statement from you," Stillwell said.

"Okay," I replied as if I really had a choice.

"In the meantime, I'll have the boat towed to the marina for the state forensic team to go over."

"Might I make a suggestion, Sheriff?"

"Sure."

"It might be a better idea if you post a guard on the boat and leave it right here for the forensic team?"

"Why? Is there something you're not telling me?"

"No. They might want to do a little diving around the boat in case some evidence was tossed overboard. Leaving it here will give them a point of reference or a starting point for an underwater search."

"Oh." Stillwell said thoughtfully. "That's not a bad idea."

I watched as he turned to one of his deputies and gave him instructions not to let anyone on board except the state forensic team and the coroner, and not to touch anything. After that he helped me into his motorboat.

"I'm going to have to check your hands for powder residue."

"Sure," I said as I sat down and held my hands out.

Stillwell swabbed my hands with a pad then placed it in an evidence bag. He put the bag in his shirt pocket then nodded at the deputy.

The deputy started the motorboat and pulled away from the sailboat. I closed my eyes and put my hands over my ears. The sound of the motor didn't do anything to help my headache. I didn't know if Stillwell wanted to talk to me or not, but he apparently decided I was hurting too much to talk to him over the noise of the motorboat.

AS SOON AS WE ARRIVED at the dock where the Sheriff kept his boat, I was helped off the motorboat and into a squad car. Stillwell drove me directly to the local hospital where I was taken to the emergency room.

A doctor took a look at the cut on the back of my head, and then examined the cut on my cheek where Martin had gotten in his first and only good punch. He also looked at the cuts on my knuckles. He decided the cuts on my hands and face didn't need anything more than to be cleaned and dressings put over them. He also decided my head wound needed to be cleaned and a dressing applied, but he felt an X-ray was in order to make sure there was nothing serious such as a concussion.

A pleasant young nurse cleaned my cuts and dressed them. She then got a wheelchair and took me to X-ray. When we were done there, she took me to a room. The doctor had suggested that I be kept overnight for observation.

I was a little reluctant to stay overnight, but it couldn't hurt any. Besides, the woman and "The Cowboy" would be long gone by now, anyway. Once I was settled in and lying comfortably in a hospital bed, Sheriff Stillwell came into my room.

"How you feeling?"

"Not too bad considering. Has the state forensic team shown up?"

"Yes. They're going to do an underwater search just in case something was tossed over the side. By the way, the powder residue test was negative."

"Good."

"Are you feeling like answering a few questions?"

"Sure," I replied.

I watched him as he pulled a chair up closer to the bed. He sat down, took a pad and pencil out of his pocket then looked at me.

"Tell me what you know about all this. You might start with how you got on the boat and why you were there."

There was no question that it was time to fill him in on everything leading up to being on the boat. My career was at stake as well as my freedom, and I was going to need his help to prove I didn't kill Jonathan.

I began by telling him what little I had found out about Bonny Ford or Bonny Johns, whatever her name was. I also told him about what my friend at the State Crime Lab had told me about the blood samples we had found in the shack. From there, I told him what I had done, who I had talked to, and anything else I had not told him before. I also told him about the *Crystal Blue,* that I had talked to the owner and that Bonny what's her name was on it illegally.

"You might want to have a little talk with the guy who owns Smooth Sailing Marina," I suggested.

"How's he involved in this?"

"He let Bonny and Martin use the boat without Mrs. Jones permission. If I'm not mistaken, it makes him an accessory to any crime committed while they were using the boat. Other than that, I don't think he's involved in the kidnapping or the death of Jonathan. You might want to see if he is involved in renting other boats without the owner's permission."

"I'll look into it."

"By the way, Mrs. Jones told me that she is prepared to press charges once I'm finished with my investigation. She told me I could act as her representative. Once the state forensic team is done with the boat, I will be pressing charges on her behalf."

"Do you think that's wise?"

"What do you mean?"

"Those involved in Jonathan's death might come back to the marina to hide out. If I arrest Tom Harden, they will know you're on to them," he said. "If I don't do anything, they might come back here to hide out if they think you've moved your investigation somewhere else."

"You might have something there. They would be stupid to come back here, but then criminals are not the smartest people in the world. That's why they get caught. I don't think they will come back here, but I'll hold off on charging them for now just in case."

"What's next?"

"I've got a feeling they will return to Denver. I think they have a place somewhere in the Denver area where no one knows them, especially this Bonny person."

"I'll keep my guys on their toes and, hopefully, if they return we will see them," Stillwell said.

"Great. I'll keep you posted on what I find in Denver."

"Good."

"I take it you're not going to charge me with killing Jonathan."

"Not at the moment. First of all, I don't think you killed him because, if you had planned to kill him you would not have come to see me and tell me about him.

Secondly, I don't have any real evidence that you shot him. I'm sorry, but I will have to keep your gun as evidence for the time being."

"I understand. I have another."

"I'm sure you do. I'll leave you to get some rest for now. If you think of anything you forgot to tell me, give me a call. In the meantime, I'll keep an eye out for Martin and Bonny, and I'll keep an eye on Tom Harden and his marina."

"Thanks. Will you let me know what the state forensic team finds on the *Crystal Blue* or in the lake near it?"

"You think there might be something of importance in the lake?"

"Maybe, but it's just a guess. It sure wouldn't hurt to have them take a look."

"Good point. Talk to you later," Stillwell said as he stood up.

"By the way, you might keep a lookout for my sailboat. The last I saw it, it was anchored about a hundred yards from the back of the *Crystal Blue*. You might also look at Smooth Sailing Marina. I saw Jonathan's SUV parked behind one of the buildings.

"I'll have my guys check around for it."

"One more thing, I would appreciate it if you didn't let it leak out that Jonathan Endicott was found dead. I would like to tell his parents before the whole world knows it."

"Sure. Is that who you are working for?"

"I can't say, you know that," I said with a grin.

"Maybe not, but I can guess," he said with a smile. "I'll talk to you later."

"Sure enough," I said as I watched him leave my hospital room.

AS THE DOOR TO MY ROOM CLOSED, I lay in bed and stared at it. There had been one thing I hadn't mentioned to Stillwell. I didn't mention the visit I received from Captain MacDonald of the Denver Police Department when I wasn't at the condo. I had no idea what Mac wanted, but at the moment I didn't want Sheriff Stillwell to know about it before I did. I would have to give Mac a call as soon as I could.

There was one other call I would need to make as soon as possible. I began to think a visit to Walter and Mrs. Endicott would be much more appropriate. Telling them their son was dead was not the kind of message that should be delivered by phone. It was certainly not the message I'd hoped to bring them.

As I laid there thinking about what to tell them, I heard someone lightly knock on the door. I had not been expecting visitors and I was sure the nurses would simply open the door and come in.

"Come in," I said.

I had to admit I was surprised to see Lora peeking around my door.

"Are you up for visitors?" she said shyly.

"Sure. Come on in."

"How are you doing?"

"I'm doing okay. I've got a bit of headache, but otherwise I'm fine. How are you doing?"

"Pretty good. I wanted to thank you for making me come here. I guess I was hurt worse than I thought."

"You're welcome."

"I - - ah - - heard Max was killed on your boat. Did you kill him?" she asked.

"No. I didn't kill him, and he was not killed on my boat. Someone killed him and dumped his body on my boat to make it look like I killed him.

"I'm sorry, but I had to know if you killed him or not."

"It's okay. Can I ask you a question?"

"What's that?"

"Would you have returned to him if he was still alive after the beating he gave you?"

Almost as soon as I said it, I wished I hadn't. I could see tears starting to well up in her eyes.

"I'm sorry. That was not very kind of me. I hope you can forgive me for being so insensitive of your feelings."

She looked up at me. I could see a hint of a smile of forgiveness, but it was clear I had upset her.

"I'm a little tired. Maybe I should go back to my room now," she said without answering my question.

"Okay," I replied.

I knew I had upset her with my thoughtlessness. As I watched her leave my room, I thought about people in bad relationships. I've heard all the reasons for staying with an abusive partner, but I will never completely understand why someone would allow it. I had no sympathy for Max Butler. As far as I was concerned, it was inevitable that he would end up beaten half to death or killed by someone he abused or by someone who cared about the person being abused by him. The only thing I was glad of was that I had not been the one who killed him.

It was getting late and I was feeling tired. My head was feeling better, but a good night's sleep would be the best medicine for me right now. It had been a long day.

I closed my eyes. My first thoughts were of Lora and what she would do now. I couldn't help but feel a little sorry for her. I only hoped she would seek help in resolving her problems before she found herself in another abusive relationship.

It wasn't long and my thoughts returned to what I was going to say to Mr. and Mrs. Endicott. I had no idea what it would be like to lose an only child. It had to be devastating.

The headache was getting to be just a dull discomfort. I must have been very tired as I soon drifted off into dreamland.

CHAPTER TWELVE

I woke early in the hospital, but then everyone was awakened early in the hospital. Those dutiful nurses have to get all the vital signs taken and recorded before the doctors make their rounds. And breakfast has to be served and the remains picked up as well.

"Good morning, Mr. Blackstone. How are we this morning?" the young nurse asked with a bubbly smile as she prepared the electronic thermometer to stick in my ear.

"I don't know about we, but I'd be a lot better if I didn't have to wake up so early."

"At least you're alive to wake up. That's a good start to any day," she said as she took hold of my wrist.

She had a point. If I had been hit much harder I might not have been around to see the morning. My headache was gone, but the area on the back of my head assured me that I was not going to be wearing a hat anytime soon. The fact that I couldn't wear a hat didn't really bother me because I rarely wore one.

I looked up at her and watched her face as she took my blood pressure. She was no great beauty by the world's standards, but she wasn't bad looking, either. She had mousy brown hair cut in a very practical style. It looked like it was easy to take care of and still looked good. She wore very little makeup, but then she didn't really need much. I noticed she glanced at me and smiled, then turned back to watch for my blood pressure reading on the monitor. She had a very pleasant smile.

"Now that wasn't so bad, was it?"

"No. Tell me, do you have any idea how long I will be a prisoner before they let me out of here?"

"Why, Mr. Blackstone, you don't like it here?" she asked with a grin.

"Not really, but I can assure you it is nothing personal."

"I'm glad to hear that. All the results from your tests are in. Once the doctor reviews them, he will decide if you can be discharged."

"You're not going to give me a hint as to my possibilities of escaping from here with his blessing, are you?"

"I'm afraid not. You'll just have to wait until he comes to see you."

"Any idea when that might be?"

"He usually makes his rounds on the ward about eight, but it might be later or it might be earlier."

"Is that eight in the morning or eight in the evening?" I asked jokingly.

"That depends on whether he has a golf game this morning or not."

I had to admit she had a sense of humor. I had already decided if he didn't show up by ten or so, I would be gone. I had too much to do and too many people to see to spend my time lounging around in a hospital bed that cost more than an overnight at the Grand Hotel on Mackinac Island, including meals.

"Nurse?"

"The name's Joan. What can I do for you?"

"Joan, I was wondering if my cell phone is with my clothes?"

"No. It is in the safe."

"Would it be possible for you to get it for me?"

"I'm afraid not. If you want to make any calls, you will have to make them using the phone next to your bed. Cell phones are not allowed in the hospital."

I looked at the phone for a minute knowing full well what it would cost to use it, and then laid back until she left the room.

I REACHED OVER, picked up the phone and placed a call using my calling card to Captain MacDonald at the downtown precinct in Denver. It took a little while to get through to him.

"Captain MacDonald."

"Mac, this is Peter Blackstone."

"It took you long enough to get back to me."

"I'm sorry, but I've been unable to call you until this very minute. I understand you stopped by to see me. Have you got something of interest for me?"

"I thought you might like to know that Jess Nolan was shot in the head with a small caliber gun, a .22 caliber to be more accurate. He was shot at close range."

"That much I already knew."

"But you didn't know the killer used a towel, a pale blue towel, to muzzle the noise. The M.E. found small pieces of blue cotton cloth in the wound."

"That explains why I didn't hear the shot."

"We found the towel stuffed down alongside the seat of the car he was shot in. It was between the door and seat. The towel also matches perfectly with the towels we found in Jonathan Endicott's house."

"Oh, really?"

"Really."

I found what he had told me interesting. Someone other than Nolan and I had been in Jonathan's house on that afternoon. I had to wonder who. Was it "The Cowboy", Hank, or maybe the woman? There was no doubt in my mind both of them were capable of murder.

"You don't suppose Jonathan shot him? We haven't been able to find him," Mac asked.

"I found him. I know where Jonathan is."

"Where is he?"

"He's on a slab in the Summit County Corner's office."

"When did that happen?"

"Yesterday, or more correctly put, late last night."

"What happened?"

"He was shot twice in the chest at very close range."

"You know who killed him?"

"Not yet, but I sure hope to find out."

"Did he have something to do with your investigation?"

"He was my investigation."

"I don't understand. You want to explain?"

At this point there was no reason to keep Mac out of the loop. He had to know what was going on. He could be a great deal of help to me and maybe I could help him. I had two murders, three if I counted Max Butler. I had no idea what Max had to do with any of it, but he was murdered during my investigation so I couldn't rule him out completely.

I took the next twenty minutes or so explaining what I had been working on and who was involved as far as I knew. The only thing I didn't tell him was who I was working for, but there was little doubt he could figure it out. I separated what I knew from what I could prove, which was very little.

"I take it you have not notified the Endicotts about the death of their son?"

"Not yet. I hope to get out of the hospital later this morning. I need to - -," I said.

"Hospital?" he asked interrupting me. "What are you doing in a hospital?"

"While I was trying to get Jonathan off the boat, someone hit me on the back of the head. When I woke up, the Summit County Sheriff was arriving on the scene, and Jonathan was lying dead on the cabin floor of the boat. He had been shot twice with my gun."

"Is the Sheriff pressing charges?"

"No, not yet. He doesn't think I killed him. This is one time when I'm glad I talked to the local Sheriff about my investigation before I started nosing around on his turf. In fact, Sheriff Stillwell has been working on it with me, a little.

He helped me gather some evidence from an old shack where Jonathan had been held captive."

"What's your next step?"

"As soon as I get out of here, I'm going to the State Crime Lab and pick up reports on all the evidence I had them check out for me. I then plan to come by and see you so we can go over it together. Maybe we can come up with something to help each other on this one."

"I was going to suggest that you stop in and see me."

I knew exactly what he meant. He meant if I didn't, I could plan on him coming to haul me in to have a long and very serious talk. It would be much better for me to go to him than for him to come after me.

"Any idea when I can expect to see you in my office?"

"No, not really. I have to wait to get released from the hospital. As soon as that's done, I'll have to get all the evidence I have here together, then stop at the lab for the reports on that evidence.

"Oh. There's one other thing I need to do as soon as I get back to Denver."

"What's that?"

"I have to tell Mr. and Mrs. Endicott about the death of their son before it hits the news."

"You want me to talk to them? I'll want to visit them anyway."

"I would appreciate it if you would let me talk to them first."

There was a long silence on the phone. I really hoped he would not go see the Endicotts before I had a chance to talk to them. I wanted to get on Jonathan's computer and see if there was anything in it that would help me find his killer.

"Okay. But if you don't stop in here soon, I won't wait."

"I'll call John in the crime lab and tell him to send you copies of all the reports on the evidence I gave him. You can go over it while I'm visiting the Endicotts. Since I don't know when I will get out of here, how about we get together first thing in the morning to go over the evidence?"

Again there was a long silence on the phone. I got the feeling he wasn't interested in waiting that long. He had agreed with me so far. I could only hope he would continue to play along with me.

"Okay. I expect to see you in my office no later than nine o'clock tomorrow morning. Is that clear?"

"Yes, very clear. I'll be there."

"Okay."

"One other thing. Did you take a look at Nolan's loft?"

"Sure. What about it?" Mac asked.

"Did you search Jonathan's house?"

"Yes. What are you getting at?"

"You might want to check out the fancy electronics in Nolan's loft and see if they were purchased by Nolan or Jonathan."

"You think Nolan might have stolen them from Jonathan's house?"

"If they were not stolen from Jonathan, then someone has a matching set of fancy electronics just like the ones in Nolan's pad. According to Nolan, they both had similar TVs and stereo sets, but that may not have been the truth."

"I'll check into it."

"Okay. I'll see you tomorrow."

"Right."

I hung up the phone and immediately called John at the crime lab and asked him to send copies of the reports on all the evidence to Captain MacDonald. He said it would be no problem. He would send them by courier within the hour. After my brief conversation with John, I hung up the phone. There was nothing else for me to do now but to wait for the doctor to give me the okay to leave.

Time passed by very slowly. While I waited for the doctor, I let my thoughts wander around freely in my head. I began to realize I had not given much thought to Max Butler.

I had no idea what he had done for a living except to beat up on young women and probably weaker men. I hadn't mentioned him to Mac. I wasn't sure why. What part had he played in it? Was he killed in an attempt to get the Sheriff to get me out of the way? If he was, it didn't work. I wondered if he was involved in any of it.

MY THOUGHTS WERE QUICKLY interrupted by the door to my room swinging open. I glanced up and saw the doctor walking in. He had a big smile on his face. It reassured me there was a good chance I would be released.

"Well, Doc, how am I doing?"

"Not too bad. You took a pretty nasty blow on the back of your head, but there doesn't seem to be anything seriously wrong. Maybe a slight concussion, but nothing to worry about."

"That's great. When do I get out of here?"

"I think you can leave as soon as you're ready. However, I would like you to take it easy for a few days."

"By take it easy, you mean I shouldn't get into any fights?"

"I wouldn't recommend it," he said with a slight chuckle. "What I really mean is you should rest a bit more than you usually do. Maybe take an afternoon nap for an hour or so, go to bed a little early and sleep in a little later than normal."

"Other than that, I can do pretty much what I feel like?"

"I wouldn't suggest you overdo anything for at least the next couple of days, but that's about it."

"Okay."

"I can give you a prescription for something for pain if you want, but I would prefer you didn't take anything unless you really are hurting."

"I usually get by on aspirin. Would that be okay to take if I need something?"

"That would be fine if you can tolerate it."

"That's what I usually take for a headache or most aches and pains."

"Good. I don't think there is any need for me to see you again unless you have some difficulties. If you like, I can send your medical records to your own physician."

"No. I'll be going back to Denver today, but I will be back in a couple of days. I'll check in with you and pick up my records then. I don't really have a regular doctor."

"That would be fine."

"So I can go?" I asked as I stood up alongside the bed.

"Yes, but I'd suggest you change into something more suitable for the outside world," he said with a grin. "That hospital gown doesn't cover your backside very well."

"Right, Doc," I said with a chuckle.

As soon as he left, Joan came into my room. She had a plastic bag with my belongings in it.

"Here are your things. I'll take you down to the discharge desk as soon as you're ready."

"I'll be ready in 10 minutes."

Joan smiled and left the room. I sat on the edge of the bed and began pulling my clothes out of the bag. I found it strange to have a holster on my belt and no gun to put in it. I took it off the belt and stuffed it back in the bag.

As soon as I was ready, I went to the door. Joan was standing next to the nurse's station. I saw the wheelchair in front of it and I knew it was for me.

"Great. I get a free ride?"

"You get a ride. I'm not so sure you will think of it as free once you get the bill for your stay with us."

"I know what you mean. But since I'm paying for it, I'll take the ride."

I sat down in the wheelchair and let her wheel me to the discharge desk. As soon as I was finished with the paper work, I went to the front lobby and placed a call to the Sheriff's Office.

"Summit County Sheriff's Office."

"Yes. This is Peter Blackstone. Is the Sheriff in?"

"Yes. One moment, please."

I was immediately put through to Sheriff Stillwell.

"Hi, Peter. How's it going?"

"I've been released from the hospital. I was wondering if I could get a ride back to my condo. I wouldn't ask, but I want to talk to you before I head back to Denver."

"Sure. I'll be there in about ten minutes."

"Great. I'll be in the front lobby."

"I'm on my way."

I hung up the phone and sat down where I could see out the front doors. My thoughts once again turned to Max Butler. He was the one inconsistency in the investigation that I couldn't figure out. Based on what I had been told, I could not see how he was connected to Jonathan. As far as I knew, he didn't even know any of those who were connected to Jonathan's disappearance and subsequent death. I guess I was hoping Sheriff Stillwell could shed some light on it for me.

IT ONLY TOOK STILLWELL about five minutes to get to the hospital. When I saw him drive up, I went out to meet him. He waited in the car while I got in.

"What's up," he asked.

"First of all I need a ride to East Shore Estates."

"I know where you live," he said as he pulled away from the front of the hospital. "What is it you wanted to talk to me about?"

"What did you find out about Max Butler?"

"Not very much. We know he was killed somewhere else and his body dumped on your boat. We know he was shot with a high power rifle, probably a .30 caliber. Other than that, we don't know much."

"Could it have been a 30-30?"

"Sure. Why?"

"Remember the picture I showed you of Hank Martin outside the shack?"

"Yeah."

"Could it have been the rifle he was holding? I believe it was a 30-30 Winchester."

"It could have been. I've known Martin to beat up a guy now and then if provoked, but never to shoot anyone."

"It wouldn't be much of a step up to shoot a man."

"That's true enough."

"Do you know of any connection between Martin and Butler, even a little connection?" I asked.

"No. Not that I can think of off-hand."

"Do you know if they knew each other?"

"I doubt it, but I don't know for sure. Martin is just about what he looks like, a cowboy. He works hard when he can get work which is what makes him strong. He isn't very bright. He seems to like to live in the past when cowboys worked hard and played hard, and didn't always play by the rules. I hear he is a good cowhand.

"Butler is a different story. He was not like Hank at all. He was a city kind of guy. He didn't work if he could figure out how to keep from it. He was impressed with himself and got his muscles working out at a gym. He also fancied himself as a ladies man," Stillwell explained.

"Any idea how he made his living?"

"Not really. I think he mostly lived off women. I've heard there are a couple of middle aged women who kept him in spending money in exchange for favors now and then, if you know what I mean," he said as he glanced over at me.

"I get the idea."

"Why all the questions about Max? You got something in mind?"

"I was just trying to see if there was some connection between him and the case I've been working on."

"I don't see one," he said.

"I don't either."

We didn't have much to say the last few miles to the East Shore Estates. I guess we were both thinking.

He turned into the drive of East Shore Estates and stopped in front of the building my condo was in. I looked over at him. I wasn't sure what to say.

"I'll keep in touch with you on what the State Forensic team comes up with," he said.

"I'd appreciate that."

"I'll see you back here soon?"

"I'm not sure when, but I'll be back. When I get back, I'll give you a call to let you know."

"Great. Take care of your head," he said with a smile.

"Will do. Thanks for the ride."

Sheriff Stillwell simply nodded and I closed the door. I stood there and watched him as he drove off. As soon as he was out of sight, I went inside. I packed up everything I thought might be important for MacDonald to see and loaded it in my vehicle. I then took off for Denver.

CHAPTER THIRTEEN

I arrived at the State Crime Lab in Lakewood shortly before eleven. The receptionist told me that John was very busy and didn't have time to talk to me right now, but he had left an envelope for me. As she handed me the envelope, she also told me that copies of the reports had already been sent to Captain MacDonald by courier.

I opened the envelope and found reports on all the evidence John had processed for me along with the photos. I thanked the receptionist and left the building.

As I walked out to my vehicle in the parking lot, I looked to see if the Chevy pickup was anywhere around. I didn't see it so I got into my vehicle, set the reports on the seat next to me and drove out of the lot. My first stop was the home of Walter and Mrs. Endicott.

I arrived at the Endicott home in Cherry Creek a little before noon. I couldn't see any vehicles in the drive, but the garage doors were closed. There was a chance Walter wasn't home, but I felt what I had to tell them was too important to wait any longer. I would have to take my chances that they would let me look over Jonathan's computer.

I pulled up in front of the house and sat there for a couple of minutes mentally figuring out what I was going to say if Walter was there. While thinking about it, I took my spare gun out of my briefcase and slid it into my sport coat pocket. I sort of wished Sheriff Stillwell had not kept my regular gun, but understood why he needed to keep it.

I opened the vehicle door, went up to the house and rang the doorbell. I looked around as I waited for someone to come to the door. My attention was quickly drawn to the door when I heard the latch click. The door opened and the young Hispanic woman I had met before answered the door.

"Good morning," I said. "I would like to speak to Mrs. Endicott, please."

"Come in, Mr. Blackstone."

I smiled and stepped inside.

"I'll tell her you are here."

"Thank you."

I watched her as she left the foyer. I couldn't hear anything so I had no idea who might be in the house.

Mrs. Endicott came into the foyer from the living room. She smiled as she walked toward me.

"Good morning, Mr. Blackstone. I hope you have some news for me."

"As a matter of fact I do. Could we maybe sit down in your study?"

The smile faded from her face. I got the impression I had in some way foretold her that the news I had was not good news.

"Yes," she replied, her voice had taken on a serious tone.

She hesitated for a second looking into my eyes before she turned around and lead me to the study. Once inside, she sat down and graciously pointed to a chair for me to sit on.

"It is not good news you bring me, is it, Mr. Blackstone?"

"No, I'm afraid not."

"Is Jonathan dead?" she asked, her eyes pleading with me to tell her that he was alive.

"Yes, Mrs. Endicott. Jonathan is dead."

She didn't say anything for sometime. She just looked at me as if she found what I told her too hard to understand. I could see a small tear start to slowly roll down her cheek.

"Does Walter know?"

"Not yet."

"Thank you. A mother needs to know these things first."

I wasn't sure what she meant. Maybe she needed time to be alone with her thoughts. I wasn't sure.

"Where is Jonathan now?"

"He's at the Summit County Coroner's Office."

"Do you know who killed him?" she asked, her voice breaking up with grief.

"Not for sure."

"But you have an idea who it is?"

"Yes, but I'm afraid I can't prove it. I could use a little help from you."

"Of course. What can I do?"

"I would like your permission to take a look at Jonathan's computer, the one he has in his room here."

"Do you think it will help?"

"I really don't know, but I would like to give it a try."

"I guess it would be all right. You know he has another computer at his home?"

"I'm afraid that computer is gone. It was stolen along with some of his other electronics."

"You mean someone broke into his house and stole his things?" she asked, a surprised look on her face.

"Yes. I have the police looking into it."

"Oh. Why would someone do that?"

"I don't know. I'm hoping to find out from his computer here. Would it be all right if I take a look at Jonathan's computer now?"

"Yes. I think it would be okay."

"Will you be okay?"

"Yes. I need to call Walter."

"Could I ask you to do me a really big favor?"

"What is it?"

"Could you delay calling Walter for maybe an hour or so?"

"Why? He needs to know about Jonathan."

"I'm sure he does, but he might get angry with me for not being able to save Jonathan. If that happens before I have a chance to look at what is on Jonathan's computer, he might cause me to lose valuable evidence that would help me find the killer of your son."

"I see your point," she said after taking a moment to think about it. "I guess it wouldn't hurt to wait an hour to tell him."

"Thank you. I'll get started, if you don't mind?"

"Please. I'd like to be alone for a few minutes."

"I understand."

I stood up, left the study and went upstairs to Jonathan's room.

AS I STEPPED INTO JONATHAN'S room, I quickly noticed nothing seemed to have changed. The armoire that held his computer stood in the corner with the doors closed. I opened it and got one hell of a surprise. There was no computer in the armoire. The scanner, monitor and the printer with a fax were there, but the PC unit was gone.

Why was it gone? Who would want what was in it? My thoughts turned to Mrs. Endicott. I had gotten the impression she didn't know it was missing. If she had known it was gone why would she give me permission to look at it? I wondered if Walter knew it was gone.

I took a minute to step back and look at the armoire. My mind was filled with questions. What was on the computer, or what did someone think was on the computer that made someone steal it? What would Jonathan have on this computer he might not have on the one taken from his home?

That last question made me think of something else. Who would know he had two computers, one at his home and one at his parents' home? I could think of several people right off the top of my head who would know. Nolan, Jonathan's parents, and possibly the one who had shot Nolan were four that I could think of who might know.

There could have been more, but not anyone I could think of at the moment.

As I sat there on the bed looking at the armoire and thinking about what might have been on the missing computers, I noticed something under a shelf. I had to bend down in order to see it better. It was dark red and looked like a piece of plastic. It was thin and about three to four inches long and it didn't seem to belong there.

I stood up and walked over to the armoire. I knelt down and looked up under the keyboard shelf. At the back of the shelf was a black metal clip hooked to the bottom of the shelf. The clip was holding a red plastic computer disk. At first it didn't seem like a very safe place to hide a disk, but as I thought about it I realized it had worked. Whoever had taken the computer had apparently missed seeing the disk.

I took the disk off the clip and looked at it. There was nothing written on the disk label to indicate what it contained. Not having a computer to put it in and open the files, I slipped it into my pocket.

If there was one hidden disk there might be others. I searched the entire armoire from top to bottom, front and back and underneath, but found nothing more. I continued searching the entire bedroom, but found nothing else that might help me find the killer of Jonathan.

A quick glance at my watch told me I had been there about as long as I dared. If Mrs. Endicott had called her husband, I could expect him to arrive at anytime now.

After making sure everything was back where it belonged, I closed the armoire. I went downstairs to the study and found Mrs. Endicott sitting on the sofa next to the phone. It was obvious from her red eyes she had been crying. She looked up at me.

"Did you find anything that will help you?" she asked, her voice soft.

"No. I didn't find anything, but thank you for letting me look."

I decided I would say nothing about the missing computer for the time being. I would wait until I had some idea of what was on the disk.

"I called Walter. He should be home anytime now."

"Would you like me to wait until he gets home?"

"Thank you for offering, but that won't be necessary. I already told him."

"I guess I'll leave if you don't need me."

"Will you still look for Jonathan's killer?" she asked.

"Do you want me to?"

"Yes. I know Walter's temper. He will be upset with you for not being able to save Jonathan. I know you tried. I also know he didn't do everything he should have from the very beginning to make it easier for you to find our son. Walter will probably blame you for it, but don't you worry about it. I'm sure you did your best. I don't care what Walter says, I want you to find the person who killed our son, and I'll see to it you get paid for it."

"Thank you. I will keep you posted on what I find."

"I should be thanking you. At least now we know where our son is."

I didn't know if there was anything else to say to her. As I left, I thought maybe I should have told her about what happened on the boat, but then maybe it was better this way. For all she knew, he was dead when I found him. For the time being it was enough. One day I would sit down and tell her the whole story, but for now I needed to find his killers.

I got into my vehicle and drove away. As I turned at the end of the street, I saw Walter drive by. I don't think he saw me. He was looking straight ahead. I felt a little sorry for him.

THERE WAS A HAUNTING FEELING in the back of my mind that said Walter was involved in it somehow. The only problem was I didn't know how, but I intended to find out. Right now I needed information on Walter and his business. I had no idea if his business practices had anything to do with Jonathan's abduction or not, but I was going to find out. At the moment, I had no other leads. The best place for me to get information about a local businessman was at the library, and that was where I headed.

It was shortly after noon when I arrived at the Denver Public Library. As I got out of my vehicle, I looked around for the Chevy pickup that had followed me earlier. I let out a sigh of relief when I discovered it was nowhere in sight.

As I walked across the parking lot toward the library building, I realized I was getting hungry. There was a little café just down the street that had very good noon specials. I decided to walk down the street to the café and get a bite to eat before diving into my research on Endicott, Inc.

Since I had been followed, I paid closer attention to everything going on around me as I walked down Broadway. I wanted no surprises. As it turned out, it was a peaceful walk that gave me time to think.

As I entered the diner, I noticed a young woman that I had seen before. Her name was Lisa. The last I had heard she was working at the library. I wasn't going to disturb her, but she looked up and saw me. She smiled and motioned for me to join her. I walked over to her booth.

"Hi, Lisa. How are things going?"

"Pretty well. Would you like to join me? I've already ordered."

"Sure. How are things going with the policeman you were dating?" I asked as I slipped into the booth across from her.

"I still see him once in a while, but it has kind of cooled lately, if you know what I mean."

"Yes. Unfortunately, I know exactly what you mean," I said.

"You still a PI?"

"Yes. Are you still at the library?"

"Yes."

"Are you working this afternoon?"

"As I matter of fact, I am."

"Maybe you can help me. I'm doing some research again."

"Is it an investigation you're working on?" she asked.

"Yes, it is."

At that moment the waitress showed up. I placed an order and watched her as she walked away.

"Who are you investigating this time?"

"I'm just looking for some background information on one of our local businessmen. I'm not really investigating him, I'm looking more into who his partners are," I said because I didn't want her to get the wrong idea.

"That sounds interesting," she said with a smile. "I can help you with it."

"I'm hoping you can."

Her meal came and I sat back to give her a chance to eat while it was hot. It was only a couple of minutes later that my meal showed up. That was one of the advantages of ordering the daily special. It was usually ready faster than other items on the menu.

As we ate, I noticed she kept glancing at her watch. A quick glance at my watch made me think she might be running late on her lunch hour.

"Are you in a hurry?"

"I don't have a lot of time. I have to get back to work. It took longer to get my order than I thought it would," she said.

"I can save you a little time. As soon as you're done eating, go ahead and go back to work. I'll pick up the tab for you."

"You don't have to do that," she said looking across the table at me.

"I want to. Besides, I will need a lot of help when I get to the library. It will be my way of expressing my appreciation for your help."

"Thank you," she said with a smile.

She finished eating and thanked me again before heading back to work. I watched out the window as she hurried toward the library. As soon as she was out of sight, I finished my meal.

When I was finished, I paid the bill and went back to the library. Once in the library, it didn't take me but a few minutes to find Lisa.

"Hi again," she said as I walked up to the counter. "You ready to get started?"

"I guess so."

"You mentioned you were looking into the partners in a business. If you tell me what business you're interested in, I can look up everything we have on them for you."

"What I'm interested in knowing is who are the partners or major shareholders in the Endicott auto dealerships? It goes by the name Endicott, Inc."

"All of them?"

"Yes, please."

"Are you interested in anyone in particular?"

"Not at the moment. Once I find out who the partners or major shareholders are I might be."

"Okay. I would guess the best place to start would be the business's Articles of Incorporation. That should give you the names of all those involved in the corporation."

"That sounds good. Do you have that kind of information?"

"Not here, but I can access it on the computer. It will take me a little while."

"How long is a little while?" I asked.

"Maybe an hour. Is there anything else you would like while you wait?"

"I'd like anything you can find on Walter Eugene Endicott. I believe he is the principal stockholder in Endicott, Inc."

"I'll get you started on that, and then I'll get the Articles of Incorporation for you."

"Good. I'll just sit over there," I said as I pointed to a large empty table.

"Things have changed a lot since the last time we worked together. It will be faster if you come with me. We have these new computers with articles from all the local newspapers in them. It's much faster and easier than looking everything up in the paper. I'll show you how it works."

I FOLLOWED LISA into a small room. There was a table with a computer on it and a comfortable looking chair. I sat down and she showed me how it worked. Although I was not fond of computers, it was as easy as she said it would be.

I began scanning through the list of newspaper articles on Walter Endicott and Endicott, Inc., until I came to the first article mentioning the incorporation. I brought the article up on the screen. The article had a couple of pictures with it of where the deal had been publicly announced. The announcement had been held in front of one of the Denver dealerships. After a minute or so of trying, I was able to enlarge one of the newspaper photos. Walter and his son, Jonathan, were in the front row. I was able to identify Nolan in among the salesmen in the background. There were a couple of faces other than most of the salesmen that I didn't recognize, but there was one I did. His name was Jacob Wiengart.

Wiengart was an accountant. He had been connected to a racketeering investigation a few years ago. I couldn't remember if any charges were ever filed against him.

Seeing Wiengart in the picture got me to thinking. I remembered something Walter had told me when we first met. It had to do with his business attorney. I began to think that a background check on both might prove interesting.

I continued my search of the newspapers over the past couple of years. I came upon another name that rang bells with me, Joseph Bartlett.

Joseph Bartlett was smart, well educated, resourceful, and had a number of very loyal enforcers. As far as I knew, he had never been arrested although he had been questioned several times. He was the kind of guy who got where he was by forcing people to give up what he wanted without much of a fight, usually through extortion, trickery and deceit.

I had to wonder if Bartlett was involved in Jonathan's kidnapping. I wanted to know what he had been up to over the past few months.

It was about that time, Lisa came into the room. She had a big smile on her face and some papers in her hand.

"I got a list of the officers of Endicott, Inc. I hope it is what you wanted," she said as she held out the papers.

"That's what I want," I said. "Thank you."

I took the papers and began looking them over. One name jumped out at me. It was Joseph Bartlett. He was listed as one of the corporate officers. I found it interesting. I would have bet he was trying to buy Walter out and Walter was not cooperating with him. I remembered Walter had said he owned a little over half the stock in the corporation and the entire dealership in Fort Collins. I would not put it past Bartlett to have Jonathan kidnapped in order to get Walter to relinquish his holdings in Endicott, Inc., including the dealership in Fort Collins.

I looked up at Lisa and smiled. She had provided me with a starting point at least. What I needed now was to find out how Bartlett had gotten his hands on any of the Endicott, Inc. stock.

"You do good work."

"Thank you," she replied with a smile.

"Is there some way I can get copies of a couple of the articles here?"

"Sure. All you have to do is return to the summary page," she said.

"Summary page?"

"Yeah. Let me show you."

Lisa leaned over my shoulder and pressed a couple of keys. The next thing I knew I was at the page listing all the articles dealing with Endicott, Inc., on the screen again.

"Which articles do you want copies of?"

I pointed to three articles. She put the little arrow on each one of them, and then clicked the mouse.

"They're printing. It costs ten cents a sheet."

"That's fine."

While the articles were printing, she explained what she did to get them. As soon as they were done, I thanked her for her help, gathered up the pages and took them to the checkout desk. After paying for the copies, I left the library.

CHAPTER FOURTEEN

LEAVING THE LIBRARY, I walked directly to my vehicle. It didn't take me long to get back to my office. As I pulled into the underground parking, I kept an eye out for the Chevy pickup. The last thing I wanted was to be surprised. I didn't see it anywhere.

I went to my office and sat down behind the desk. I began looking at the papers I had gotten from the library. Bartlett seemed to be the big investor in Endicott, Inc. I wondered how much of the stock he had, but more importantly I wanted to know how he got hold of it. Walter didn't strike me as the type to want to share his business with anyone.

The next few hours went by rather quickly. When I got done reviewing the papers, I found I still didn't know much more than I had suspected. If I was right, there was more to Jonathan's kidnapping than simple extortion for money. My next move was to pay a visit to Walter Endicott. When I started looking into Jonathan's disappearance, Walter had kept some valuable information from me. I could only guess what else he had kept from me.

I took a look at my watch and saw it was almost six o'clock. From what I had been told, Walter should be getting home about now. There was a good chance that he was already at home with his wife grieving over the loss of their son. I could think of no better time to visit with him and his wife. Maybe if she was there, he would open up a little. I not only wanted to know who had killed his son, I wanted to know why they killed him.

I WENT DOWN TO THE PARKING GARAGE in the basement of the building. Just as I was stepping out of the elevator, a shot rang out and a slug slammed into the cement wall not more than a few inches from my head. I got a quick look at the truck that the shot had come from as I dove for cover behind a car. I quickly drew my gun. I heard the sound of tires squealing in the garage and stood up in time to see the black Ford pickup with big oversize tires and chrome rims pull out of a parking space and race toward the exit. I fired two rounds at the back of the pickup. One of them smashing threw the rear window, but I wasn't sure if I hit anyone.

As the pickup sped out onto the street, it was hit broadside by a car. The front of the low car nosed under the truck's side causing the driver of the pickup to lose control and the pickup to rollover on its side. It looked like it was again struck by a car coming from the other direction, but it was not hit hard.

I ran out of the garage with my gun in hand. As I approached the pickup, I kept my gun at the ready and worked my way to the front of the pickup. I could see two men inside the pickup through the broken windshield. They were both trapped inside. One of them was moaning in pain, but the other one was just lying under the driver. He wasn't making a sound or moving. There was no doubt they were not going anywhere.

I slipped my gun into my holster and turned toward the car that had caused the pickup to turn over. The driver was a young woman. She had a few minor abrasions from her airbag and was shook up a bit, but otherwise looked okay.

"You all right?" I asked.

"I think so," she replied.

"Don't move. Just stay right there until the ambulance gets here."

She didn't say anything. She simply nodded her head slightly.

I ran around back of the pickup to check on the other driver. When I got to him, he was out of his car and looking at the front of it. It was apparent he had not hit the pickup very hard, if at all. The front of his Cadillac was hardly scratched. He hadn't even hit it hard enough to release his airbags.

"What the hell's going on here?" he demanded. "And why the hell are you shooting at these guys?"

"I'm the guy they were shooting at in the first place."

"Wait 'til I talk to my attorney. I'll have your badge."

I couldn't help but smile.

"First of all, I don't have to explain a damn thing to you. Secondly, you can't take from me what I don't have."

The expression on his face was priceless as it soaked into his pea sized brain what I said. His mouth fell open and his eyes got big.

"I'm not a cop, so sit down and shut up. When they get here you can tell them what you saw, until then I've injured people to look after," I said then turned and walked away.

"You're not a cop?" he asked in surprise.

I didn't bother to turn back around and reply. The young woman was in a lot more need of help than he was. All he was interested in doing was suing the city. It made me think he was probably a lawyer who made his living suing people.

I walked up to the woman. She was still sitting in her car.

"How you doing?"

"Okay, I think."

"There will be an ambulance along in a few minutes. They will check you out."

"Thank you. That pickup came out of nowhere. I didn't even see it until it was too late," she said looking at me with eyes asking me to believe her.

"I know. I saw the whole thing. It was not your fault. And don't worry. I'll be here to tell the police everything."

"Thank you," she said as she tipped her head back against the headrest, closed her eyes and let out a sigh of relief.

I walked back over to the pickup and looked inside. The driver seemed to be coming around. He opened his eyes and looked at me, but didn't say anything.

"Don't move," I said as I pushed my coat back so he could see I had a gun.

I took a minute to look over the two men in the pickup. They were carrying guns, but that was no surprise. They were dressed in western shirts, jeans and from what I could see they had on cowboy boots, yet neither of them was Hank. My gut feeling was they were probably working for Hank.

It wasn't long before the police showed up. The first officer on the scene walked up to the pickup and looked at me.

"You again," he said.

"Yes, me again."

I recognized him from the other day at the alley behind Jonathan's home.

"You going to explain what happened this time, or do I have to call Captain MacDonald again?"

"Call Mac, but I'll tell you about it this time. First call for an ambulance."

"There's an ambulance on the way. It should be here any minute now."

"Good. There's a woman over there that is hurt, but she's doing okay for the moment. There's at least one hurt in the pickup, the driver. The other guy looks like he might be dead. They're not going anywhere until the rescue squad gets here to pry them out. You might like to know they're both armed."

The officer looked at the men in the pickup. As he did, he put his hand on his gun. With his free hand, he called for another ambulance and a rescue truck.

"You might want to check on the woman. Oh, there's a guy on the other side of the pickup who claims to be involved, too. He said he ran into the pickup after it turned over. He's already screaming about suing. He's not hurt, just mouthy. His fancy Cadillac has a couple of scratches on the front bumper. I'm not even sure they are from his hitting the pickup. He may have already had them."

"Thanks. I'll check on the woman."

"I'll keep these two company for you."

"Thanks," the officer said.

The officer walked around to the other side of the pickup, while I leaned against the hood of the pickup and waited. It wasn't long before an ambulance showed up. Mac showed up a couple of minutes after that.

When the ambulance crew arrived to check on the injured, I stepped back and got out of the way. The woman was taken away first. The two in the pickup were pried out and placed on stretchers. One of them was dead. The other guy was in pretty serious condition and in no condition to talk.

I noticed the officer had taken two pistols off the guy on the bottom and one from the driver. He looked up at me and smiled. The look on his face told me that he was glad I told him about the guns.

"I thought we were going to meet tomorrow morning?" Mac said as he walked toward me.

"I sure as hell didn't plan this."

"What can you tell me?"

I took a minute or so to give Mac a brief explanation of what happened.

"Any idea why they took a shot at you?"

"Not really, but I must have stepped on someone's toes."

"Any idea whose?"

"No, but I must be getting close to something."

"You said you fired a couple of rounds at them. Any more than that?"

"No. Just two shots. Both of them went into the pickup. One threw the tailgate and probably lodged in the back of the driver's side seat. The second one took out the rear window. I think it hit the passenger. It may have been what killed him."

"It was what killed the passenger. The other guy wasn't shot. His injuries were the result of the car flipping the pickup. What about shots at you?" Mac asked.

"Only one. It hit the concrete just to the left of the elevator door. They fired once and then split."

"Okay. I'll take it from here."

"Any idea who those two are?" I asked.

"Not at the moment, but I might have an idea by the time you show up at my office in the morning."

"Good. Am I free to go?"

"Sure. I'll talk to you in the morning."

"Okay."

It was now close to eight o'clock. I was beginning to feel tired and was starting to get a little bit of a headache. I remembered what the doctor had told me and decided he was right.

I walked back into the garage. As I passed the elevator, I could see some of the people from the forensic unit looking at the wall where the bullet had struck. They were looking for evidence. With the concrete wall, they would be lucky to find anything but a few bullet fragments.

I got into my vehicle and headed for home. It didn't take me but about fifteen minutes to get to my apartment. Even though I was tired and there was a dull ache at the back of my head, I still kept an eye out for the green Chevy pickup with the dark tinted windows.

As I turned into the drive and went around the back of the apartment building to the garages, I remembered I was originally headed for Endicott's home in Cherry Creek. With the way I was feeling it would have to wait until tomorrow.

Once inside my apartment, I took a couple of aspirin. I was a little hungry so I fixed myself a bowl of tomato soup with a few crackers on the side.

By the time I finished the soup, it was only about nine o'clock. I went into the bedroom. I was so tired at that point I simply took off my clothes and crawled into bed. It wasn't but a few minutes and I was asleep.

I HADN'T SET THE ALARM when I went to bed, but I woke up to a gray morning and to the sound of rain on my window. I rolled over and looked toward the window. It seemed like the perfect morning to close my eyes and go back to sleep, but I had an appointment with Captain MacDonald. It was an appointment I didn't want to miss. The last thing I wanted was to make him come and find me. I didn't want to piss him off by not showing up on time. I needed him on my side.

If I got up now, I would have time to fix myself breakfast and still get to Mac's office on time. I swung my legs over the side of the bed, sat up and rubbed the sleep from my eyes. The first thing I needed to do was take a shower to get myself fully awake.

After a shower and shave, I got dressed then fixed my usual breakfast. As soon as I was done, I left my apartment and drove to my office where I picked up the items I wanted Mac to see. I left the office and headed for the first precinct. It was only a few blocks from my office. It would have been an easy walk, but I planned to go see Walter Endicott immediately after I was done at Mac's office, plus it was still raining.

As I left the parking garage for the first precinct, I noticed the same Chevy pickup that had followed me before. Since I was going such a short distance, I figured I would simply let him follow me. In fact, he could follow me into the police parking lot for all I cared. I didn't know who it was, but Mac would know about him very shortly.

The pickup stayed fairly close even though the traffic on Broadway was not heavy. I had to smile to myself when I thought about the guy following me.

As I pulled into the police parking lot, the Chevy pickup went on by the entrance. I drove to the area reserved for visitors and parked. I saw the pickup pull up at the curb along the street outside the police parking lot as I got out of my vehicle. I had no idea what his plans were, but it was obvious he was trying very hard to keep an eye on me. The only questions I had were who was he and who was he working for?

I TOOK MY EVIDENCE and other items and walked to the precinct building. Once inside, I went directly to the sergeant's desk.

"Hi, Pete. How are you doing?"

"Pretty good, Frank. How's the wife?"

"Same as always. Pushing for me to retire."

"I'm here to see Captain MacDonald."

"He's waitin' for you in his office. He said to expect you."

"Thanks," I replied, then headed toward Mac's office.

I tapped on the door and was immediately told to enter.

"I see you're on time," Mac said without getting up from his desk.

"I try to be."

"Let's sit over at the table," he said as he stood up. "We can spread out a little better there. Would you like a cup of coffee?"

"Sure. Black, please," I replied as I sat down.

While Mac was getting me a cup of coffee, I spread out some of the photos I had taken as well as some of the other information such as the forensic reports. I decided I would wait for Mac to make the first move. By letting him start things off, he would be setting the tone for our discussion.

Once we had covered everything he wanted to go over, I would bring up anything left of interest to me.

"Looks like you have a lot of stuff there," Mac said as he set a cup of coffee in front of me. "There anything in there might interest me?"

Mac sat down across the table from me and took a sip of coffee. I noticed he was looking over the photos and other papers on the table.

"I think so. Where would you like to start?"

"Let's start with the pictures. I've already gone over the stuff from the crime lab you had sent over."

"Okay."

"Is this the shack you talked about?" he asked as he picked up the photograph.

"Yes. The guy with the rifle is Hank Martin. He's someone you might want to be looking for. He was involved in the kidnapping of Jonathan Endicott. I'm not sure if he was just helping the woman, or if he was an active participant in the actual kidnapping itself. I had a fight with him just before I got hit on the head from behind. He's pretty tough. He may have killed Jonathan, but I suspect the woman did the actual killing.

"He's also being looked at as a suspect in the killing of a woman beater by the name of Max Butler. Sheriff Stillwell wants to have a talk with him," I said.

"Has this Butler guy got anything to do with Jonathan's kidnapping?"

"I haven't found any connection to the kidnapping so far. The only possible connection I've made up to now is Butler might have been killed by Martin. But why is still something we haven't figured out. Butler was shot with a high power rifle, a .30 caliber. If you notice in the picture of Martin, he is holding a 30-30 Winchester. Don't know if it's the weapon that killed Butler. No ballistics and no rifle."

"I should probably get an APB out on this Hank Martin. Since you had a fight with him on the boat Jonathan was found dead on, we can arrest him as a material witness, if nothing else."

"That would be good. At least it would get him off the streets for a little while. Oh, by the way. He might also be known as "The Cowboy".

"I also have a couple of pictures of the woman on the boat. As best I can figure, she's the leader in the kidnapping, but I think she's working for someone else," I said.

"What makes you think that?"

"Nothing more than a hunch right now. I've had a tail the past few days. Don't know who he is, but he drives an old green Chevy pickup with rusty chrome wheels. You don't have someone on my tail, do you?"

"Why would I? I know where to find you."

"That was my feeling," I said.

"You think it might be this Martin guy?"

"Could be, but I haven't gotten close enough to see the driver's face. He has dark tinted side and rear windows on the pickup."

I went over all the evidence I had collected with the help of Sheriff Stillwell. Then I talked to Mac about what I knew, which was very little. Then I talked to him about what I thought or suspected, which was a lot. The one thing I left out was what I found in Jonathan's room at Endicott's home in Cherry Creek, namely the red computer disk. I hadn't had a chance to look into the files on the red disk, but I knew someone who could help me with it.

We spent a good deal of time talking about what I thought this whole kidnapping was about. Mac seemed to want to agree with me, but since I had little or no proof there was very little he could do to help me, at least for now.

"I don't know how much help I can be to you. Without any kind of proof that a law has been broken, my hands are pretty well tied. The death of Jonathan is in Sheriff Stillwell's jurisdiction. It's damn hard for me to get search warrants or pick up anyone for questioning without something solid to go on. Now if he was kidnapped here and you can prove it, then I'll certainly get involved officially. Unofficially, I'll help where I can."

"I understand. It might help if you can pick up Martin, but I doubt he would talk. I understand he is a pretty hard cowboy. I'm still trying to find out who the woman is. I got this idea in my head she lives here in the Denver area," I said.

"What makes you think that?"

"For one thing, she knows this town pretty well. She knew where to find Jonathan, but she may have had a little help with that from Nolan."

"You think Nolan was involved in the kidnapping?"

"Nothing I can really prove, but yes. I suspect him of getting Jonathan and the woman together in the first place. I think it was a setup from the very beginning to get money out of Walter Endicott."

"What's your next move?"

"I was going to have a talk with Walter Endicott last night, but I didn't get to it. I'm planning on going over there and having a talk with him as soon as we're finished here."

"Have you told them about Jonathan yet?"

"Yes. Well, I told Mrs. Endicott yesterday afternoon. I didn't talk to Walter. He wasn't home. I want to talk to him about a few things I discovered yesterday at the library," I said.

"At the library?" Mac said with surprise.

"Sure. It's a great place to find out things, like who are the principal stockholders of Endicott, Inc. I think this kidnapping has something to do with Endicott, Inc."

"That would be good to know if what you think is true."

"I'm going to have a talk with Walter Endicott about his stockholders. I want to know how he came to let a guy like Bartlett get his hands on so much of his stock."

"He can't pick and choose who buys his stocks," Mac said.

"In this case, he can. Endicott, Inc. stock is not available on the open market."

"I see. That makes a difference. Did Endicott need cash?"

"I'm not sure, but it's beginning to look that way."

"Let me know what you find out. If that stock was obtained by extortion, we might be able to get Bartlett on racketeering and extortion," Mac said thoughtfully. "I'd like nothing more than to put him away. Up to now I've been unable to get anything solid on him."

"I'll keep you posted."

"You want me to go with you when you talk to Endicott?"

"No, I don't think so. I think it would be better if I talk to him alone. He might talk to me where he wouldn't talk to the police. But if I don't get anywhere with him, maybe you could take a run at him."

"Okay. Let me know how it comes out," Mac said.

"I will. If we're done here, I'll get on with what I have to do."

"We're done. You take care out there. Let me know if you need anything."

"I will. Thanks for your help, Mac" I said as I stood up to leave.

"You're welcome."

CHAPTER FIFTEEN

I left Mac's office and headed out the door. While I was still on the steps of the precinct building, I could see over most of the cars parked in the lot all the way to the street. The Chevy pickup was still parked at the curb. I could see there was someone in the pickup, but couldn't make out who it was.

I smiled to myself as I walked toward my vehicle. As I got in, I began to wonder if it was a good idea to have him following me to Endicott's home. If he was working for Bartlett it might prove to be a problem for Walter, and I had no wish to make things any harder for him than absolutely necessary.

Since I had lost my tail before, I figured it might be a little harder to lose him again. But one advantage I had was my vehicle was more agile than his pickup.

The more I thought about it, the more I was beginning to think it was time to find out who was tailing me. It would be helpful if I could find out who was paying him to do it. It was not going to be easy to get him to talk. If he was working for people like Bartlett, it would be in his best interest to keep his mouth shut. His life expectancy was not very long if he talked.

I reached down, started my vehicle and drove out of the police parking lot onto the street. I made it a point to stay within the speed limit. He followed me at a respectable distance considering the traffic. I didn't bother to change lanes in the hope he would. There was no need for that. I wanted him to follow me, at least for the moment.

I led him to an area of town where there were narrow alleys and a lot of businesses. As I drove around a couple of blocks, I began to look for parking spaces that would work for my plan. It took me a few blocks before I saw it. There was a parking space near a corner and another one right at the corner, but none along the street behind me. I took the parking space away from the corner. If my plan worked, he would drive by, park at the corner and wait for me to return to my vehicle.

I pulled into the parking space and watched him as he drove by. I held my breath in the hope he would pull into the parking space at the corner. If he did, I could carry out my plan. If he didn't, then I would have to try something else.

It looked as if my luck was changing. He pulled into the parking space at the corner. I smiled to myself. It was time to put my plan into action. I got out of my vehicle and went into the furniture store on the corner. The guy would most likely not follow me into the store. It would be too easy for me to spot him there. I was counting on him staying in his pickup.

I waited for a moment or two to see if he was going to follow me into the store. When it was clear that he wasn't coming in, I hurried to the back of the store and went out through the storeroom to the loading dock in the alley. I looked around to make sure he had not decided to check to see if I was going to go out the back. Luckily he hadn't.

I jumped down off the dock into the alley and worked my way around to the corner. I then moved to the front corner of the building and peeked around it. He was still sitting in his pickup. He was turned in the seat so he could see the store entrance out the rear window. He was watching for me to come out of the building. He was probably wondering what business I had in the store.

He was parked only about twelve to fifteen feet from me. It was further than I had hoped for, but not so far that I couldn't surprise him if I moved quickly. It was also nice of him to have rolled down the passenger side window. At first I thought I might have to smash it to get to him.

I drew my gun from my holster and held it down alongside my leg. After making sure there was no one to get in the way, I dashed out from the corner of the building to the side of the pickup and stuck my gun in the window. I suddenly found myself face to face with "The Cowboy".

"Well, well. We meet again."

I could tell by the look on his face that he was surprised to see me. He had expected me to come out of the front of the furniture store. His look of surprise quickly turned to a disgusted look. He glanced down at the seat. A quick glance at the seat of his pickup showed me that he had a six gun lying next to his leg.

"You ain't Hopalong Cassidy. I wouldn't try anything stupid. You might be fast with a gun, but not fast enough that I can't blow a hole in you if you reach for it. Now don't make any sudden moves, Hank, I tend to get nervous. You don't want me to get nervous," I said.

"Very slowly and very carefully, reach over with your left hand and pick up your gun with just two fingers. If you do anything else or make a sudden move, I'll blow a hole in the front of your pants big enough that you won't have to worry about your next date," I said as I pointed my gun at his crotch.

At least he wasn't stupid. He held the gun out to me by his thumb and forefinger. I took it and slipped it in my belt under my coat.

"I want the keys to your pickup."

He hesitated for a second, but seemed very willing to honor my request when I pulled back the hammer of my gun.

"Now, why are you following me and who hired you to do it?"

"You think I'm going to tell you that?"

"To be honest, no, not really. To get that information out of a guy like you, I would have to do something really illegal, like shoot your kneecaps off. I'm tempted, but I don't need the headache it would cause right now. Tell you what, you tell whoever hired you that if I find you on my tail again, we're going to have a real meeting of the minds, you understand what I'm telling you?" I said.

"Yeah, I understand," he said.

The tone of his voice was that of a very angry man. I was sure it was because I got the drop on him. He probably thought he was too good to let that happen.

"I sure would like to hear what your boss has to say about this, but I have more important things to do."

I thought about telling him the cops were looking for him, but decided against it. I couldn't see any reason to give him even the slightest advantage.

"You'll be sorry you pulled a gun on me," he said.

There was no doubt in my mind what he meant.

"Have a nice day. And just remember, this could have been your last," I said, then smiled.

I turned around and went back to my vehicle. I got in, drove around the corner and into the alley. The first dumpster I came to, I rolled down the window and tossed his gun and his keys into the dumpster. Then I was off to Endicott's home.

I DROVE INTO THE DRIVEWAY of the Endicott home shortly before noon. I noticed the large Cadillac I had seen Walter driving parked in the driveway. There was a good chance he was home. I got out of my vehicle, walked up to the door and knocked. It was answered by Walter.

"You've got a lot of damn nerve showing up here. What the hell are you doing here?"

"I came by to have a little talk with you. It's rather important."

"So was my son. You were hired to find him and you failed."

"Not true, Walter. I found him. I just wasn't able to get him away from where he was being held before they killed him."

"It's all the same to me. He's dead and you're still walking around," he said angrily.

"That's true, but if you think about it, and think really hard; you might realize you have to take some responsibility for the death of your son," I said sharply.

I hadn't come here to get into a pissing match with him, but I needed his undivided attention. With as much anger as he was directing toward me, I needed to get him to focus on himself for a bit. He could be angry with me all he wanted later.

Walter's expression changed very quickly. He turned pale as a ghost. I got the impression he knew what I was talking about, but was afraid to say anything. I even got the feeling he wondered how much I really knew.

"Who is it, Walter," Mrs. Endicott asked as she stepped into the foyer behind Walter.

"Oh, it's you, Mr. Blackstone," she said as soon as she saw me. "How nice of you to drop by."

Walter turned and looked at his wife. I don't know what was going through his mind, but it was clear his wife was not upset with me. It was also clear that Walter was not happy that she seemed to be glad to see me.

"Won't you please come in?" she asked.

"If it's okay with Mr. Endicott," I replied as I looked at Walter.

"Of course it's okay," she said. "Please come in. Walter?"

"Yeah, sure," Walter managed to say.

I walked past Walter and followed Mrs. Endicott to the study. Walter followed along behind like a little kid who was upset that things were not going his way. Once in the study, Mrs. Endicott motioned for me to sit down. She sat down on the sofa. I half expected Walter to sit down beside her, but he sat in a chair near the end of the sofa.

"Have you found out anything about who murdered our son?" Mrs. Endicott asked.

"No, not really. However, I am a little disturbed by some of the things I have uncovered. I was hoping Walter could help clarify some of them for me."

"Me?"

Mrs. Endicott turned and looked at her husband. The expression on her face led me to believe she wondered what I had found out. It also made me think she was wondering what more he had kept from her.

"Walter?"

"What?" he replied sharply?

"Mr. Blackstone would like to talk to you."

Walter looked at me and then let out a big sigh. I got the feeling he had come to realize his secrets may have contributed to the death of his only son, and he could no longer hide them from his wife. His eyes seemed to be pleading for me to understand.

"Walter, do you know who Joseph Bartlett is?" I asked.

"Yes. I know him."

"He's one of the officers of your corporation, isn't he?"

"Yes."

"Did you know who he was before he got involved in your corporation?"

Walter hesitated to answer. He looked at his wife as if he wished she was not in the room right now.

"Yes. Yes, I knew him before he bought in."

"Yet, you let him buy in, didn't you?"

"Yes."

"Why?"

"I needed the money and I had no place to turn."

"Would it be fair to say you knew you were making a deal with the devil?" I asked.

"Walter. What is he saying?"

"Mrs. Endicott, Walter got himself involved with a man who is, shall we say, less than honest and less than honorable."

"You mean, he's a crook?"

"That would be correct. I believe Bartlett used extortion and your husband's need for cash to get a foot in the door of Endicott, Inc. And correct me if I'm wrong, Walter, but after you formed the corporation, Bartlett wanted controlling interest in it, and possibly controlling interest in your Fort Collins dealerships, as well. Am I right?"

Walter just looked at me. From the look in his eyes I was sure I had hit the nail on the head.

"Walter, is he right?"

"Yes, damn it. It never would have happened if you hadn't had to have this damn house."

"Walter!" she said with surprise.

"This damn house cost me a small fortune. We had been happy in the old house for years, but you insisted we move up. I never wanted this damn place."

The look on Mrs. Endicott's face was one of shock. Walter looked like he wished he had never said anything.

"Walter, how did Bartlett find out you needed money so badly?"

"What?"

"How did Bartlett find out you needed money so badly?"

"My attorney and my accountant came to me one day and told me I was running very low of cash, and that I had a big problem with cash flow. They told me I needed to do something to improve my cash flow, or I was going to lose some of my dealerships and probably my house."

"After they told you that you were in dire need of cash, I'd be willing to bet they said they knew someone who could help. Right?" I asked.

"How'd you find out?"

"A lucky guess mostly. What happened after they told you about the cash flow problem?"

"My attorney suggested I incorporate. It would bring in some fresh money. He said it would be easy to do and I could still keep controlling interest."

"Did he have a suggestion of who might have the kind of money you needed?"

"No. But my accountant said he knew a guy looking for a good investment. He said the guy could probably come up with the money needed to keep the business on its feet if we could convince him it was a good investment."

"So it was your accountant that actually brought you and Bartlett together?" I asked.

"Yeah."

"Your accountant wouldn't just happen to be Jacob Wiengart?"

"Yes," Walter replied, the look on his face showing some interest in why I knew that.

"Did you ever do a background check on Wiengart?"

"No. He came highly recommended by my attorney."

"This is one time when you should have checked him out for yourself. Did you know your accountant has been arrested several times and has been connected to several less than honest business deals and less than honest business people in the Denver area?"

"No."

"He has never been convicted of a crime, but that doesn't mean he wasn't involved in some.

"I'm sure you will want to get rid of your accountant as soon as we get this cleared up. You might also want to rethink keeping your attorney, as well," I added. "I don't know much about him, but a background check into his activities might very well be in order."

"Can you do that?" he asked, the tone of his voice suddenly showing some willingness to cooperate with me.

"Yes. But before we get into that, I want to know why you took more money out of your business account and said your son took it?"

"I took it in an effort to get that woman to let my son go."

"I understand that, but why did you say Jonathan took it?"

"I had to. If Bartlett found out I had taken it, he would have - - -."

"He would have killed you?"

"He might have, but he might have hurt Abby," he said as he looked at his wife. "I couldn't stand that."

"Did he threaten to harm your wife?"

"He didn't come out and say it, but it was very clear what he meant."

"I've got a couple of things I have to look into. I want you to stay at home for the next couple of days. And I don't want you talking to anyone."

"Won't that cause suspicion?" Mrs. Endicott asked.

"I don't think so. Most people would expect the two of you to stay home and grieve. They would not expect Walter to go to work at least until after your son's funeral."

"He's right, Walter. I think we should do what he says."

"I would hope you would, this time. Is there anything else you've left out?"

"No," Walter said.

"Are you sure? Look what happened the last time you didn't tell me what I needed to know."

"We've told you everything we can think of."

"Okay. If I call here, I expect you to be here. Do you understand?"

"Yes."

"I'm going to have another talk with my friend on the police force and see what we can do to keep this quiet for a little while longer."

"Is that necessary?" Walter asked.

"It is now. Once Jonathan was murdered, it became a case for the police. I plan to stick around to help find out who killed him and how we can get your dealerships back in your hands."

"Do you think you can do that?"

"I'm not sure, but we're going to try."

"Thank you," Walter said, obviously feeling there might still be hope.

I left Walter and Abby in the study. I didn't know how things were going to work out for them, but they had some serious talking to do. I only hoped they talked. Walter had kept too many things from her already.

When I got to my vehicle, I turned and looked at the big house. That big fancy house made a statement, but it was all a lie. I got in my vehicle and headed for the police station. I needed some more information on Bartlett.

AS I DROVE TOWARD the downtown area, I began to realize I needed to get something to eat. It was going on twelve-thirty. I decided I would swing by my apartment and get a sandwich before going to the police station. Besides, Mac would most likely be out to lunch anyway.

I pulled into the parking lot of my apartment, parked in front of my garage and went inside. Once in the kitchen, I began fixing my lunch. As soon as it was ready, I sat down and picked up my phone. I placed a call to Jennifer at home. I was sure she would be home for lunch today.

"Hello."

"Hi. It's me."

"Hi, me. How are things going?" Jennifer asked with a slight giggle in her voice.

"Not too bad. I have a question for you."

"What do you need now?"

"I need you."

"Oh, really?" she said with a pleasant tone in her voice.

"Yes."

"How bad do you need me?"

"So bad that I need you for two things."

"And what two things do you need me for?" she asked.

"The first is I need you to have dinner with me and maybe spend some time with me after dinner."

"That I can do, and with pleasure I might add. What else?"

"The other is I need you to help me find out what is on a computer disk I found."

"Peter, are you ever going to need me just for me?"

"God, I sure hope so."

"So do I, but it's taking you a long time. This is going to cost you?"

"Okay. How much?" I said without hesitation.

One thing I knew was when she said it was going to cost me, it was usually something I wouldn't mind doing anyway. I doubted it would be any different this time.

"More than pizza out of the box while we watch television, I can tell you. It's going to cost you a very expensive dinner in a very nice restaurant - of my choice."

"Not a problem. Where would you like me to make reservations?"

"I would like to eat at – ah – let me think. I got it. I would like to eat at The Briarwood Inn in Golden."

"Well, if anyone says you don't have good taste, I'll certainly tell them they're wrong."

"Is that a problem for you?" she asked as if she might have asked for a little too much.

"Not at all. What time?"

"Seven o'clock tonight? It would give me time to get home and get dressed up nice."

"Seven it is. I will be there with bells on," I said.

"Might I suggest you leave the bells at home?"

"Are you sure? I have some great bells."

"I'm sure."

"Okay," I said, trying to sound as if I was hurt.

"See you about seven?"

"I will be on time."

"You better be," she said.

"Love you," I said.

"Love you, too."

As I hung up the phone, I smiled to myself. She was one sexy lady and I was sure she would be dressed in her very best. She had a very sexy black dress that hugged her shapely body. She liked to wear it, and I had to admit she looked absolutely stunning in it. I'd have to get my best suit out for dinner tonight.

As much as I liked to think of her in her black dress, I had other things to turn my attention to for now. I finished my lunch and left my apartment for the downtown police precinct. Fifteen minutes later I turned into the police parking lot.

CHAPTER SIXTEEN

As I walked up the steps in front of the precinct, I glanced back toward the street, looking out over the parked cars. I smiled to myself when I saw the old Chevy pickup parked on the street near the entrance to the parking lot. I turned and went inside the building. Frank was at the sergeant's desk as usual.

"How's it going, Frank."

"Good. You back again so soon? What do you need this time?"

"I need to talk to Mac again."

"He's busy, but he should be finished in a little while."

"Okay. I'll wait."

I sat down on a bench that ran along a wall in front of the Sergeant's Desk. I leaned back a little to relax.

While I waited, I looked around. There were several civilians in the room. One was an old lady who looked like the world had come to an end. There were two teenagers who were looking a bit worried as if they had gotten themselves in trouble and were going to have to pay the time for the crime. Other than the few in the room, it was pretty quiet. I didn't figure it got real busy until evening and probably on weekends.

I heard a door open down the hall from where I was sitting. I glanced down the hall in time to see Mac come out of his office with a couple of other officers. He had apparently been having a meeting about something. As soon as the others had gone off to do what they had to do, Mac walked down the hall toward me.

"You want to see me?"

"Yes. I need a little information."

"Come on in."

I followed Mac into his office and closed the door behind me. He motioned for me to have a seat as he walked around behind his desk and sat down.

"What do you need?" he asked, getting right to the point.

"I need a little information on Bartlett."

"Sure. Did you get to have your talk with Endicott?"

"Yes. He told me Bartlett had more or less forced his way into Endicott, Inc."

"Is there enough evidence to build a case against Bartlett for extortion or racketeering?" Mac asked.

"I don't think so. I think Walter is scared to death. I doubt he will talk to the police."

"That's understandable. Whoever is after his company might very well have been the ones to kill his son. I think that would make me a little nervous."

"It would be for most people. The only way we are going to get Bartlett is to get someone to roll on him."

"Got any idea as to who that might be?"

"Actually, I have a couple, namely Endicott's attorney and his accountant," I said.

"What makes you think either of them will roll on Bartlett? He doesn't like that to happen."

"Don't know, but they might if they thought their livelihoods and their freedom were in jeopardy."

"We can give it a try. What do you want me to do?"

"I would like you to invite them to come in for a little chat," I suggested.

"That's it? A little chat?"

"They're not likely to say anything that would help, but you can bet Bartlett will know about it before they leave the precinct," I said with a smile.

"I get it. You want Bartlett to start sweating."

"It wouldn't hurt. We'll have to keep an eye on them after they leave here."

"True. Let me think about it. You still want the file on Bartlett?"

"Yes, but I'm not sure what I'm looking for. I guess I'm grasping at straws at the moment."

"I'll get it. You can look at it here," he said as he stood up.

I watched him leave the room. Mac returned with the file on Bartlett in just a couple of minutes.

"By the way, did you manage to figure out what the woman's name was that was involved in Jonathan's kidnapping?" I asked.

"Not yet. I have a couple of guys working on it from the pictures you left with me. They're looking at mug shots and checking computer files using the woman's description."

I nodded that I understood, then opened Bartlett's file and began going through it. The only thing I found was he had a long record of being arrested for a number of different things, but he never served a day in prison. He had never been found guilty of anything other than a traffic violation three years ago. He had been suspected of being involved in extortion, murder, money laundering, drug distribution, and prostitution, but nothing had ever been proven. Since Bartlett had used extortion to get a grip on Endicott, Inc., that was what my investigation would focus on, at least for now.

After I finished with Bartlett's file, I decided it was time for me to go. I had all the information on Bartlett I could get. What I needed now was proof, and I didn't have it.

I left the precinct for my vehicle. As I walked down the steps, I looked for the pickup, but it was gone. I wondered if Hank got a little nervous sitting out in front of a police station for so long.

IT WAS GETTING ON TOWARD mid afternoon. I had a few things I needed to do before I picked up Jennifer. One of those was to make reservations for dinner. Since it was a weekday, I didn't think it would be too hard to get them.

I decided to return to my office and make the reservation from there. When I got there, I found the door was open. I quickly drew my gun and went inside. After making sure there was no one in my office, I put my gun away and began looking around.

Someone had literally torn the place apart. The drawers to my desk had been pried open and emptied on the floor, the bookshelves didn't have a single book left on them, and even the coffee table with the coffee pot, sugar bowl and creamer had been turned over, the coffee pot was broken. All the files from my file cabinet had been taken out and tossed around the room.

I had no idea what they were after, but I didn't keep much of interest there anyway. I had learned a long time ago not to keep anything important in my office. It was too vulnerable to anyone who wanted to break in. I had a room on the floor above my office where I kept files I didn't want anyone to see locked in a big steel safe. Any current cases I was working on, I kept in a drawer built in the bottom of my sofa when I was gone. It was built in such a way that it was undetectable even if the sofa was turned over.

I quickly checked the sofa and found my hiding place had not been disturbed. That being the case, I knew they had not found anything that would be worth their trouble.

The only thing I could think of that anyone might want was the red computer disk I had found in Jonathan's room at his parents' home. Since I didn't think anyone knew I had the disk or that it even existed, I had doubts about what they were looking for. I had left the disk at my apartment neatly wrapped in a plastic bag and hidden deep inside a canister of sugar in the kitchen.

The more I looked around the room, the more it became clear they weren't looking for anything. They were simply trying to send me a message. I could only guess at what the message was, and my guess was I should let my investigation into Endicott, Inc. die, and die quickly.

Cleaning this mess up was going to take a long time. I could see no reason not to take Jennifer out to dinner and clean it up tomorrow morning. Besides, it would probably take most of the morning to clean it up.

I picked my phone up off the floor and set it on the desk. It took me a minute or two to find the phone book, but I found it under a bunch of papers. After looking up the number of The Briarwood Inn in Golden, I called and made reservations for tonight.

Once that was done, I sat down and looked at the mess. I decided I wouldn't call the police. I would dust the place for prints myself and give what I found to John in the crime lab. Maybe he could come up with who had torn my office apart. I was pretty sure I didn't have to have fingerprints to know who had done it, but having some proof might go a long way in making sure I nailed the right guy for it.

I left my office and went upstairs to my storage room. I got what I needed and returned to my office, then dusted for prints. As soon as I was done, I put the fingerprint cards with the prints pressed on them in an envelope and addressed the envelope to John Farrell at the State Crime Lab in Lakewood with a note telling him what they were.

Once that was done, I dropped the envelope in the mail slot next to the elevators on my way out. When I got home, I showered and dressed for my date with Jennifer. Just before leaving, I took the disk from the sugar canister and slipped it into my inside suit coat pocket.

I ARRIVED AT JENNIFER'S a few minutes before seven. When she opened the door, I smiled at her. She was wearing the sexy black dress. It almost took my breath away.

"Good evening, Miss Taylor."

"Good evening, Mr. Blackstone."

"I have come to fulfill your desire to have dinner at The Briarwood in Golden. Are you ready to go?"

"Yes, I am."

I held my arm out and she slipped her arm in mine. I walked her to my vehicle and opened the door for her. As soon as she was in the Tahoe, I ran around to the other side, got in and started for Golden.

"This is a nice car," she said as she looked it over.

"Don't get too used to it. I have to give it back when I'm done with the case I'm working on."

"I take it it's one of the perks."

"Yes, but you have to admit it's a pretty nice perk."

"You look nice in a suit," she said. "You should wear one more often."

"You look very nice in a dress. In fact, you're down right sexy."

"Thank you," she said with a smile.

It took us a little while to get to Golden. There was a bit of traffic, but that was nothing unusual. Although we were a few minutes early for our reservation, we were seated at a table in a corner right away. Within a few minutes we had our meals ordered and had a glass of wine in front of us while we waited.

"What is this about a disk?" Jennifer asked as she looked at me from across the table.

"I found a plastic computer disk I believe has something to do with the case I'm working on. I would like you to help me find out what's on the disk. It may be nothing, or it may point to who is involved in what I'm working on."

"I can probably help you with that. What are you working on?"

"I believe I told you I was looking for a missing young man. Well, he is no longer missing, he's dead."

"Oh, my God."

"I'm sorry. I shouldn't have said anything. I didn't want to spoil your evening."

"It's all right. I know you do things like that. Are you looking for who killed him?"

"Yes. But for now, let's not talk about it. Let's enjoy our evening together. Shall we?"

"Okay," she said with a slight smile.

I knew it was too late. The thought I was looking for a killer would still be in the back of her mind. We spent the rest of the time at The Briarwood Inn talking about little unimportant things. Although we always enjoyed each other's company, it was not as it should have been. When we were finished with our dinner and had an after dinner drink, we agreed we should go back to her place and check out the computer disk.

After I had paid for our meal and left a tip, we got up and left the restaurant. We got in my vehicle and headed back to Jennifer's apartment. The ride back was quiet.

She sat looking out the windshield with her hand resting on my leg. I glanced over at her. She seemed to be deep in thought.

"Honey, after this is all over, I'll make it up to you."

"That's not necessary. I always enjoy being with you."

I guess there was nothing else to be said. We drove the rest of the way in silence.

BY THE TIME WE GOT BACK to Jennifer's apartment, it was getting on toward eleven o'clock. As I got out of my Tahoe, I noticed the headlights of a vehicle go off about a half a block back down the street. I couldn't see what kind of a vehicle it was, but I had seen it following us for sometime. I hadn't said anything to Jennifer as I didn't want to worry her.

I walked around my vehicle and opened the door for her. She must have noticed I was not giving her my undivided attention which she deserved, and she was right. I was looking past her hoping to get some idea of who it was.

"What's the matter," she said with a slight smile. "You saw something, didn't you?"

"Yes. We've been followed," I said with a smile.

"Is it anything I should worry about?"

"I don't know. Let's go inside, then I'll check it out."

"Okay," she replied as she slipped her arm in mine.

Jennifer was one smart woman. She knew it was important that she didn't do anything to make the person following us think we knew he was there.

Once inside her apartment building, we went directly to Jennifer's apartment. She unlocked the door and started to go inside.

"Wait. Stand aside," I whispered.

I didn't have to tell her twice. She stepped away from the door while I drew my gun from under my suit coat. I opened the door slowly checking between the door and the door frame in case someone was dumb enough to hide behind the door. It was clear so I went on inside. Without turning on but one light, I went from room to room to make sure no one was inside her apartment waiting for us. When I was sure it was clear, I motioned for her to enter.

"Stay inside and lock the door behind me. Don't open it for anyone but me or the police, and don't come out. If you hear any shots fired, call 9-1-1 immediately. And hold on to this," I said as I took the disk from my suit coat pocket and handed it to her.

She bit her lower lip and nodded that she understood. I closed the door and waited to hear her lock it. As soon as I heard the door lock, I moved to the back of the apartment building and went out the back. I moved among the bushes to the corner of the building. Once at the corner, I hid in the bushes while I waited to see if whoever had been following us would come to the building and try to get in.

The night was quiet. It had rained earlier in the day and it was cool. There was no wind making for a very quiet evening. About the only things I could hear were the sounds of traffic off in the distance and my own heart beating.

Suddenly I heard what sounded like a twig snap as if someone had stepped on it. It was immediately silent again. It wasn't until a car drove by on the street out front that I got a glimpse of someone moving along the side of the building next door. I waited to see what he was going to do.

The shadowy figure rushed across the narrow opening between the buildings, then moved around behind a bush. He was now up against the apartment building where Jennifer's apartment was. I was hoping he would come to the rear of the apartment building, but if he didn't, I could confront him where he was or in the hall if he went in the front way.

He slowly began moving along the building toward me. The only thing I saw that would help me identify him was the cowboy hat he was wearing. It was dark colored, probably black. That fact alone led me to believe I was going to be confronting Hank Martin again. I still wasn't a hundred percent sure who the guy was, but I got an idea of his size from the shadows. There was no doubt in my mind it was "The Cowboy", even if I didn't see his face. I could think of no one I would like to confront more than him.

I knelt down for better cover from the bush I was hiding behind and watched him as he moved on by me. When he started to step around the corner of the building, a light from an apartment lit up his face enough for me to see him clearly. It was Martin, all right, and I was getting tired of him following me. I also didn't like the idea he was sneaking around my girlfriend's apartment building.

It was time we had it out. I stepped out from behind the bush to confront him.

"You'll never learn, will you?" I said, just loud enough for him to hear me.

Martin froze in his tracks, then slowly straightened up. He started to turn around, but he did it very carefully. He was probably sure I had a gun on him and he would have been right. The look on his face showed how angry he was that I had caught him following me, again.

"You're a damn slow learner, Hank," I said.

"Yeah, well, you're a dead man. You're just not smart enough to know it," he spit out.

"Who you working for?"

"You don't really think I would tell you?"

"No, not really. I haven't decided what I'm going to do with you, but beating the hell out of you certainly comes to mind."

I couldn't help but see the slight grin come over his face. I was sure he would like a good old fashioned fist fight.

"If you didn't have that gun, it would be a pleasure to have you try," he said.

"But I do have the gun. And I have you sneaking around this apartment building. So if I were to shoot you, I could most likely get away with it by saying you were a burglar. What do you think about that?"

"You wouldn't dare. Besides, you don't have the guts to shoot a man while he's facing you."

"I'm not like you, Hank. I don't have to gun someone down from behind with a rifle, like you did to Butler," I said hoping to find out if he actually shot Butler.

"I didn't kill him, but even if I did you couldn't prove it. If I had killed him, I would've done it so the last thing he saw was my face. He would know who and why he was being killed."

"So if you didn't do it, who did?"

He smiled as if to say, 'I'll never tell'.

"I got a feeling I know who killed Butler. It was the woman you've been hanging around with, wasn't it?"

He just stood there looking at me. I could see by the look on his face I had probably guessed right.

"She killed him using your 30-30 Winchester, and you put him on my boat. Am I right?"

"You'll never live long enough to find out," he said with a hint of confidence in his voice.

The way he said that and the way he looked led me to believe he might not be alone. It got me to wondering where his partner was. If it was the woman, she was as deadly as anyone I had run into for a very long time.

"Where's your partner?"

I wasn't sure what my situation was, until I heard the sound of movement coming from behind me. I dove to the left and rolled under a bush as a shot ran out. I returned fire in the direction where I had seen a muzzle blast out of the corner of my eye, then moved deeper into the shadows. I looked at where Hank had been standing to make sure he wasn't going to join in the fight. I saw him lying on the ground only a short distance from me. It was obvious he had been shot, but I didn't know how badly he had been hit.

A second shot rang out and I saw Hank's body jerk. He had been shot again. I turned and pointed my gun at the bushes where I had seen the muzzle blast, but didn't return fire. If whoever was shooting was shooting at Hank, they could be on my side. The only question was who was it?

I heard someone running away. It was at that moment I became convinced as to who had been shooting and who they were shooting at. The first shot may have been intended for me, but when it hit Hank things changed. I would have bet the second shot was to make sure Hank didn't talk, and the best way to make sure was to kill him.

I got up and moved over to Hank. He was still alive. In the dark, I couldn't see how badly he was injured.

"Hank. Hank."

"You can't get rid of me that easy," he said with a hint of pain in his voice.

He thought I had shot him. I had heard the shot go by me that hit him. The second shot was intended to kill him. He was hit, but it didn't sound like it was very serious.

"I'll get an ambulance."

"That's damn nice of you."

It was clear he would survive his gunshot wounds. The question was will he survive very long after he recovers from them. Either way, I needed information and there was no time like the present to see if I could get him to talk.

"I didn't shoot you, Hank. Your partner did," I said as I moved up next to him.

"Why that bitch," he said angrily.

"What's her name?"

"Bonnie Tillman."

He spit out the name as if it had left a bad taste in his mouth.

"Who's paying you to follow me around and why?"

"I ain't telling you that."

Even shot he was not going to cooperate completely. I had to try and make him.

"How much do you like your left knee," I said as I put the barrel of my gun against his knee.

"You wouldn't dare," he said defiantly, but it was clear he was afraid I might just shoot him.

"I've got all night. Who's got you tailing me?"

"I'm not telling you," he said looking at me and gritting his teeth.

"You are a slow learner, but than you already know that."

He coughed and looked up at me. I could see the hate in his eyes. He wanted more than anything to kill me.

"You didn't answer my question."

He just looked at me. I wasn't sure what to do. I didn't need the hassle of shooting him although I was tempted.

I made the mistake of looking away from his face for just a second. He may have been shot, but he was far from out. He grabbed for the gun, but I held on to it. As I hit him alongside the head we rolled over, but he didn't let go of it. He hung onto my gun hand with both hands as we wrestled for it. I was able to roll over again and get on top of him.

We continued to struggle for the gun. I still had a firm grip on it even though he was trying to get it away from me. Using all my strength I pinned his hand down on the ground next to his head with the hand I had the gun in. With my free hand I started punching him in the face, one blow after another until he didn't resist any more.

Breathing hard, I sat back on my heels and looked down at him. After taking a minute to catch my breath, I rolled off him and stood up. In the dim light from a window of the apartment building, I could see his face was bloody.

As he groaned and started to move, I stepped back just in case he had regained enough energy to continue the fight. He sat up and looked at me, but there was no fight left in him.

"You going to tell me who hired you to follow me, or do I have to beat on you some more?"

Just then I heard the sound of sirens coming closer. As he started to speak, I stepped back which put me in the shadows.

"I'm not going - -

A single shot range out. Hank's eyes got big as he looked up at me, then he fell backwards on the ground. I wasted no time in ducking down behind a bush. I heard a noise near the front of the building and saw a shadow for only an instant. It was not enough time to identify who it was, or to take a clear shot. Within a couple of seconds, I heard the squealing of tires and saw a pickup roar by in front of the building. It was the same pickup Hank had been driving. I had not seen who had fired the shot, but it was most likely Bonnie Tillman.

There was little doubt in my mind the shooter was gone. I moved out from behind the bush. I walked over next to Hank, reached down and put my fingers on the side of his neck. He was dead. There was nothing to do now by wait for the police. I had no doubt they had been called the moment the first shot was fired.

TWO BLACK AND WHITE units squealed to a stop in front of the apartment building. The officers from one car started for the front door, while the officers from the second car started running around to the back of the apartment building. The first officer running around to the back of the building spotted me and stopped suddenly.

"Over here," he called out to the others.

The officer already had his gun in his hand as he started toward me. He must have seen my gun. He stopped suddenly, raised his gun and pointed it at me.

"Drop the gun," he yelled.

I immediately dropped my gun and put my hands on my head. He was quickly joined by his partner. Together, they moved in on me, being very careful to keep me covered.

"Turn around," the one officer said.

I did as he ordered. He walked up behind and put me in handcuffs. As soon as I was in handcuffs, the first officer's partner bent down and checked Hank for a pulse, then looked up and shook his head.

"Looks like you've got a lot of explaining to do, mister. You want to tell me what happened here?"

"Sure. But could you call Captain MacDonald first?"

"Why?"

"He knows what I have been working on. I'm a PI and I have a permit to carry a gun. My license and permit are in my inside coat pocket."

"That may be so, but you don't have a permit to shoot somebody."

"I didn't shoot him," I said in frustration.

"What are you doing here?" the first officer asked while his partner reached inside my coat.

"He's a PI, all right. Here's his permit to carry."

"It don't matter. He still doesn't have the right to shoot someone. We'll take him in and let the detectives sort it out."

I looked at the first officer and quickly decided he was one of many cops who don't like PI's. I could also see it wasn't going to make any difference what I said with the exception of one thing.

"I want an attorney. I'm not saying another word."

"I don't care what you want. You're under arrest for murder."

I didn't say anything. I stood there waiting for them to take me to their patrol car and on to the police precinct in their district.

I saw Jennifer come out of the front of the apartment building just as they were stuffing me in a patrol car. The look on her face was that of someone who couldn't believe what they were seeing. She looked like she was about to run over to me, but I shook my head. Like I said before, she was one smart woman. She turned and went back inside.

CHAPTER SEVENTEEN

I was taken to the fourth precinct and put into an integration room. A detective by the name of Juan Sanchez came into the room and looked at me.

"You're Peter Blackstone, right?"

"Right, and that's all you're getting until I get an attorney."

"The arresting officer said you wanted him to contact Captain MacDonald. Is that right?"

"Yes."

"So you will talk to Captain MacDonald, but not me?"

I could see what he was trying to do. He was trying to get me to talk to him about what was happening. It was time to clam up and stay that way until my attorney or Captain MacDonald arrived.

"Why did you shoot that man?"

I didn't even look at him. I just sat there looking at my hands on the table in front of me. Time went by slowly. Detective Sanchez continued to ask me question after question and I continued to say nothing. He knew that once I asked for an attorney, the integration was over until council was present. That small fact didn't seem to bother Sanchez. Even my refusal to answer him didn't seem to deter him from asking. I guess he thought I would get tired of not answering him and blurt out something he could use against me. The only problem was I had no intention of saying a word.

Sanchez must not have had anything else to do because he kept at me for several hours. At times he yelled at me and sometimes he even threatened me, but I didn't say a word. At least he was smart enough not to hit me or even touch me.

There was little question that the officers who arrested me didn't bother to call Mac. Nor had they or Detective Sanchez bothered to call for, or allow me to call for an attorney. That was defiantly against the rules.

It had reached a point where I could now say anything I wanted and my attorney would get it thrown out of court. But I could see no reason to talk now. The longer it went on the more resolve I had not to talk.

It was about four in the morning when Sanchez finally gave up. I was taken to a cell and locked up. I wasted no time in lying down and doing my best to get some sleep. There was no doubt in my mind they would get me up early and start in again, but it would still do them no good.

I DIDN'T KNOW WHAT TIME it was when the jailer came to the cell and unlocked the door. They had taken my watch when I was arrested along with my other personal belongings.

"Time to get up hotshot. Detective Sanchez wants to visit with you again."

I turned over, looked at him, then sat up on the edge of the bunk. I was feeling a little stiff after such a short night on a hard bed and after my fight with Hank.

"What time is it?"

"What do you care? You ain't goin' nowhere," he replied.

I didn't say anything he could hear, but I said to myself, 'that's what you think'. I got up off the hard bed and straightened up as best I could. I was still in the same clothes I had on the day before, namely my suit minus my belt and tie. I probably looked like a guy who had spent the night in a drunk tank after an evening of celebrating, which was pretty close to how I was feeling.

The jailer had me turn around, then handcuffed my hands behind my back. He then led me back to an interrogation room. When I entered I wasn't sure if it was the same room I had been in last night, but it really didn't matter. They all looked the same to me.

Once in the room, the jailer had me sit down, took one handcuff off one of my wrists and hooked it to a heavy metal ring on the edge of the table. The table was bolted to the floor.

After making sure it was secure, he left me alone to wait until Sanchez felt I'd been there long enough to loosen my tongue. He had no idea how long he was going to have to wait for that to happen. He finally decided to show up. I was almost sure it had been at least an hour later. Needless to say, I was tired and hungry, but I still wasn't going to say a word.

"You get a good night's sleep?" he asked with a slight grin.

He looked like he thought his comment was funny. I didn't answer him, but I was sure he could see I didn't think he was one damn bit funny. The only redeeming thought I had was he would find out just how funny I thought he was when I filed a formal complaint regarding his treatment of me, and his failure to contact an attorney for me or let me contact my own attorney. The City of Denver took a very dim view of officers not allowing a person under arrest to exercise their right to legal council.

"What were you doing at that apartment building?"

I didn't respond to his question. I didn't even bother to look up at him. Instead, I took the same posture I had taken last night. I simply looked at my hands on the table in front of me.

"Who were you there to meet?"

Again, I said nothing. I could tell it was getting to him by the sound of his voice.

"You damn well better talk to me. If you don't, I'll have your PI license pulled along with your permit to carry a weapon."

Now that made me look up at him. As I looked at him, I just shook my head in disbelief. He had to be dumb as dirt to think that would make me talk. He didn't have the authority to take my PI license, or my permit to carry a gun. He was blowing smoke and he knew it.

"You damn well better start talking."

I could see he was getting a little short tempered. To make his point, he slammed his fist down on the table only inches from my hand, but I didn't move. Just as his hand hit the table, the door behind him opened.

"Get the hell out of here," he said before turning around to see who had opened the door.

The look on his face was priceless when he realized who had come in. Standing behind him with a very stern look on his face was Captain MacDonald. Sanchez's Lieutenant, William Summers, had followed Mac into the room.

"Would you like to explain yourself, Sanchez?" Lieutenant Summers asked in a tone that demanded a response.

"Well, sir. I'm – ah - I was just trying to make him talk, sir."

"Is this the way you let your detectives carry on an interrogation?" Captain MacDonald asked Lieutenant Summers.

"No, sir. This is not what my men are supposed to do when interviewing a suspect."

"How long have you been here, Peter," Mac asked.

The look on Sanchez's face when Mac called me by my first name was one I wished I could have gotten on camera. He looked like the world as he knew it was crashing down around his ears, and there was nothing he could do about it. He was very close to right.

"Since last night, somewhere around eleven-thirty or so," I replied.

"Why didn't you call me, Peter?"

"I asked the officers who arrested me to call you last night. They refused. I also told Detective Sanchez, as well as the arresting officers that I wanted an attorney."

"Has your attorney been here?"

"Nope."

"Have you talked to an attorney?"

"Nope."

"He hasn't said anything to anyone," Sanchez said, suddenly realizing that may not have been the thing to say.

"Did he ask for an attorney, Sanchez?" Mac asked.

Sanchez looked at me then back at Mac.

"Well, -ah-," Sanchez mumbled.

"It's not a difficult question. Did he or did he not ask for an attorney?" Mac demanded.

"Yes, sir. He did," Sanchez replied rather sheepishly.

"If he asked for an attorney, then why isn't his attorney here? And why are you still questioning him?"

Sanchez didn't reply. He was searching for something intelligent to say, but I doubted anything came to mind.

"Well!"

"Because we didn't call one," Sanchez finally admitted.

"You are dismissed. I expect to see a complete report on my desk by the end of the day. I want everything that was done and said from the time Mr. Blackstone was arrested until this very minute. It will be in your best interest to make that report as accurate as possible. Do I make myself clear?"

"Yes, sir."

"Now get out of here. You will be very lucky if Mr. Blackstone doesn't file a formal complaint against you. And I wouldn't blame him if he does."

Captain MacDonald and Lieutenant Summers watched as Sanchez turned and left the interrogation room. It was the first time I had seen Mac so angry. As soon as Sanchez was gone, Mac looked at the lieutenant.

"I'll have a talk with you later. Now leave us alone and I don't want anyone listening in on the intercom. Do I make myself clear?"

"Yes, sir."

I watched as the lieutenant left the room. As soon as he was gone, Mac got a key and took the handcuffs off me. He then sat down across the table from me.

"You still want an attorney, Peter, or are you willing to talk to me?"

"I'll talk to you. I would have talked to you last night if they had gotten hold of you. Hell, I would have talked to them if they hadn't been so hell bent on convicting me without a shred of evidence. If they didn't call you, how did you know I was here?"

"Jennifer called me first thing this morning. She told me what she could about last night. She said you had been arrested. It took me a little while to find out which precinct you were at.

"Have you had anything to eat?"

"No."

"You want something? I can get you coffee and a doughnut."

"That would be great. I haven't had as much as a glass of water since they arrested me."

Mac got up and went to the door. He stuck his head out and told someone to get two cups of coffee and some doughnuts. He then returned to the table and sat back down.

"You want to fill me in on what happened last night?"

"Sure."

I spent the next hour drinking coffee, eating doughnuts and telling Mac what happened. I began from the time Jennifer and I arrived back at her apartment building after dinner. I took it step by step up to the time he came into the interrogation room this morning.

"I don't know who shot Hank, but my best guess would be the woman. It sounded like he might have been shot with a rifle. By the way, I did get one thing out of Hank before he died. He told me the name of the woman. I think she shot him to keep him from talking. Her name is Bonnie Tillman. I can't say for sure, but I think that might be her real name," I said.

"I'll run a check on her. You ready to get out of here?"

"Yeah. I need to call Jennifer and tell her I'm okay. I'll also need to get my vehicle."

"Your car is still in front of Jennifer's apartment. They were going to tow it in and impound it while they looked for evidence, but I told them to leave it alone. I'll take you over there to get it," Mac said.

"Thanks."

We left the interrogation room and went down the hall to the property room. The sergeant inside the property cage handed me an envelope and a paper to sign. I emptied out the envelope to make sure everything that was taken from me last night was there. The only thing that was missing was my gun.

"Where's my gun," I asked the sergeant.

"We have to keep it. It was involved in a shooting."

I looked at Mac for some help. He shrugged his shoulders and said, "There's nothing I can do. You did fire it."

"I want it back as soon as ballistics is done testing it."

"I'll see to it you get it back," Mac said. "Come on, I'll take you to get your car."

I FOLLOWED MAC OUT TO HIS CAR and got in. He got behind the wheel and we left the fourth precinct parking lot for Jennifer's apartment. I watched as Mac placed a radio call to records.

"I want everything you can find on Bonnie Tillman, that's T-i-l-l-m-a-n, Bonnie with an i-e. I want it on my desk when I get there."

"Yes, sir. It'll be waiting," the person on the other end said.

As soon as Mac signed off, he looked at me.

"When you get cleaned up, come by the office. We'll see what they have on this Tillman woman."

"I'll be by this afternoon."

As he drove, we talked a little more about what we thought was going on. We still didn't have anything on Bartlett. I was hoping once we found Tillman that would change. The one thing I couldn't let go of was my thought that the kidnapping of Jonathan was somehow connected to Bartlett's attempt to take over Endicott, Inc. I still had no proof to support it, only what Walter Endicott had told me.

When we arrived in front of Jennifer's apartment, I started to get out, but stopped when Mac spoke.

"Have you got another gun?"

"Yes, I do, but if I don't quit leaving them with different police departments all over the state, I'm going to run out pretty soon."

"That's right. I forgot that Sheriff Stillwell has one of your guns."

"I think that one will be a little harder to get back since it actually killed someone. I seriously doubt the one at the fourth precinct will be linked to anyone. I should be able to get it back in a couple of days, unless Sanchez decides to keep it longer because he's pissed at me."

"That isn't going to happen if he wants to keep his badge. I'll personally see you get it back soon."

"Thanks, Mac, and thanks for the ride."

"No problem. See you later."

I got out of his car and stood on the sidewalk while I watched him drive away. I then turned and went inside the apartment building.

I KNOCKED ON THE DOOR to Jennifer's apartment. The door flew open and before I could say a word, Jennifer had her arms around my neck and was kissing me as if I had been gone for months.

"Wow," I said as she let loose of me long enough for me to take a breath. "If I'd known I was going to get this kind of greeting, I would get myself arrested more often."

"Come in," she said as she almost dragged me into her apartment. "I've been worried about you. I got hold of Mac. Did he come by to see you?"

"Slow down. I'll tell you everything."

"I ran over to your place and got you a change of clothes in case you came by here first. I'm glad I did."

"I'm glad you did, too. I could use a shower and shave. Do you mind?"

"No. Would you like me to wash your back?" she said softly.

"That would be very nice."

I could hardly refuse an offer like that. We went into her bathroom, quickly got rid of our clothes and stepped into her large shower. I'm not sure how much cleaning of each other we did, but we did do a lot of hugging and kissing.

The next thing I knew we were curled up together in her bed. We made love as if we had not seen each other in years, then fell asleep in each other's arms.

I had only gotten a few hours of sleep last night. With the loving, the warm shower, and the warm body next to me, it was easy for me to fall asleep.

WHEN I WOKE, I found myself alone in a dark room. Jennifer had closed the drapes when she left so I could get some much needed sleep. I wondered where she had gone.

I heard the phone ring. It only rang twice before it stopped. I figured she answered it as quickly as she could in the hope it didn't wake me.

After a brief moment, I heard the faint sound of footsteps coming toward the bedroom. The door opened slowly and Jennifer peeked in.

"It's all right. I'm awake," I said.

"I'm sorry to disturb you, but there's a phone call for you."

"Who is it?"

"A Sheriff Stillwell from Breckenridge."

"I wonder how he got your number and how he knew I was here." I said. "Tell him I'll be right there."

Jennifer held up her portable phone. I smiled at her as I sat up and reached out for it.

"Sheriff Stillwell, how's it going?" I asked.

"Not too bad. I'm sorry to disturb you, but Captain MacDonald said I might be able to reach you at this number."

"Did he tell you anything else?"

"No, but when I told him I had some good news for you, he suggested I call you right away."

"What's the good news?"

"The woman you've been looking for, it seems she has shown up in Frisco. One of my officers spotted her. He followed her and saw her go into an apartment building near the lake."

"When did he see her?"

"A couple of hours ago. She was headed west on interstate 70 and got off at the first Frisco exit. He followed her to an apartment building, but had to drive on by as there was no place for him to stop without being seen."

"I guess you were right. She went back to Frisco," I said.

"But she didn't go back to the boat. As far as we can tell, she hasn't left the apartment since she arrived."

"Is there some way you can keep an eye on her without being seen?" I asked.

"I put one of my officers in a plain car and in plain clothes in a motel across the street from the apartment building. He has been watching the car and the building since shortly after she arrived."

"Good. I'll be back up there later this afternoon. Can we meet somewhere?"

"We can meet at the motel on the southwest side of the first west bound Interstate 70 exit into Frisco."

"Great. I have to meet with Captain MacDonald, in a little bit. I'll call you as soon as I get into town," I said. "By the way, Sheriff, you can cancel your APB on Hank Martin. He was killed last night."

"What happened?"

"Let's just say Bonnie Tillman shot him to keep him from talking to me. It looks like Bonny Johns's real name is Bonnie Tillman. I hope to have more on her when I get there."

"Great. I look forward to visiting with you again."

I shut off the phone and sat there looking at it. I was beginning to think I was wrong about Tillman having a place in Denver. It was beginning to look like she had a place in Frisco.

The other question that kept cruising through my mind was what was her connection to Bartlett? There had to be some connection, otherwise everything I believed would fall apart. It didn't seem to make any sense that the kidnapping was unrelated to the extortion.

My thoughts were disturbed by Jennifer when she stuck her head in the door.

"You ready for something to eat?"

"Yes. I could eat a horse."

"I don't have a stove big enough to cook a horse. Would a nice steak with a few trimmings do?"

"It would do just fine."

"Then you best get dressed. It will be ready in a few minutes. Oh, the disk you left with me, it was sort of a diary of Jonathan Endicott's relation with a Bonnie Ford."

"Was there any mention of a guy by the name of Bartlett?

"No. It was mostly about Bonnie Ford and how much he loved her."

"By the way, the woman's real name is Bonnie Tillman, and she probably murdered him."

"Oh. I didn't know," she said with a shocked look on her face.

"I'll explain it all after I get dressed."

After getting dress, I sat down and enjoyed a very good meal with Jennifer. We talked about what I was going to do. She asked if she could go with me to Frisco. I had to tell her no. There were just too many unknowns to have her with me. I felt it would be too dangerous for her.

After we finished eating, I kissed her and left for downtown to visit with Mac. I wanted to know what he had found out about Bonnie Tillman before I headed back to Frisco.

I LEFT JENNIFER'S APARTMENT and drove to the first precinct downtown. Mac was waiting in his office when I got there.

"Did you get some rest?" he asked.

"A little. Do you have anything for me on Bonnie Tillman?"

"Sure do. Some of it you might find interesting."

"Fill me in."

"Take a look for yourself," he said as he pushed a file folder across his desk toward me.

I picked up the folder and opened it. As I did, I looked across the desk at Mac. He was tipping back in his chair as if he expected it to take me awhile.

I looked at the file. It was pretty long. It seemed Bonnie Tillman had a long rap sheet starting out when she was in her teens. A quick check showed she was now forty-one years old.

At first I didn't see anything I hadn't expected. She had been in trouble for all kinds of things. She had been arrested for prostitution and on a few drug related charges when she was young. From what I could see in her file she had graduated to more serious crimes. She had served a couple of years in the women's penitentiary for attempted extortion and burglary.

Seeing the charge of extortion grabbed my attention, especially when I noticed a second charge of extortion including a charge of kidnapping, but it never went to trial. It showed the name of Hank Martin as a possible accessory. That one reminded me of something John had said about a case involving a guy called "The Cowboy". The interesting thing about it was the file didn't say why it never went to trial.

"Say, Mac. Do you know why this second charge of extortion and possible kidnapping never went to trial?"

"The victim of the kidnapping refused to press charges against her, and his parents withdrew their claim that she and Martin had extorted money from them. The DA ended up having to drop the case."

"I wonder if we are going to have problems with that, too?" I asked.

"Maybe, but we found Hank's pickup. It had her fingerprints on the gearshift knob and the steering wheel which means she drove it. We also have Hank's gun and her fingerprints are on it as well. Ballistics proves Hank was shot with his own rifle. We have a pretty good case for her having killed Hank. Did you notice who the attorney for Tillman was?"

"I saw his name, but I'm not familiar with him. Who is he?"

"He was Bartlett's attorney as well."

"No kidding. That seems like a big mistake to me. That just might be our connection between Tillman and Bartlett," I said.

"I thought you might think so. What's your next move?"

"I'm heading back to Frisco. Stillwell called me and said Tillman returned to Frisco and is staying at an apartment up there. Stillwell plans to watch her for a little while to see what she will do. He's been watching her since this morning."

"I'm going to want to talk to her."

"I figured that. If we grab her, I'll let you know. I don't think Stillwell wants her to get away this time."

"Okay. Keep me posted. Tell Stillwell I'll come up if he needs some help."

"Will do. I think I best get on the road."

I left Mac's office and headed for the parking lot.

As soon as I got in my vehicle, I headed for the interstate and on to Frisco. It was a little less than a two hour drive to Frisco.

CHAPTER EIGHTEEN

I arrived at the Best Western Motel in Frisco at around four-thirty in the afternoon and went directly to the lobby. I placed a call to the Sheriff's Office. Stillwell told me there was an officer in the lobby wearing tan slacks, a blue shirt and dark blue blazer. He described the officer to me. I took a quick look around the lobby and saw the man fitting the Sheriff's description sitting on a chair behind a large plant looking out the window.

"I see him."

"I'll be there in about fifteen minutes."

"Is he expecting me?"

"Yes, but he had instructions not to approach you, but to let you come to him so he didn't have to leave his post."

"Okay. I'll go talk to him. See you in a bit," I said, then hung up.

I walked over to the officer sitting by the window. He was watching the apartment building across a vacant field from the motel. It was about two hundred yards away. It was a good distance, but there was nothing in the way. I also noticed he had good binoculars.

"Excuse me, but are you one of Sheriff Stillwell's deputies?"

"Don Yeats. You must be Peter Blackstone."

"Right. Anything going on?"

"Not at the moment," he said as he turned back to watch. "Our suspect went in the apartment building over there by the lake this morning, but I haven't seen her come out."

"Anyone else go in?"

"There's been three or four people go in and out of the place, but none I recognized. Her car hasn't moved."

"By chance did you see a woman and a man leave the apartment building together?"

"No. Not so far."

"Have you been away from this window at all since you arrived here?"

"Only once, but I had a relief. He said no one went in or out will I grabbed a bite to eat and made a pit stop. I was gone maybe twenty minutes, but my relief was here all the time."

"You've been here every minute, except for when you were relieved?"

"Right."

"Good. Do you need a break?"

"I could sure use a pit stop. I've had a lot of coffee," he said with a grin.

"I'll take over for a few minutes."

"Thanks," he said. "You see that car, the silver four door parked next to the red convertible?

"Yes."

"That's the car she arrived in."

"Okay. Looks like a rental car."

"What makes you say that?"

"Just a guess, but it looks a little conservative for someone like her."

"Maybe. I'll be back in a few minutes."

I didn't respond. He left for the restroom while I slipped into his chair. I had often found surveillance to be the most boring part of being a PI, sitting and waiting for something to happen.

It wasn't very long before Yeats returned. He stood behind me and looked out the window.

"Anything happening?"

"Not so far."

"You have any idea what we're looking for?" Yeats asked.

"Not for sure, but I have a picture of a guy. I want you to take a good look at it and see if you recognize him."

"Sure."

I reached in my coat pocket and took out a picture of Joseph Bartlett that I got from Mac. He looked it over, but I couldn't tell by the expression on his face if he knew who it was.

"I don't know who he is, but I've seen this guy," he said thoughtfully. "I saw him just a little bit ago."

"Where?"

Yeats looked up from the picture and looked out the window toward the apartment building for a moment before turning to look at me.

"I saw him go into the apartment building with some other guy. He went in about - - ah - - twenty minutes ago."

"What did the other guy look like?"

"A little bigger than your guy. Muscular, dark hair probably six foot two or three, two hundred and thirty to two hundred and forty pounds."

"Did they come back out?"

"I think so."

"Did either of them come out alone?"

"Your guy came out of the apartment building and walked back to his car. He was followed by the big guy just seconds later. The thing I found interesting was they had come in the same car, but left in different cars.

"Your guy got in the same car they came in, a Lincoln Town Car. But the bigger guy got in a different car, a little sporty car. When they left the parking lot, the bigger guy followed your guy."

"What direction did they go? Did they go back toward the interstate?"

"No. As a matter of fact, they both took the road into town."

"What's going on?"

I turned to see Sheriff Stillwell. He had a puzzled look on his face.

"I think we should go find Bonnie Tillman. Joseph Bartlett and probably one of his enforcers went into the apartment building, but when they came out they took different cars. I think one of them took Tillman's car, but she wasn't in it."

"You think they were here to see Tillman?"

"More likely here to kill her to make sure she didn't talk to us. That seems to be Bartlett's pattern. While I was in Denver, Captain MacDonald showed me Tillman's file. We found a connection between Bartlett and Tillman."

"Do you think it's a good idea? We might lose her."

"We may have already lost her. Let's go," I insisted.

I turned and headed for the door. I ran out of the motel to my vehicle while Yeats and the Sheriff ran to their cars.

DRIVING AS FAST as traffic and circumstances would allow, I drove to the front of the apartment building, stopped in front, jumped out and ran into the building. I stopped at the mailboxes in the lobby just long enough to find out which apartment Bonnie might be in. There it was, Bonnie Tillman. She lived in apartment six. It didn't take me but a few seconds to figure out where apartment six was located. By that time, Yeats and Stillwell had caught up with me.

I started running down the hall toward the apartment with Yeats and the Sheriff hot on my heels. I drew my gun from under my coat on the run.

As I approached the door, I could see it was standing slightly ajar making it so I could see inside, but only a little. I stopped and leaned up against the wall. Stillwell and Yeats followed suit. I put my fingers over my lips to make sure they didn't say anything, then moved slowly toward the door.

When I got close to the door, I thought I could hear a noise. It sounded almost like someone crying. I moved closer to where I could see in the room a little better, but I still could not see anyone.

Reaching out, I slowly pushed the door open further. There was no one in the living room, but I could see into one of the bedrooms. I could also hear someone moving around.

As she passed by the door, I got a glimpse of Bonnie Tillman. She seemed to be scurrying about in the bedroom. I moved further into the living room. I could see her packing a suitcase, and she was doing it rather quickly. It was obvious she was getting ready to run.

Since I knew what kind of a woman she was, I thought it would be a good idea if I was very cautious around her. It was my feeling she had already killed at least two other people and possibly three. I moved up close to the bedroom door and gently pushed it open, then stood there with my gun pointed at her. She had her back toward me.

"Going somewhere?" I asked.

She stopped moving then slowly straightened up, but didn't turn around. Her back was stiff and her shoulders tense. I had no idea if she had a gun or not, but I wasn't about to risk it.

"Put your hands out to your sides and slowly turn around."

"You wouldn't shoot a woman," she said without moving.

"Just as quickly as I would step on a black widow spider," I replied with authority.

"How's your head," she asked, then she started to slowly turn around.

She must have thought I was alone. The confident grin disappeared from her face when she saw Yeats and Stillwell standing in the door with their guns on her. Instead, her eyes got big and the fight within her seemed to dissipate as if she had the wind knocked out of her.

I got a little surprise, too. She had been crying. The reason she had been crying was easy to see. She had a bruise and a cut on her right cheek, a cut and swollen lip, along with bruises on her arm where she had obviously been grabbed and held with considerable force. She had been worked over pretty well.

"Your boyfriend do this to you?"

"No. I fell," she said sharply.

"I guess I would say that, too, if my boyfriend was Joseph Bartlett and he came to visit with one of his apes."

The expression that came over her face assured me that I was right.

"Bartlett never touched me."

"I'm sure he didn't. He just watched while his enforcer did it for him. There's no need to lie. We saw them come in here and we saw them leave."

"You can't prove anything. And I don't have to talk to you without a lawyer."

I smiled, then looked over my shoulder at Stillwell and Yeats.

"Would you mind leaving us alone for a few minutes?"

Stillwell looked at me for a moment as if he was trying to decide if it was a good idea.

"What are you doing?" she asked, the look on her face showing a bit of fear and a lot of concern. "You can't even question me without a lawyer."

Stillwell turned and left the room. He went out into the hall taking Yeats with him. As soon as I was sure they were out of the room, I looked at Bonnie.

"There is one thing wrong with your statement about a lawyer. You see, I'm not a cop. I'm not required to honor your rights. I'm the guy you smacked on the head while I was trying to rescue Jonathan Endicott from the *Crystal Blue*. I deserve a few minutes alone with you.

She had the look of fear in her eyes. The beating she had already had helped convince her that she might be in for another one.

"Now, I'm going to tell you how it is. You have to remember I saw you on the *Crystal Blue* when I was there to rescue Jonathan. That puts you at the crime scene where Jonathan was killed. By the way, we also have you for stealing the *Crystal Blue*. For your information, that is grand theft which will be easy to prove and will get you a lot of years in jail."

She didn't say a word. She just looked at me as if she was wondering what else we might have on her.

"We also have your fingerprints on Hank's rifle which makes for a pretty strong case that you shot him. Ballistics shows it was Hank's rifle that was used to kill him. And there's a witness who saw you when Hank was killed, namely me. Then there are your fingerprints on Hank's pickup which you used to flee the scene of the shooting. That makes it murder one.

"In addition to everything else, we also have you for assaulting me. We don't have you for killing Butler, yet. But that's just a matter of time. Sheriff Stillwell hasn't finished reviewing all the evidence, yet.

"So you see, there is a needle with your name on it waiting for you at the women's prison. Now, I might be able to get the DA to take the death penalty off the table if you agree to tell us what part Bartlett played in all this."

I could see she was mulling over everything I had said in her head. It took awhile, but she was not as dumb as she might appear. She had a lot to think about if she was going to save her own skin, and I was sure that was her main interest at the moment.

"What do you want from me?"

"I want to know why you kidnapped Jonathan?"

"You already know that."

"Maybe, but I'd like to hear it from you."

"For money."

"I don't believe you. There was more to it."

Her eyes told me she was wondering just how much we really knew. It was probably more than she expected us to know.

"You've got a record. It won't do you one bit of good to lie. It will only make things worse. You keep lying and you will get the death penalty. In fact, I'll work very hard to see you do, unless you cooperate with me."

"We – ah – we kidnapped Jonathan in order to get as much of old man Endicott's money as possible."

"Why?"

"So he would have to borrow more."

"Why did you want him to borrow more? On second thought, you tell me if I'm wrong. So Endicott would have to sell off more of his stock in Endicott, Inc., to Bartlett?"

"Yes."

"Bartlett was trying to get complete ownership of Endicott, Inc., wasn't he?"

"Yes, but the damn old fool wouldn't let go of it."

"So you kidnapped his son."

"Yeah. And it would have worked if you hadn't interfered."

"Why did you risk being caught by getting hold of a boat you had to know belonged to someone else?"

"That was Hank's idea. He said the guy who owned it had died and no one would be around to use it. He thought it would make it more difficult for anyone to sneak up on us if we were out on the lake. He also said if it got too hot, we could weight Jonathan's body, and dump him overboard. He said it made for a quick and easy way to get rid of the body, and it would take them weeks or even months to find him, if they found it at all."

"If that was the case, why did you keep Jonathan in the old mining shack?"

"That was Hank's idea, too. Actually it was his first idea. We moved him back to the boat later. He said we could hide him there while we negotiated with the old man.

That way they wouldn't be able to prove a thing. We had to move him back to the boat when you showed up at the shack."

"You were waiting for me to try to rescue him from the boat, weren't you?"

"I figured you'd try something, and I was right."

"Who shot Jonathan?"

That question brought me nothing but silence. I was sure it had been her idea in order to get me out of the way. The only thing she didn't count on was the Sheriff not arresting me.

"You shot him with my gun, didn't you?"

"I'm not saying anything else until I have a lawyer."

"Okay, but you've said enough. You see, it doesn't matter if you actually shot Jonathan or not. You were there when he was shot, you participated in the kidnapping that led to his death, and you stole a very expensive boat to hold him captive on which shows premeditation and thought."

She just stood there looking at me. There was nothing she could do. She had already confessed to everything important.

"I have just one other question for you. Where did Bartlett and his enforcer go?"

She looked at me as if she had already lost everything. In fact, she had. She had lost her freedom, and to me that was everything.

She let out a long sigh, then said, "They went to burn the *Crystal Blue.*"

"Why?"

"Bartlett said he couldn't take the chance that there was any evidence left on it. He plans to burn down the entire Smooth Sailing Marina with the owners in it to make it look like an accidental fire. He doesn't like loose ends, and Tom Harden and Bill Harden are loose ends."

"Stillwell!"

"Yeah."

"Get your men and the fire department over to Smooth Sailing Marina. Bartlett is going to try to burn it down. Yeats, cuff her and take her to jail. Don't let her out of your sight, not even for a second."

Stillwell and I headed for his car leaving Bonnie in the custody of Yeats. As Stillwell jumped in his car, I got in the passengers seat. While he drove, I got on the radio and called for the fire department and for back up.

WE WERE THE FIRST TO ARRIVE at the Smooth Sailing Marina. There were no signs of a fire. I could see the *Crystal Blue* tied at the dock. We got out of the car, but stayed behind it. There were too many places they could hide for just the two of us to search.

"We better wait for back up," Stillwell suggested.

"Good idea. Keep your eyes open. They probably know we're here."

Staying behind the police car with our guns drawn, we watched the marina. Waiting was hard, but it gave us time to think about how we were going to search the entire marina, the boat storage buildings and the boats. It also gave them time to figure out how to get away. The only good thing about the situation was we could hear sirens approaching which meant we were getting reinforcements.

AS THE REINFORCEMENTS drew closer, Stillwell got on the radio directing them to what areas of the marina he wanted them to cover. The unfortunate part of the whole thing was we didn't have enough deputies to cover all the out buildings. They focused their attention on the largest boat storage building and the building containing the office and store. If Bartlett and his enforcer had seen us coming, they could have slipped out of the office building and hid in any number of places in the four outbuildings.

Stillwell opened the trunk of his car and got out a bullhorn. He put it to his mouth and spoke slowly and clearly into it.

"Okay, Bartlett. You and your enforcer come out with your hands in the air."

Suddenly, there was the sound of a single pistol shot. Everyone ducked down behind their cars. It took a few seconds for us to realize that the shot had not been fired at any of us. The shot had been fired inside the office and the store.

"Stillwell, I think we better try to get in there."

He didn't say anything as he thought about what I had suggested. After a few seconds or so, he nodded his head. He turned and looked at one of his nearby deputies and signaled him to cover us, then turned back to look at me.

"Ready when you are," he said.

I nodded then jumped up and ran from behind the car toward the front of the building. When I got to the building I hugged the wall only a foot or so from the door for a couple of seconds before signaling Stillwell to come. He ran toward the building, stopping against the wall on the other side of the door.

Since the door opened away from me, it was necessary for me to go in first. I nodded to him that I was ready. He reached over and pulled the door open. I charged into the store part of the building immediately taking cover behind some shelves filled with small parts for boats. Stillwell followed behind taking cover behind another set of shelves on the other side of the aisle.

As soon as he looked like he was ready, I peeked around the end of the shelves. I didn't see anything at first, but when I was getting ready to work my way to the next row of shelves I saw what looked like a boot. It was behind the next set of shelves.

I looked over at Stillwell and pointed at the boot. He looked and nodded. I motioned for him to keep an eye on it while I moved down the row of shelves to the other end.

When I got to the end of the shelves, I checked around to see if I could see anyone. I didn't see anyone or hear anything. I carefully moved to the next set of shelves then peeked around the end of them. Lying in a pool of blood was Bill Harden. He had been shot once in the head. He was dead.

I slipped back to the first row of shelves where Stillwell could see me. I moved down the row of shelves to the aisle.

"It's Bill Harden boot, and he's dead," I whispered. "He was shot in the head. I didn't see Tom Harden."

"What now?"

"I think we should work our way to the office."

"Okay."

I moved back to the end of the shelves and began moving from one row of shelves to the next. Stillwell moved from one row of shelves to the next, but at the opposite end of the shelves. It wasn't long before we were at the last row of shelves between us and the office.

The next move would put us up against the wall in front of the office. I quickly moved to the wall staying as low as possible. It was very quiet, too quiet. I couldn't hear anything coming from the office.

Stillwell moved up next to me, but he didn't say a word. I motioned to him that I was going to move to the door, and when I got there, he was to cover me while I opened the door. He nodded that he was ready and understood what I wanted him to do.

I crawled to the door. After glancing back to make sure he was ready, I jumped up and jerked open the door. I rushed in with my gun ready, but there was no one in the office.

When I looked over at Stillwell, he was standing outside the office with his gun pointed at the window in front of him.

He was ready to shoot threw the glass if anyone tried to shoot at me. He looked over at me and shook his head then moved to the door.

"They must have gone out the back," he said.

"I wonder if they have Tom Harden with them."

"Do you smell something?" he asked.

"GAS, RUN!"

Stillwell and I ran for the door of the store as fast as we could. I got to the door just a few steps ahead of Stillwell. We had run about twenty feet out of the building when the place exploded. I knew what I had smelled was propane gas. A trap had been set for anyone who came into the office. We had escaped by only seconds and had ended up with our faces in the dirt.

I rolled over and looked back at the building. It was fully engulfed in flames, at least what was left of it. I noticed Stillwell lying on the ground. He wasn't moving. I went to him. He was still breathing. The explosion had knocked the wind out of him, but he was coming around.

"You okay," I asked.

"Yeah," he said as he looked up at me.

He was short of breath, but we both knew our problems were not over. As I started to help him up, another shot rang out kicking up dirt only a foot or so away. While we were scrambling to the safety of one of the patrol cars, a couple of the deputies returned fire to give us cover. We made it to the car.

Once safely behind the patrol car, Stillwell ordered his men to stop shooting. He took a couple of deep breaths then stood up behind the car.

"Where did the shots come from?" he demanded.

"That little building down by the dock," one of his deputies replied. "You want us to get him out of there?"

"Stillwell, the guy down there by the dock is probably Bartlett's enforcer. My guess he's there to cover Bartlett's escape and to set fire to the *Crystal Blue.* You need to keep him pinned down there and don't let him get near the boat," I said."

"You think Bartlett has already gotten away?"

"Yes, and he's probably headed back to the apartment to kill Tillman. He has no way of knowing she isn't there."

"You might be right."

"When he finds out she's not there, he will run and we may never find him."

"You're probably right. Take one of the patrol cars and get back to the apartment building. See if you can get him there. Take one of my deputies with you. We'll get this guy," Stillwell said.

I didn't take the time to respond. As I headed for one of the patrol cars, I grabbed one of his deputies and told him he was going with me. The deputy I grabbed happened to be the one I had a couple of run-ins with already.

He didn't say a word. He had been behind Stillwell and myself and had heard our conversation. The deputy got in behind the wheel while I got in on the passenger side. He drove while I checked the shotgun attached to the dash to make sure it was ready to use.

"We going to need that?" he asked keeping his eyes on the road as we sped toward the apartment building.

"I don't know, but it's always nice to have more firepower than you need. Sometimes just a good show of force is all you need."

CHAPTER NINETEEN

WHEN WE ARRIVED at the apartment building, I saw a car parked behind my vehicle. The fact that it was parked crooked made me think it was probably Bartlett's car.

"Park behind my vehicle," I told the deputy.

He pulled up behind my vehicle. We jumped out and ran into the apartment building. I tossed the shotgun to the deputy and drew my pistol out from under my coat. We headed straight to Tillman's apartment, being careful when we rounded corners we didn't run into Bartlett.

As we came around the last corner, Bartlett was coming out of the apartment. We didn't have time to react. He fired a quick shot from the apartment door while I scrambled for cover. The deputy fired a blast from the shotgun at Bartlett forcing him back into the apartment.

"Go around outside and make sure he doesn't escape out a window," I told the deputy.

I watched him as he ran for the door. It was time for me to get Bartlett's attention.

"Bartlett, you've got no place to go. We have you pinned in the apartment. You might as well give up."

There was nothing but silence for a minute or so. I wasn't sure what he was thinking, until I heard glass break. It was almost immediately followed by the sound of a shotgun blast from outside. That shot assured me the deputy had the windows to the apartment covered.

"I told you there was no way out. Now give it up."

There was nothing but quiet for what seemed like forever. Finally, Bartlett decided he had something to say.

"You've got nothing on me I can't beat in court. I've killed no one."

"Toss your gun out and come out with your hands in the air."

I waited to see if he really believed what he had said. It took about a minute or two before he tossed his gun out into the hall. He slowly walked out of the apartment with his hands in the air. The confident look on his face turned to one of confusion.

"I know you. You're not a cop," he said in disgust.

"No, but you are under arrest just the same. You see, I'm working for Sheriff Stillwell. He happens to be a little busy right now getting your enforcer down at the marina. Let's go."

The halls in the apartment building were fairly narrow. As he started to move past me toward the front door of the apartment building, he made a sudden move toward me. The only problem for him was I was ready for it. As he lunged at me, I sidestepped him and buried the barrel of my gun deep in his gut. It immediately bent him over. I had knocked the wind out of him. He went to the floor in a heap banging his head on the wall as he went down.

While he was trying to catch his breath and making an effort to get to his hands and knees, I was picking up his gun. Since he was already on the floor, I could see no reason to let him get up.

I kicked his hands out from under him causing him to fall face down on the floor, again. I knelt down putting my knee in the middle of his back while I searched him for any other weapons. He had none.

About that time a guy stuck his head out of his apartment door to see what all the commotion was about. His timing couldn't have been better.

"Excuse me sir. Would you be so kind as to go out in front and ask the deputy sheriff standing out there with a shotgun to come in here, please?"

He looked at me for a second and glanced at the gun I had pointed at the back of Bartlett's head. He decided it would be a good idea to do as I asked. He took off down the hall at a run. Within seconds, the deputy came running down the hall.

"You got him."

"I need your handcuffs."

He gave me his handcuffs and I put them on Bartlett. Once he was secured, I stood up.

"He's all yours deputy. Put him in your car."

The guy from the apartment was standing in the hall watching with his mouth hanging open. I felt I needed to say something to him.

"Thank you for your help, sir," I said, then turned and walked out of the building.

When I got outside, the deputy was standing next to his car. Bartlett was hunched over in the back seat. The deputy looked like he was waiting for me.

"He's all yours. Take him to jail and lock him up."

"Mr. Blackstone, I want to thank you. Whether you know it or not, I've learned a lot from you. Thanks again."

"You're welcome. Remember, not everything is as it appears."

"I'll remember," he said with a smile.

"I'll follow you to the jail. Maybe Stillwell will be back there by then."

The deputy nodded, then got in his car. I got in mine and followed him back to the county courthouse where the jail was located.

WHEN WE PULLED INTO the parking lot, there were several patrol cars there. It made it a good bet that they had gotten Bartlett's enforcer at the dock.

I parked my vehicle and went inside. Sheriff Stillwell was in his office. He was on the phone. He saw me and motioned for me to come in. I went into his office and sat down in a chair in front of his desk. I couldn't help but hear part of his conversation.

"Sure, Mac. I'll tell him," I heard Stillwell say.

He was talking to Captain MacDonald.

"Blackstone just came in. Do you want to talk to him?"

There was a moment of silence before Stillwell spoke again.

"Okay, I'll tell him. Talk to you later."

Sheriff Stillwell hung up and looked across his desk at me.

"Mac would like to see you when you get back to Denver. He said there was no hurry. He has one of your guns and would like to return it to you. He was also glad to hear we got Bartlett, his enforcer and the girl. A pretty good day as far as I'm concerned."

"I'll have to agree with you."

Did you find Tom Harden?"

"Yeah. He was in one of the outbuildings with his throat cut."

"To bad."

"Yeah. I want to thank you for all your help."

"I want to thank you for not tossing me in jail when you found me on the *Crystal Blue*. I have just one question for you."

"Sure."

"Can I have my gun back?"

"Sure. I'll have one of my deputies get it for you."

After making my statement regarding the capture and arrest of Bartlett and getting my gun back from Sheriff Stillwell, I got in my vehicle and headed for the condo at East Shore Estates.

IT WAS GETTING RATHER LATE when I drove into the parking lot of the condo. I began thinking about what had happened to my sailboat. I had been too engrossed in other things to even think about it until now. I decided to walk down to the dock. As I walked out on the dock, I saw my boat securely tied in one of the berths belonging to Marcy.

"Hi, Mr. Blackstone."

I turned to see Hudson coming toward me.

"Hi. Say, do you know how my boat got back here?"

"Yeah. I was out sailing, you know, checking out a boat for one of my clients, when I saw your boat. I knew it was yours, after all I had seen it enough times. I towed it back here and tied it in its berth. I didn't know what happened to you, but I figured you'd be back. If you weren't, the sheriff would be looking for it."

"Thanks for bringing it back. What do I owe you?"

"Nothing."

"Thanks again."

"You're welcome. How you coming on your investigation?"

"It's finished."

"Will you be leaving soon?"

"Maybe. I might stick around for a couple of days to do a little sailing before I go back to Denver."

"Okay. Maybe I'll see you around. If you need some help cleaning up your boat, I'd be more than happy to help."

"I'll keep that in mind. And thanks again," I said as I shook his hand.

He simply smiled, turned and went on down the dock. I returned to the condo.

AS I OPENED THE DOOR to the condo and went inside, I was hit by the smell of something cooking. It smelled very good. My first thought was Marcy had come out in an effort to see if our relationship might change a little.

I walked across the living room and looked in the kitchen. Standing in front of the stove was Jennifer. I couldn't help but notice how domestic she looked. I kind of liked it.

"Hi," I said as I leaned against the door frame.

Jennifer turned around and looked at me. A big smile came over her face.

"You hungry?" she asked.

"Hungry for you," I said as I moved toward her.

Jennifer stepped up in front of me and put her arms around my neck. I put my arms around her narrow waist and pulled her up against me. I leaned down and kissed her hard on the lips. It was a long passionate kiss.

She leaned back, looked up at me and smiled.

"Dinner will be ready in a few minutes. Would you like to take a shower before dinner?"

"I think that would be a good idea. I smell like propane fuel and smoke. Would you like to take a shower with me," I said hoping she would.

Jennifer looked at me, then turned her head and looked at the meal on the stove. She looked back at me and smiled.

"It's one of your favorites, my thick beef stew. I could put it in the oven on low to keep it warm. It needs to cook a little longer anyway."

"Sounds good to me."

I waited until she shut off the burner on the top of the stove and put the pot of stew in the oven. She then slipped her arm around me as we went to the bathroom.

It was well after dark before we were sitting at the table eating her stew. It was delicious. The long wait for dinner didn't hurt the stew or my appetite one bit.

"Are you going to take me sailing on your boat before we have to go back to Denver?" she asked.

"How long before you have to go back to work?"

"I've got three days off."

"Sure. Would you like to spend those three days here with me?"

"I thought you would never ask," she said with a smile.